When his father died, David Mulk⟨…⟩ ney to come home and run the fa⟨…⟩ He is driven by personal demons ⟨…⟩ ⟨…⟩y tragedy to see it through, despite his love of teaching and the ongoing drought and debt.

When David meets the new local doctor Martin James, there is a meeting of minds and dark pasts. Martin is intrigued by David's closed demeanour and makes an effort to reach him. They strike up a friendship, able to understand the pain in each other's past. When David discovers that Martin is gay, he feels duped and betrayed, but the revelation forces him to confront what it means to love someone and how sometimes we don't get to choose.

SOMETHING ELSE

Alicia Thompson

A NineStar Press Publication

www.ninestarpress.com

Something Else

© 2021 Alicia Thompson
Cover Art © 2021 Natasha Snow

This is a work of fiction. Names, characters, places, and incidents are either the product of the author's imagination or are used fictitiously. Any resemblance to actual persons living or dead, business establishments, events, or locales is entirely coincidental.

All rights reserved. No part of this publication may be reproduced in any material form, whether by printing, photocopying, scanning or otherwise without the written permission of the publisher. To request permission and all other inquiries, contact NineStar Press at the physical or web addresses above or at Contact@ninestarpress.com.

ISBN: 978-1-64890-407-3

First Edition, October, 2021

Also available in eBook, ISBN: 978-1-64890-406-6

CONTENT WARNING:

This book contains sexually explicit content which is only suitable for mature readers, deceased parent, deceased sibling, death of a child, death of a prominent character, animal death, homophobia, homophobic slurs, no HEA.

For Matthew

Prologue

David sat in the pew with the Wilson family. He fingered the imitation leather cover of the prayer book—familiar but not. He hadn't touched one since he'd been confirmed. When the service was over everyone filed outside, the only sounds the creaking of seats and the reedy punctuated notes of the organ ushering them out of the church.

The coffin had preceded them, borne on the shoulders of the Barry boys and four other relatives of the family who had come from out of town. The congregation pooled at the front step of the church in respectful hesitation as arrangements were being made at the hearse. The smell of Brylcreem and moth-balls was palpable.

Mrs Wilson stood near his elbow. "Such a waste." She wiped her eye with a finger wrapped in the corner of a handkerchief and delicately blew her nose. She looked down to the family gathered near the hearse, a woman with her three teen-aged children. "Bad enough as it is…"

Her husband shook his head and wiped his mouth, muttered, "Silly bugger," and stalked off towards the car.

The words echoed in David's head. Manse Stevens was the second man in the area who had taken control of the last thing he had any say in. Another farm to be sold up for nothing.

At the cemetery David had reached his limit. He slipped away from the crowd moving towards the burial site. He'd never been good with seeing boxes lowered into sharp-edged holes. Instead, he weaved between the streets and alleys of stone until he was standing in front of some brown blocks of polished granite. The tips of his fingers traced the carved letters on one of them, rubbing away any cobwebs and blown dirt. Crouching down, he placed his palm on the bottom corner of the slab. He didn't know how long he'd been there, his head bowed, when he heard approaching footsteps. He looked up to where Jodie stood at the end of the row. Not meeting his eye, she gestured towards the gate with her hand.

"Heading off…now, if you…"

He rose to his feet. "Yep. All right."

Chapter One

He'd felt the pull, but there was no pain. Yet. Only the livid blood running through his fingers, dropping to the ground like seed. Grabbing his wrist, he ran back to the cab of the ute, found a rag in the glove box, clutched it in his hand. The fleshy part of his palm just below the thumb was beginning to throb.

He walked back to where the cows were chewing the hay he'd torn apart. Shaking out that last biscuit with his good hand, he found the culprit. A jagged piece of fencing wire. Bastard. Better him than one of his cows.

By the time he'd driven through three sets of gates and juggled numerous gear changes, the pain was like a blade pushing through his palm to his wrist. He consoled himself that in his own experience the smallest wounds often hurt the most.

He ransacked the cupboard under the bathroom sink and found cotton wool and a roll of bandages. No Dettol. Reefing everything out onto the floor, he found a small can of antiseptic spray rolling around the back of the shelf. It was rusted and useless.

Still clutching the dirty rag in his hand, he headed out to the kitchen. He wasn't much into hard spirits, so the ancient cooking brandy used for his mum's Christmas cakes would have to do.

Back in the bathroom he slowly pulled away the rag. It grabbed where it had stuck to the wound and fresh carmine welled up through the rusty-brown muck. He turned on the tap and before he had time to think about what was coming, thrust his hand under. It was times like this he realised how limited his repertoire of swear words actually was. Catching him once, his mother had said, "That's a lovely conjugation, dear, now take it outside before I belt you round the head."

He could now see the extent of the damage: a gutter of open flesh, torn to a long triangle at the end, black in its depths. He glanced at the brandy bottle. *Shit.* He hugged it to him and unscrewed the lid. He was about to pour it when he chickened out and took a big slug instead. Then another. Gritting his teeth, he poured the rest into his hand.

Fang lay where he'd been left, staring through the screen door on the front verandah, his head on his paws, his ears pricked. The tan dots above his eyes gave him a perpetually surprised look. An anguished howl roared down the hallway. He lifted his head and waited.

He woke up several hours later on the couch shivering, cradling his bandaged hand to his chest. His hand felt like it had grown to the size of a pumpkin. His head was ready to split open and his throat was sore. Bloody brandy. May as well have eaten Ratsak. He swung his legs to the floor, but his knees gave way and he felt dizzy. After a few deep breaths he made it to the bathroom and took some aspirin. And promptly vomited them into the toilet.

He splashed some water on his face and looked in the mirror. Ugly as. He took a few more deep breaths. "Okay, all right." He opened the screen door and Fang scrambled to his feet. "Lassie would've gone for help by now, you useless mutt." He leaned down to rub the dog's head and they got in the ute together.

The forty-kilometre trip took longer than usual as he forced himself to concentrate on the road ahead. He passed the school bus before crossing the Mill Bridge. Not so many kids on that bus these days. Fewer families, fewer kids. More single guys like himself. You couldn't blame the girls for wanting better jobs in town or moving to the city. His sister had upgraded boarding school for uni and never looked back, and when his dad had died, his mother hadn't waited long either.

The town of Bruce wasn't anything pretty to look at. Flat, with the red-roofed houses sprawling out till they ran out of energy. The town was a main street with a hardware store and bus depot at one end and a Woolworths at the other. Dr Jacobs was in a leafy street parallel and behind. Surgery hours would be over, but he felt confident of rousing the old man up. A man his age didn't get up to too much at the end of the day.

He rolled down the window an inch. Fang settled down in the driver's seat and watched him as he tried to tuck his shirt in with one hand. He walked under a rose trellis, up a narrow brick path, and knocked on the heavy green door with the lion's head knocker. Its clatter seemed to echo through the house. He heard a door open and then there was the delicate pulse of classical music.

When the door finally opened, all he could think was, *who the fuck are you?* Before him stood a thin young man with a high forehead partly covered by an unruly fringe. But what took him aback were the deep-set eyes. Dark blue and compelling.

"Sorry, I was after the doctor."

"I am the doctor. Dr James. Martin James." He held out his hand but let it drop when he saw the bandaged hand. "Ah."

"I've never seen anyone but Dr Jacobs my whole life."

The doctor arched an eyebrow at him, and his thin lips looked like they might smile but didn't. "Well, he'll be back in six months if you'd like to wait till then."

Right. Those dark eyes held his and he felt he was being turned into a private joke somewhere in their depths.

The doctor took in his dusty boots and exhausted features and inclined his head towards the surgery. "You'd better come round the front." He walked past him and pulled some keys from his pocket. When he realised he wasn't being followed, he turned back and said, "If you're willing to take a punt, that is."

Once in Dr Jacobs' surgery he relaxed a little. He watched this new man open cabinets and extract bandages, cotton wool, scissors, and bottles. "So, where's Dr Jacobs?"

"On holiday. I'm covering for six months."

"Jessie had enough, then?"

The doctor glanced round and smiled. "I guess so."

Mrs Jacobs was always saying that being married to a country doctor was harder than being one as you never got a holiday. She never seemed to see the irony of saying this to farmers' wives.

The doctor had taken a seat and pulled a pad towards him. "Sorry, I didn't get your name?"

"David. David Mulkerin. Property's out on the Fullerton Road." He explained what happened to his hand.

The doctor scribbled some notes and put his pen down. "Okay. Let's take a look."

He held out his hand, palm up, on the desk between them. With the doctor bending over his hand and gently beginning to unravel the bandage he could look at his face unobserved. Cheekbones to cut bread, as his sister would say. Sandy eyelashes. He felt a second uncomfortable wave of déjà vu since first encountering those eyes. He swallowed it down and tried to focus on what was going on.

Long girlish fingers wove the bandage under and over, under and over.

"Hands like that, you must be a piano player."

He didn't look up from his task. "Flute, actually, but only for a short while. Why, do you play?"

Something in his tone made him bristle. "Yeah. Yeah, I *do*, *actually*. We're not all yokels out here, y'know."

The doctor paused to look up at him. "Is that right." His smile seemed genuine.

There was a brief moment of pleasure as the cool air of the surgery hit his newly exposed skin, but it was soon replaced with the pain of being pressed and stretched.

"Jesus, man. Why didn't you come in straight away? This will need some serious embroidery. Look at it. It's already weeping pus. Have you heard of septicaemia?"

"It's just a cut. I didn't wanna make a fuss," he mumbled into his collar while the doctor turned away and rattled metal in a tray.

"You macho types toughing it out." The doctor sighed and shook his head.

The anaesthetic hurt more than the actual stitches, but he wasn't going to let on if it killed him. He stared over the doctor's shoulder, trying to focus on breathing.

"So, where're you from?"

"Sydney."

Like it wasn't obvious. "So, what made you want to come out here then? I hear they pay good money to get doctors out into the country."

"I did a long stint in casualty at St Vincent's during my training. Saw a lot of things I wouldn't wish on anyone. It wears you down after a while."

"Be around some real people for a change."

The doctor looked up. "The people I saw in casualty are about as real as they get."

"I didn't mean—what I meant is country people are different."

"They are that."

He stumbled on, sure he had offended. "I lived in Sydney for a while. Did my degree at New South."

"We must just have different definitions of what constitutes 'real' then." He pulled a stitch in and it grabbed, drawing a gasp. "Sorry. Nearly done."

Once he had painted him with antiseptic, rebandaged his hand, and given him a tetanus shot, the doctor made some more notes on his pad. "I'd like to take another look at it next Thursday. You said you're on a property. How are you going to manage with one hand? Are you married? Do you have family or hired help?"

He opened his mouth and shut it again. The answer was D, none of the above, but if he said this it was bound to encourage interference. It was bad enough having Jodie dropping in all the time.

"Yeah, ah, the neighbours are good."

The doctor paused in his writing to look at him. He nodded thoughtfully. "Okay. Here's a script for some painkillers if it gives you any trouble, and here's another for some antibiotics. Make sure you take the whole script. But I'm warning you, if you start trying to do any heavy work and burst those stitches, next time I'll whack you in a full cast."

David looked down at his hand.

"David? I'm serious."

The doctor followed him out to his ute. "What's your friend's name?"

"Fang."

"A bit vicious, is he?"

"Nah. More likely to fang you to death with his tongue."

"You sure you're okay to drive?"

"Yeah. My left does all the work. She'll be right."

As he cranked into second, he glanced in the rearview mirror. Dr James was still standing on the nature strip, his arms folded, watching him.

Chapter Two

He squinted into the light and held his watch in front of his face. He let his head collapse back on the pillow. It was already 8:00 a.m. Those painkillers had really knocked him out. Downing them with a few beers may also have helped.

His hand throbbed like a bastard and he stank. He was about to jump under the shower when he remembered. He felt like a right idiot trying to shower with a plastic shopping bag ballooning on his mitt. After nearly castrating himself trying to wrangle his jeans on, he was ready for his next challenge.

Three instant porridges in a bowl were soon whirring around in the microwave while he tapped his spoon on the countertop. He eyed the bananas in his fruit bowl longingly. The porridge was sickly sweet. *How do people eat this shit?* His mother had always fed them up on salted oats soaked overnight. Then they would have cream skimmed off the day's milk and a little brown sugar which soon turned to syrup. A starving man couldn't afford to be fussy, his mother would say, but she had always fed them well.

He took his mug of tea out to the front verandah and sat on the step. So many jobs to do and he was bloody helpless. Feeding his animals was non-negotiable, but he reckoned he could still do that. Even if it did take twice as long. He'd have to call Dan about that fencing job. It would have to wait. He could do his year-end accounts with one hand, he realised glumly. Just thinking about the tide of red numbers awaiting him tightened his gut into a knot. He could spend some time on hold to Telstra. Visit Ethan and haggle over his overdraft again. He could spare a week. Maybe the doctor could take out the stitches next Thursday.

Dr Martin James, eh. He stared down the driveway without seeing. He felt foolish now, reacting the way he had. Lots of people had dark-blue eyes. *Not like that, they don't.* And mousy-brown hair. Common as muck. *What about the cowlick though, eh?* But it was more than that. It was just as much his gentle demeanour. The inner quiet he seemed to have. And the small pursing of the lips that dimpled his cheek. Thank god he'd only smiled. If he'd grinned or laughed…the shock of seeing his brother, as a grown man before his eyes, had nearly undone him.

He must have sat there for some time, steeped in morose thoughts, when a plume of dust rose where the driveway pinched into the side of the hill. He blinked and realised his fingers were stiff from strangling the handle of his mug. Fang bolted out from the shed and escorted the Ford Falcon up the drive with sawing barks until it crunched to a stop on the gravel. The barks were replaced with joyful jumping when a woman emerged with some plastic containers.

Jodie and Penelope had been best mates through school, but where his sister had left at the first opportunity, Jodie had stayed on. He watched her approach, her Blundstones making a soothing sound in the loose stones, wondering, as he often did, why she wasn't married. She was pleasant-enough looking, if a bit plump for a woman on the land, but girls who cooked like her were never begrudged a little extra in the haunch. He stood up as she approached, eyeing the containers.

"What the flipping heck have you done to yourself this time? Doris told Mum you'd busted your hand feeding the cows. One of 'em go for ya, huh?"

"Yeah. I was a bit late with the feed." He automatically went to take the containers off her, but she swung them away from him.

"There's a plastic bag on the front seat you could grab." She kicked open the screen door and disappeared into the house.

Inside, she'd put on a jug and was stowing items in the fridge and freezer. "There's three serves of Mum's beef casserole here. You could have pasta with it to make it go further." She looked at his hand. "Could you manage that?"

He nodded.

"And here's a carrot cake I made this morning."

He leaned against the bench, tried to fold his arms, gave up, and took a seat at the table while she fussed around making them tea. Before joining him, she poured the leftover hot water in the sink with a squirt of detergent, threw in his breakfast things, and wiped down the counter.

"So," she said, sipping her brew and scrutinising him over the top of her cup. "What's this new doctor like, then?"

He threw back his head and laughed. "Geez. You could've at least pretended to be concerned about me before screwing me for information."

"I've just loaded your fridge with food you ungrateful pig. Now, spill."

"Way too pretty to be your type."

"Who says I don't like pretty?"

"Oh, I know the kind of guys you like. Those gorillas that play pool at the Black Rock on Friday nights…vocabularies limited to about thirty words. Yeah. Wild, animalistic sex—"

She slapped his arm hard and pointed her index finger at him. "Next time I'll bang your bad hand." She was squashing a smile though. He'd sometimes take her for a night out at the pub where she could meet up with some friends while he did the same. There was a guy from out Gibson way who came in sometimes and he had the hots for her. On those nights she would come and hang around the pool table with David and place her dollar on the side cushion with the others in an effort to avoid him. He couldn't say he blamed her. The type of guy she could run rings around in her sleep.

They talked a while longer, catching up on gossip. After finishing the washing-up, Jodie took a turn around the house. "Okay," she said, returning to the kitchen with an armful of clothes and dumping them on the table. "I'll run these through when I get home. Then I can help you with the evening feed." She sorted through the items and picked up a scabby pair of jocks. "I was going to say I'd do any repairs—" She waggled her finger through a ragged hole. "—but these aren't even good enough for a duster."

"Strewth, Jodie. Leave a man some dignity will you."

"You're the one wearing them. I hope you have something better for when you're on the pick-up. What a turn-on that'd be seeing you strip down to these little numbers."

He went to swipe them off her, but she was too quick. "Any girls I invite to horizontal folk dance are more interested in what's *in* my jocks. How do you think they got shredded in the first place?" He gave her a leery grin, whipping his hand up in time to catch the smelly bundle before it hit his face.

"Did you see David?" Jodie's mother called from the kitchen when she heard the outside door to the laundry open.

"Yeah, he'll live. Being a one-armed bandit is going to drive him mad, but he'll be fine."

Her mother muttered something she couldn't hear and then, "He should come over for dinner tomorrow night."

Jodie dropped David's smalls into a bucket with some soap flakes. She added some other socks and dusters that had accumulated in the basket and then headed into the kitchen to put a kettle on.

"So, what does he have to say about the new doctor?" Nellie didn't look up from the trousers she was repatching.

"Not much. Men never notice anything. Reckons he did a good job on his hand though."

"Well, that's good. I'm surprised you haven't seen him round the hospital yet."

"He's been there a few times. Evenings though. I'll get to meet him when I change to night shift." She took the steaming kettle out to the laundry.

According to Sarah he was roll-your-tongue-out gorgeous. A bit on the quiet side. And definitely not arrogant, which was unusual enough. Not that she was interested in that way, but some decent eye candy was always appreciated.

She rolled and squeezed the soggy bundles in the bucket, noting with satisfaction the darkening colour of the water. It was weird imagining David stooping to such domestic tasks, but he seemed quite content to "do" for himself. Of course, he always trotted out the old chestnut about there being no single girls around. She was well sick of hearing that. There was a nurse or two she worked with who had made eyes at David at the pub on a Friday night to no effect. Or none they'd been game to share with her, at any rate. She had been relieved, but she still wondered. She was sure one day he'd snap out of it and realise he only had so much time to have a family. It would make all the difference if he had a wife and children to focus on instead of whatever else he mulled over all those nights alone. A narky voice inside her head chipped in that having a family hadn't interfered with Manse Stevens' thought train. She paused in her ringing out of a sock. But that was different. He was…older.

She pushed the thought from her mind as she refilled the bucket with clean water. Still, that scene in the cemetery the other day had unsettled her. It had been a rare moment, seeing him vulnerable and serious when he always went out of his way to clown and be the blokiest bloke in the room. It was a never-ending source of frustration for her that even when they were alone it was impossible to get him to be real; his suit of armour was now part of his skin after all these years. Seeing him so still with his forehead pressed to the cold stone made her realise you just never get over these things. It was always there under the surface, a mere thought away. It seemed almost unreal to her given it all happened before she was even born, and maybe even more so, given she herself had never lost any close family, but of course she knew all about it from her mother. She certainly never raised it with David.

As promised, Jodie returned around half four with his jocks and socks neatly rolled and folded.

"Cutting it fine. I nearly left without you."

"Don't get your pee in a froth. There's heaps of time."

He smiled as her black bun bounced towards his bedroom. She'd picked that saying up from him.

They loaded up the hay and David took off down the driveway. Jodie refused to have Fang crawling all over her, so he was standing on the hay, his barking only interrupted when a bump in the road made him lose his balance.

Jodie turned to look behind them and then back at David. "Where are you going?"

"Down to the end paddock. I like to go along by the creek."

"But there's all those gates. Round past the dam—"

"I always go this way."

He felt her frowning at him, but he kept his eyes squarely on the road ahead. After a moment she sighed and turned her face to the road. "Well, if I'd known that I would've come a bit earlier, wouldn't I."

The light was already murky when they pulled up and the surrounding hills had progressed from purple to black. Tendrils of chill wove through the air and a more solid cold rose from the ground. Fang plonked himself down at a distance, eyes darting everywhere, ready for anything. The last of the cows were ambling up as they got out of the cab.

"Here." He threw her a pair of gardening gloves.

"What are you going to wear?"

"I'm just dragging them off the tray. You can break them up. There's a Stanley knife in the glove box."

They worked in silence, focusing on the task at hand. After scattering the last biscuits, she came and stood with him to watch them eat.

"They're looking pretty good."

"Yeah. Got enough hay to last till the end of winter. As long as we get some rain by the end of the month to bring in the new feed, I'll be right."

On the drive back they both stared ahead into the beam of the headlights. David flicked on the reverse lights for her to close the gates. In the last stretch up to the house Jodie started rubbing her arms. "I don't know how you stand it in your house without a fire."

"I've got a bar heater in the main room. Don't use it much though. I'm tough as." He flashed a grin at her in the dark.

"Yeah, bet you impressed that new doctor, nearly ready to faint at his feet."

"He said it was incredible, me dealing with all that pain. Said apart from being a handsome bastard, I must have great pain genes. Said I should donate to a sperm bank in Sydney, you know, do my bit for evolution."

Jodie burst out laughing. "Crikey, you're full of it. If anyone told you to go to a sperm bank it would be because you're a prize bloody wanker."

"Well, yeah, that too." They were now standing in front of her car, her open door between them. He gave her a slow punch in the arm. "You're a gem for helping me out. You don't have to keep coming over, though, I'll be okay."

"You always help Dad out when he needs it. You should come over for dinner tomorrow night. They'd both be glad to see you."

While Fang was occupied in seeing Jodie off in the time-honoured fashion, David had time to duck to the shed and see about his dog's dinner, his mouth already watering at the thought of Mrs Wilson's beef casserole.

Chapter Three

The morning had been a write-off farting around with his computer and sniping at hapless technical support staff saying he *had* done what they told him to do, and it *still* wasn't working. If only he knew someone with teenagers. Perhaps he should ring up the local high school. He tilted his head to rest on the back of his chair and closed his eyes. When he opened them again, the ugly piles of paper were still covering his desk; in fact, he was sure they were breeding. As soul-destroying as it was, it had all been a ploy to put off attacking his accounts. In that, it had succeeded a treat.

It was a funny thing. He'd been pretty organised as a uni student. Got his papers in on time; got reasonable marks. He couldn't afford to muck around like the other guys who were still living at home with their meals taken care of. But papers on educational theory and critical analysis of texts were things he enjoyed. He'd been good at those. But doing his accounts was maths; maths that always seemed to result in negative unhappy answers.

He went out to the living room and squatted in front of his CD rack. Ran his finger down the titles. *Nup. Nup. Nup. Yeah, you. Jimmeh.* With the Chisel at full bore, he might just be able to get through the afternoon.

Yelling about cheap wine and poor shaving habits, he sorted his dockets into piles and employed whatever bulldog clips he could scrabble up. When he had neat stacks of bank statements, invoices, and saleyard accounts, and he'd flattened out all his crumpled receipts, he went through them again, putting them in date order. By the time he went out to give the CD another go, he was tallying everything up in his cashbook package on the PC, hen-pecking with his left index finger. His accountant would be loving him. A pity his bank manager wasn't so easily impressed.

Every year he told himself just one more year. Then he'd sell up, go back to teaching. But he couldn't bring himself to do it. There was always a reason to hold off. And now he was like a loser at the gaming table who was sure his next throw would be the winner that made it all good.

Everyone had expected him to take things over when his dad died. Everyone except his mum. She'd had enough by then. *You don't have to do this*, she'd said. *I'll just tidy things up for sale, get those young steers ready for market.*

If we sell now, we'll lose money, he'd said. After the first few years, she'd stopped saying anything. She knew it wasn't about the farm. She was the only one who understood. Penelope, on the other hand, was happy to get stuck into him. He was denying her her inheritance, wasn't he. And all for what?

"Flame Trees" was one of his favourites. He could belt that out till the cows came home. He printed off a couple of reports for Doug and attached them to the piles of papers before sliding them into some plastic RM Williams bags. He had inwardly winced when he'd seen what he had feared confirmed in black and white…or red, to be more correct. He could already see the look on Doug's face. Last year he'd made the sour joke that David's biggest asset would soon be his tax losses. He slapped out some rhythm on the two fat bags as if they were bongo drums, determined to focus on the positive. He hated paperwork and he was now done with the worst of it for another year. Thinking he heard a noise, he paused in his singing and cocked his head. *Nup.* He was feeling good, even if it had taken him all afternoon and the results were worse than last year.

The desk was now clear except for some stray paper clips and a dirty coffee cup making a long shadow. Any paperwork for the current year had been stacked in an in-tray on the shelf where their sad story could be postponed a bit longer…allowing time for that break in the weather they were all so desperate for. With a bag in each arm, singing "My Baby" at the top of his lungs, he danced jauntily out to the living room. Spinning around on *Yeah*, he nearly dropped his bags and fell over. On the other side of the screen door Dr Martin James raised his hand in tentative greeting.

"Sorry, I called out, but…"

David dumped his paperwork on the lounge and mimed that he needed to turn the music off.

"Sorry about that. Yeah, come in." He glanced at him sheepishly. "There's only one way to play Cold Chisel."

They stood facing each other for a moment. David waved his good hand as if to conjure up some conversation. "So, you…please don't tell me you drove out all this way to check up on me."

"No, I had a house call a bit further out. Thought I may as well drop by and see how you were doing. Gratis, of course," he added quickly.

David grinned. "Thought you might catch me in the act of breaking the rules, eh?" He gestured for the doctor to take a seat. "I don't know about you, but I think it's beer o'clock." He stopped and turned on his way to the kitchen. "Or are you still on duty?"

The doctor shook his head and smiled. "No, I'm done for the day, but I would like to check your hand while I'm here. I'll have a light beer if you've got any."

When he returned with two bottles hanging between the fingers of his left hand, he found his guest standing behind the lounge with his back to him inspecting his bookshelves. He turned when he heard the bottles land on the coffee table.

"You've got some great books here. Have you read them all?"

David passed him a bottle as he sat in the chair adjacent to the lounge. "Yeah, there's not much to do out here in the evenings."

The doctor raised his eyebrows and turned back to the shelves. "So, you've actually read *Ulysses*? Isn't it just a load of gibberish?"

"Nah, mate." He couldn't help a small superior smile lifting the corner of his lips. "You're thinking of *Finnegan's Wake*. That's a pile of tosh." He took a long swig of beer and smacked his lips. "So, what do you read, doctor, when you're not...doctoring?"

"Oh, crime thrillers, mostly. Relaxation material." He stretched his arms out to rest on his knees, his bottle clasped in both hands. "You can call me Martin, you know." He took a sip of beer and looked around the room. "Ah, the piano."

David glanced over to the corner of the room, the upright covered in a dust cloth, some photos on the top. He said nothing as Martin walked over to have a closer look, but he thought, *nosy bugger, aren't you.* He watched as Martin stooped to get a better look. The largest was his parents' wedding photo and next to it a formal shot of his sister making her debut. After a crystal bunch of flowers there was another wedding photo, this time his sister's. They'd been there so long he didn't even see them any more. His mouth twisted at the irony.

"None of you."

David shrugged. And none anywhere else either. "There's a few mirrors in the house." He applied his bottle to his lips.

Martin also took another mouthful of beer and set his bottle on the table. He sat and clasped his hands in front of him between his knees. The way he was watching him was beginning to make David feel uncomfortable. "Is she younger or older than you?"

"Younger. Lives on the Central Coast. Mum moved out there with her when Dad died." Before Martin could open his mouth again, he said, "And you? Where's your family?"

"I have an older brother living in Sydney, married. My father died while I was at uni; Mum hasn't remarried. I'm the black sheep of the family."

"Black sheep? You're a bloody doctor." He waggled his empty bottle in front of him. "Here, I'll get us another."

"I'd better look at your hand before I start on a second," he called out to the kitchen. "Where's your bathroom? I'll just wash my hands."

"Geez, mate, you're on light."

When they'd resumed their positions, David held out his hand over the corner of the coffee table. He held his beer in his other hand as Martin unwound the bandage. What had been fine in Dr Jacobs' surgery now felt a bit awkward in his own living room. Holding on to his beer made it feel more acceptable, somehow. The hand that firmly held his was soft and cool and he tried not to react as Martin fingered the area around the wound.

"Seems to be healing well." He ran the back of a nail lightly over the stitches. "We can probably take those out in another week." He reached for his bag.

As Martin re-dressed his hand, David again found himself examining that face. The man had barely any stubble. Looked like the type who couldn't grow a beard even if he wanted to. His neck looked like that of a girl.

"You hardly seem old enough to be a doctor."

He didn't look up. "They lower the age limit for country doctors."

David pulled at his hand. "You're shitting me."

"Of course. How old do you think I am?"

"Mid-twenties."

Martin's cheek dimpled. "Thirty-two."

"I'm thirty-six. Some days I look forty-six. Working on a farm's good like that."

"And not married."

David grimaced. "No single women, mate. Haven't you noticed? Those that finish high school without getting pregnant don't hang around long. Chasing the money in the bigger towns." He recalled his comments to Jodie. "So, what's your excuse? Plenty of girls where you come from. You'd have the nurses throwing themselves at you."

"Oh yeah. All the time." His eyes twinkled.

"But nothing stuck."

Martin shrugged. "High pressure environment. All pretty casual."

"Hmm. I thought you'd have to be pretty strict about that, being a doctor an' all."

Those dark eyes looked straight at him. It was like coming under the teacher's gaze when you'd just flicked a spit bomb. "I'm exceedingly careful."

They talked more about restaurants and pubs they knew in common, David enjoying recalling his student days. He'd been about to offer another beer when he noticed the fading light.

"Shit, I'm sorry. Gotta get and feed the cattle before it gets dark. Takes a bit longer with this." He held up his hand.

"I'll help you. I've got nothing on."

Martin insisted on loading the ute on his own, so David dragged bales up to the ute while Martin flicked each one onto his knee and from there onto the tray. David smirked to himself. He was going to dirty those nice trousers. But then, they did need some roughing up. And he didn't seem to mind when Fang jumped in the cab with them.

David glanced to the side. Fang was using Martin's thigh to stand taller and get a better view of the road. *He'll be getting a pretty good lungful of dog breath,* David thought, as his dog panted and moved around with every bump of the road.

"You'll be just about right to go to the pub tonight smelling of hay and dog. Blend right in."

Martin laughed.

It was as if someone had poked David in the chest. He focused on the road ahead and said nothing more until they got to the first gate.

Martin spent a lot of the trip looking around and asking questions. How far did his land go? How long had his family owned it? Did he always have to hand feed?

David reeled out the facts like a travel guide, happy to appease his curiosity for all things rural. Happy also to focus on practical things. Real things.

After they'd set out the feed David walked among the animals, counting them up. When he'd done the rounds, Martin was back at the ute brushing straw off his jumper and putting his jacket back on.

"Cold, eh. Not like Sydney."

"Yeah."

David watched as he dug in his pocket and pulled out an inhaler that he held up to his mouth.

"You all right?"

"Yep. It's this cold air. Pollen in the hay doesn't help either."

On the trip back, listening to his stomach gurgle, he made a tough decision.

"So, what do you normally eat in the evenings, all on your own?"

"I don't mind cooking. Maybe some pasta, sometimes a curry or a stir fry. Sometimes cheese on toast. How about you?"

"Oh, you know. Steak and veg. Sausage and veg. Chops and veg. When I'm feeling wild and adventurous, I'll do a spag bol. But I was gunna say, Jodie's mum has seen me right with some beef casserole. One serve'll stretch to two if you give me a hand with putting some pasta on."

"If you're sure you don't mind? I'd enjoy the company." Martin turned to look at him. "I have a request though."

David gave him a wary glance as he pulled on the handbrake.

"I'd love you to pull the dust cloth off that piano."

David held up his bandaged hand with an incredulous look.

"Oh, come on. Just a tinkle. It'll be fun."

Leaving Martin with the pasta preparation, David went into the living room and headed towards the piano stool. Lifting its cushioned lid released a waft of oiled wood and musty paper. His more serious collection was in a box somewhere, but there might be something here to keep them amused. He became absorbed in memories flicking through the dog-eared pages, smiling at the pencilled notes of his teacher, when Martin poked his head round the corner.

"Do you have any oil?"

After dinner David propped back the piano lid and ran a cloth over the yellowing keys. "It's going to be well out of tune."

"Perfect for a one-armed man and a flautist."

Martin placed the stool from the laundry at the treble end of the piano and sat down. Flexed his fingers and played a C major scale with his right, then his left. David raised his eyebrows as he threw the duster aside. "Not bad for a flautist."

Martin smiled. "At least pianos are straightforward." He dandled his two end fingers around E and played the clichéd opening of "Für Elise."

"Okay, okay." David mimed cracking his fingers in front of him. "You must know this then." He started rolling through the universal C-A-F-G bass known to all young piano players.

After a few bum notes on the first round Martin picked up the lilt of the treble accompaniment. David started varying his style as far as he could with one hand while watching Martin's long fingers on the keys.

"Playing a flute would've been good practise for a surgeon? Something like 'Flight of the Bumblebee' to keep you nimble?"

Martin grinned. "I guess. Mum thought it would be good for my asthma. Must be why I gave up and stayed a GP."

Getting bored with his restricted tune David started horsing around and invading Martin's playing space. After some pushing and shoving, David suddenly realised "Heart and Soul" had morphed into something else. He let out a guffaw of recognition.

"Ohh…come *on*."

"You come on. You're not keeping your end up." Martin started bobbing his head from left to right in an exaggerated fashion. "Always look on the bright si-ide of life…"

They plodded their way through some rounds of Pachelbel's "Canon" and some other simple duets David dug out of the pile, but Martin's fingers always managed to find their way home to Eric Idle. At one of these departure points, David jabbed him with his elbow.

"Oof. Just joking. Crucifixion."

By the time David saw his guest off, his head was buzzing and his good hand was aching. He'd had a laugh, it was true, but it was more than that. He'd felt free to make observations and jokes he could never have made at the pub. His old uni self had been prodded awake. He smiled to himself as he put away the dishes on the draining board. Not a bad return on half a casserole.

Chapter Four

The dirt road's corrugations shone under his high beams like some kind of moonscape. The Wilsons' property was deeper than his and their driveway took you right up to the base of the hills. The same hills that killed off his sun early on winter afternoons. It was a road he knew well. Right from the time he was a kid with his parents dragging them over for a barbeque to much later, helping Dan out on the property when he broke his leg one time. Dan had paid him back threefold when his dad died.

Heart attacks don't know anything about good timing. He'd just bought his first house. A cramped little semi in Maroubra. He'd had to renovate it straight away to make it habitable for tenants, something he'd intended to do over the years as he could afford it. The extra time meant he'd been able to stay on till the end of term for his students though. Poor beggars, having to change teachers with their HSC around the corner. He could still remember the kids in that class. They'd genuinely loved Shakespeare, and anything else he'd thrown at them for that matter, and there'd been brilliant class discussions; he liked to think it was due to his teaching, but they'd been a special group. They'd all be in their early twenties now. He shook his head in disbelief.

By the time he'd come home, his mother had made her arrangements.

"I can't stay, love. There's just too many hard memories. It's been awful, these last four years, just me and your dad knocking around the place. But he was never going to sell." She'd given him a long searching look, her eyes round and sad. "You will sell it, won't you?"

He had nodded. Said he would. And at the time, he'd meant it.

A bunch of rabbits scattered as he revved up the last slope and parked in the glare of the outside light. It was an imposing house. More of a homestead, really. He'd always loved how it glowered down the hill overlooking everything. From their verandah, which circled the entire house, you could see the red roofs of Bruce dotted on the horizon.

At the front door he stood on his heels and levered his boots off. Stumping sounds echoing down the wooden floor of the hallway told him the man of the house was on his way.

Dan reached out and shepherded him in. "Come in, son, come in. Get yourself in out of the cold. Y'all right?" Still holding his upper arm in one hand, he shook David's bandaged wrist with the other. The older man's weathered face looked up at him, genuinely wanting an answer.

"Yeah, I'm good. Just a scratch."

"Hmph. That's not what we heard. If you need anything, just get on the blower."

The warm smoke of roast lamb hit him before they even got to the kitchen. Mrs Wilson bustled over to him with a tea towel still hanging over her wrist. He'd never been able to make the transition to calling her Nellie, and certainly not Aunty Nellie like Penelope always had. She was a giant from his childhood and using her first name would just be a damned cheek. She grabbed both his upper arms and squeezed.

"Let me see that hand of yours, Davey. Doris said you looked like death warmed up when she saw you in Woolies."

He caught Jodie giving him a quick grin as she turned vegetables over in a tray of sizzling fat.

"Have you heard from your mother?"

"Yeah. Penelope's daughter has the croup."

"Oh dear. Poor little pet."

When Mrs Wilson's focus returned to dinner he walked back to where Dan was flicking through some letters on a side table.

"See ya got some rabbits."

Dan's mouth turned down. "Yesss. And that reminds me. I've had young Biddy in the lock-up these last few nights with your Fang a-courting. When he can't get to her, he barks at those bloody rodents all night."

"Shit. Sorry. I'll tie him up the next few nights. You shoulda said."

Jodie came over and put a coldie in his hand, clinking her bottle to his. The beers were kept primarily for his visits as Dan didn't drink. It was prime spoiling time when he came over and he was always like a python digesting a goat when he crawled into bed afterwards.

"Come on, sit down all of you. This is ready now." Mrs Wilson heaped his plate up with everything and poured gravy over it all, just as he liked.

"I had a visitor for tea last night."

"Socialising two nights in a row, you big floozy?"

"Mmm." He nodded at Jodie, his mouth full of lamb. He turned to Mrs Wilson and grinned. "Your beef casserole was a big hit with the new doctor."

"Doris went to see him to get her corns pared when she was in the other day. Said he's lovely. Very young though."

"Yeah, they lower the age limit for country doctors." He shovelled in more roast potato, his cheeks pulling tight when he caught her expression. "He's over thirty, actually."

Jodie's eyes were gleaming with curiosity. "So, tell us all about him. What did you talk about?"

"Can't really remember. Blokey stuff." He laughed. "We spent most of the evening mucking around on the piano."

"I didn't think you played any more?"

"Don't really. I was atrocious, even with one hand as an excuse, but he didn't seem to mind. We bumbled through some of the usual rounds and easy duets. Nothing wrong with his sight-reading. We'll be on the stage in no time."

"I always said it was a shame when you gave up your lessons," said Mrs Wilson.

After the girls had dealt with the washing-up, they brought out tea and fruit cake in front of the fire. He and Dan had been discussing their mutual fencing project and then what they'd have to do if no rain came. It was the same old ground as usual, but he always found it comforting to chew it over with Dan. From there they naturally moved on to bitching about Ethan, the bank manager.

"Makes a lot of money for doing not much," said Dan. "I swear they've sent out a trainee cuz no one else'd wanted to come out this way."

David laughed under his breath. Ethan was his own age at the very least.

Mrs Wilson had made herself comfortable in her favourite chair, ready to steer the conversation back to more interesting topics. "Did you tell David about what happened Sunday night?" Before Dan could open his mouth, Mrs Wilson continued. "Those Barry boys have been at it again. Racing down that stretch of road before you get to the Mill Bridge. Dan was coming home late from town and saw two sets of headlights coming at him. He flashed them and pulled over. They didn't even slow down! Gave him a right scare. I've been telling him to ring Charlie—"

"There's no bloody good doin' that, woman. He knows about it. He's given 'em a talking-to. Nothing else he can do unless he catches them in the act."

"Or they kill someone. He's the laziest policeman we've ever had. Wayne would've camped out till he caught them at it. Then he would have thrashed some sense into them."

The fire was making David drowsy and the next thing he knew, Jodie was jabbing him in the ribs. "Mum says you should stay. I'll make up Pete's bed for you."

"No, I'm good. I should get going."

Taking it easy as he drove over the bumpy road so as not to disturb the pile of plastic containers in the passenger seat, he started humming. When he realised what the tune was, he smiled. Tomorrow he would hunt up his old sheet music and get his "Moonlight Sonata" back into gear.

Chapter Five

The Fullerton Road didn't have a lot of curves. The land on either side was flat paddock leading to low hills. A westerly had arrived in the night and the wind now rose off the flats on its hind legs to buffet the ute, squealing through invisible gaps. Beyond the loose gravel at the edge of the road, fireweed and tussock grass cowered in its wake. It was the same everywhere he looked: grey and yellow desiccation. The winter rains had not come and now the winds of August had arrived to suck out of the ground whatever possibility of life was left. If there was anything he hated, it was wind. It leached, it thieved, it destroyed. The rattle of it under the galvanised iron roof was directly related to his father's bad temper and the hammering repetition of the word *overdraft* over dinner every night. Now it was déjà vu time once again with the solutions no further evolved than before.

Not being able to keep as busy these last few weeks, he'd been hyperaware of the slow passing of time, how it was grinding him and the farm down. Usually, he worked himself to exhaustion to avoid thinking too much. This last fortnight had given him far too much time to mull over his problems without giving him any more hope of solution than if he hadn't thought about them at all. Whoever said worry was like paying interest on trouble due was dead right. The trouble would come with or without added surcharges.

He flexed the fingers of his right hand back and forth on the steering wheel, played an imaginary scale, felt the pull of the scar. It had been strange that afternoon, watching Martin take out the stitches with the same fingers that had hesitated over his keyboard.

"Looks like you sew better than you play."

"Lucky for you." He spoke as he wrote in David's file. "You should get back to it. Would be good for the muscles in your hand."

He would think about it later. Now he had his hand back, he was itching to do everything at once, to stop all this *thinking*. And the first thing he needed to do was load that pile of new fence posts and deliver them round to Dan's.

It was almost a week before he had the energy to root around for his old music books. Four days of morning-till-dark fencing wasn't for wimps and Dan set a cracking pace. The last few evenings he'd fallen asleep on the couch watching mindless crap on the telly. The only pity of his restored hand was the meal supply had dried up and he was back on his own resources. Beans on toast and scrambled eggs had barely topped up his fuel tank, but tonight's steak had turned him into a new man.

He slid the door open on the wardrobe in the spare bedroom and sat on the bed that used to be his. He nearly closed it again on the imposing columns of stacked boxes. There was shit in there he hadn't looked at in years. Another day of back-breaking work would be preferable to going through those dust pits. He sighed, determined to go as long as it took to find what he wanted. With his luck they'd be on the bottom of the last stack.

Some boxes were transferred straight to the back room ready for the dump. Spare parts for things he didn't own or recognise any more, old moth-eaten jumpers his mother must have packed away. Then there were the stacks of old magazines and comics; he resisted the temptation to browse and put them aside for later. The second box in the next stack contained books: old uni textbooks and notes; some treasured novels he'd thought he'd lost. His enthusiasm rose with these finds and he was now pulling things out at the speed of a child under a Christmas tree. Then he stopped. The last item was covered in the face of a horse with soulful brown eyes. He had difficulty levering it out as it was the exact shape of the bottom of the box. Loose envelopes of photos slipped out. He turned the pages, but there were no surprises. He knew exactly what was in there. The album had been started when Penelope was born. There were stacks more, full of her baby pictures, far more than had ever been taken of him, but these were all his mother had left behind. He looked at the scrawny kid gingerly holding his little sister. The wary look on his face said it all, really. It was a wonder he'd been trusted to even do that. He flicked through more pages. Penelope's successive birthday cakes and parties, him sometimes hovering in the background like a ghost. Near the back, there were a few pictures of him behind the wheel of his first car. What a pimply scarecrow he'd been. He'd had to wait years to fill out the height he'd shot up to. He replaced the loose envelopes inside the cover and closed it softly. He couldn't look in those right now.

His energy had fizzled, and he still hadn't found the sheet music. He lifted the flap of the box at the bottom of the middle stack. More papers. He peeped under a few and found exercise books and under them—bingo. Thank god for that. Without investigating further, he reefed the box out and hauled it to the living room to be looked at another night. When he returned, he stacked the comics and magazines to take to the office. He hesitated over the album, about to throw it back in the wardrobe, then changed his mind and placed it on top. That was enough clearing out for one year.

Friday night was pub night. It took a while to rev up with many grabbing a quick dinner at home after they fed their animals, but by 8:00 p.m. the place would be humming. He'd missed a few now, what with his hand and work, so Jodie was champing at the bit. There was a darts comp on she said, so there would be a good crowd.

"Your mate from Gibbo'll be there." He grinned into the phone as he searched in a drawer for a pen. "If he hasn't pined away, that is."

"Oh, shut up, would you. You're like a broken record sometimes. It'll be easier to lose him in a big crowd. I was thinking, though, why don't you ask your doctor friend? Be good to get him mixing with the locals."

He was about to say, he's not *my* doctor friend, when Jodie launched into a story about one of her girlfriends who'd just had a second baby. At the end of the call she said, "Don't forget to give your mate a ring. We can pick him up on the way."

Martin had sounded pleased to be invited and David realised with a pang that sitting in his surgery all day would hardly be conducive to making friends. But would he want to socialise with people he'd seen half naked complaining about their aches and pains? Apart from his own misdemeanour, he imagined most of Martin's day was spent seeing kids and old ladies, neither of whom would be at the pub. But you never knew.

Jodie had volunteered to drive. "You can't have Mr Spiffy getting into that stink box."

"What makes you think he's 'Mr Spiffy'?"

"I've been hearing things."

When Martin slid across the back seat and said hello to Jodie in the rearview mirror, David turned to shake his hand through the gap in the seats. "I hope you didn't wash those trousers, mate. They'd be just about cured up for tonight by now."

"Ignore him, Martin. David thinks eau de cow manure is what real men are wearing this season. I bet he told you he's single cos there's no available women around."

"It's true! Jodie's the last eligible specimen under thirty-five left in Bruce only because she's fussy as. She expects me to fend off the poor moping bastards that try it on with her every week. One day I'm just gonna let one through to the keeper."

Jodie rolled her eyes at the rearview mirror. "Looks like it might be up to our gallant doctor to protect me from harm tonight."

Martin laughed. "But I was planning on hiding behind *you*!"

David turned and grinned over his shoulder. "Good luck with *that*, you tall drink of water."

★

The Black Rock was a long, low building with multiple rooms all leading into each other. When they arrived, it was already surround by utes, trucks, and six-cylinder cars and Jodie had to let the boys out first before squeezing into one of the few tight parks remaining.

"Mul*kaaah!*" Someone grabbed David by the arm as soon as they walked in. Jodie and Martin left him yarning to weave their way to the bar. She noted with amusement that being a tall stranger, Martin didn't have to wait long for a barmaid's attention. They found a single high table with one bar stool.

She hoisted herself up on the chair. "That's better. Can almost look you in the eye now. How tall *are* you?"

"Only an inch or so taller than David."

"You look much taller. You're attracting a few second looks at the hospital, I can tell you."

"Y'reckon?" He laughed shyly into his glass.

"Oh, don't give me that."

"It'll wear off once they get used to me."

They chatted more about life at the hospital, and she gave him a rundown of some of the main personalities there, who to get to know, who to avoid. In a gap in the conversation, she noticed him looking over her shoulder with amusement.

"Seems like our friend is pretty popular." She swivelled on her stool to look in the direction of Martin's nod where David was now, beer in hand, holding court to three other men, gesturing to his right hand and staggering around in a small circle like he was dying.

"It's all a big act, y'know."

"Yeah, I can see that. You wouldn't think he was the same guy talking to me about Joyce and Beethoven the other day. I'm curious to know what's under all that."

"Joyce and Beethoven?" She let out a huffy breath. "You're doing better than me then." She took a mouthful of wine and placed her glass back on the table. She slid it to and fro as she measured her thoughts.

She looked at Martin with a crease forming between her eyes. "I'm not sure if anyone knows. Sometimes I think I have a handle on him when he lets a few comments drop or you see him when he thinks you're not looking, but then he sprays you with blokey smoke and mirrors and you lose sight of what you thought you saw, wondering if it was ever there in the first place. I reckon my mum knows him better than anyone, but she doesn't let on much."

"Yeah? Why's that do you think?"

"Oh, she's very protective of him."

She felt Martin watching her from his great height, meditatively rubbing his glass against his lower lip.

She looked over at David again and then down at her hands in her lap, seeing him bowed in front of the grave, reliving the pang of worry that had jabbed her heart. She turned her attention back to Martin.

"Look," she said quietly, "just so you know…in case it becomes…relevant. David lost his little brother when he was young."

"Ohhh." A ripple of pain crossed Martin's face as he waited for her to say more.

"Yeahhh, well. It was before I was born, so I can't tell you much because no one talks about it. His sister, who is the same age as me, was the replacement child. I don't think the family ever recovered. His mum put all her energy into Penelope and David was kind of left aside after that. That's where my mum stepped in, I think. She's like that, with injured animals and the like." She gave Martin a crooked smile. "I've kind of been thinking about it a bit lately. We had a funeral some months back and I could see…well…I think it pricked at some un-healed wounds for him, if that doesn't sound too dramatic."

Martin nodded without comment. He picked the bottle up from the floor and wiggled it in her direction with a questioning look.

"I shouldn't, but go on." She held her glass out. Her eyes shot up from her glass to his face. "On pain of death, you can't—"

"Shhh. It's fine." He smiled. "I appreciate you telling me. It helps."

"I worry about him living on his own. If only he'd marry and start a family. Have some love and purpose in his life."

"The farm seems to provide him with his purpose."

Another huffy sigh. "Oh sure. And his every excuse too."

"But you love him anyway?"

"Huh. Yeah, of course. We all do. He's the life of the party. Cheers." She lifted her glass to clink with his. "Speaking of." She lifted her glass to her right as David ambled up with a big grin on his face.

"What's goin' on here, then, eh? Whatever bull twizzle she's been planting in your head, I can set you straight with later, mate."

"Oh, I think she's got a pretty square view of things." Martin's eyes crinkled at her as he took a mouthful of wine.

She gave David a look of exaggerated innocence.

"Hmph." He looked at their drinks and his expression changed. "Geez, woman, you warned him about the house wine, didn't ya? It's an ingredient of Kiwi boot polish."

Martin stooped down to the floor and came up to place the bottle back on the table.

"Oh." David met her smug expression. "Gone top grade, eh?"

"Martin said if I could only have one, it'd better be a good one."

"Right. I'll just get a top-up and we'll head in for some pool. You play?"

Martin looked at her. "Well, I can, but…"

"Come on," she said. "It's entertaining watching David make a dill of himself."

They stationed themselves near the furthest of the three tables and placed their coins in a line on the cushion. Jingling some shrapnel in his hand, David wandered over to the jukebox. She leaned into Martin and murmured, "Here we go. I hope you like 1980s Australian rock. He lives in a bit of a time warp."

David returned to where they stood in the corner singing "You Got Nothing I Want" into his pool cue.

"Happy now?"

"I will be when I boot Johnno off the table." He looked round to where a bearded man with a rat's tail was leaning towards them lining up a shot. A cheer went up as he sunk the last ball. David tapped his cue on his boot and winked at her. "I'm on."

As the game progressed, she filled Martin in on who was who.

"So is your beau from Gibson here?"

She gave him a dirty look. "No. Haven't seen him." David had just sunk a difficult shot and was wiggling his arse in time to "Hoochie Gucci Fiorucci Mama" in celebration. Martin chuckled. "So, he can play a bit."

"Oh yeah. He's pretty good. Played a lot when he was at uni."

"Next victim, please." David beckoned to Martin with his hand.

"Go on, Jodie, you first."

While she went through the motions of putting up a fight, she noted a few people coming up at various times to speak to Martin. Some seemed to be just polite nods and handshakes, others were longer exchanges. As the next load of balls clattered down onto the shelf, she came over to give Martin her cue. A stocky red-headed man she vaguely recognised was talking earnestly at him over his beer.

"…we was looking everywhere for her. You wouldn't believe it, but I found the silly kid standing on an ants' nest on our driveway…sweeping away with her toy broom. Ants crawlin' all over her and the more she was screaming the more she was trying to sweep 'em away." He grimaced and shook his head. "Tanya said it was only thanks to that cream you gave her…"

Martin gave her a private little smile as he accepted the cue. He swallowed the last of his wine and excused himself.

He took his time chalking up while David horsed around with Johnno in front of the jukebox. He leaned over and sank one off the break. She sat up a little straighter in her stool and darted a glance at David. He wasn't even watching. When the third ball plopped in, she let out a whoop that finally got his attention. When he came over to stand at the corner of the table with his hands on his hips, grinning in shock, Martin sank the rest. Johnno did a little war dance and Martin bowed to the applause. As the cue was pulled out of David's hand, he was still shaking his head and smiling.

"Not bad for a flautist, mate." He went over and shook Martin's hand.

"Flaunt it, Mulka? He wiped the bloody floor with y'son!"

"So, who brought Fast Eddie along, eh? Looks like you'll have to line up and pay for a few games like the rest of us, Mulka."

After the next game Martin tried to step down but the crowd that had gathered wouldn't allow it. David came back to sit with her, and it was all she could do not to laugh out loud.

"Shit, eh." He shrugged.

She wiggled her eyebrows at him and turned back to the game, giving Martin a thumbs-up.

"I think you kinda like him."

"He's nice. A good talker. Unlike some around here."

David folded his arms. "Well, he can find his own way here next time. Bloody stage hogger."

She snorted and he turned and gave her a look of mock surprise. "What?"

★

David swigged his beer and watched Martin walking around the table sizing up his shots. No wonder he played well. Those long arms of his reached the whole way over the table. Still. It had caught him by surprise. He smirked to himself and shook his head. *Black sheep my arse. Dark horse, more bloody like.*

After Martin beat David in a rematch, he retired with them into the corner of an adjoining room.

Despite the losses, David was feeling merry and entertained them both with stories of his old students.

"It sounds like you miss it," Martin said, wiping his eyes.

The wattage of David's smile dropped. "Yeah, I do sometimes."

"You could teach and still keep the farm, couldn't you?"

Jodie's gaze shifted back and forth between them, but she said nothing.

"Nah. Better to do one job well than two poorly."

"You prefer farming?"

David gave him a crooked smile. "Keeps me fit. Besides, I think all this technological change going on has left me behind. I can't even get my internet sorted out." He stood up and dug his hand into his pocket. "Time for some more music."

On the drive home Martin asked him about his computer problems. When they dropped him off, it was with a promise that he'd come out on Sunday and see if he could help sort them out.

As Jodie prepared to take off, David propped his elbow up on the window ledge, his fingers digging into his hair. He stared out at the road lost in thought.

He glanced back at her as she gripped the wheel at ten and two and checked her rearview mirror. She turned to meet his eye.

"Well, I *like* him."

That wasn't it. He covered his eyes with his palm pretending he was tired. It had hit him tonight when Martin had started quizzing him on why he couldn't have a foot in both camps. It was like asking some women why they couldn't have just one piece of chocolate. He was either fully in…or not. Besides, it was impossible to be a part-time farmer—a proper one, that is. Unless you were earning enormous amounts in your chambers or your surgery to finance the indulgence, usually for the tax losses, playing pretend farming cost a bomb.

Up until now he'd been kidding himself saying he had a choice. Once this or that was done or achieved, he could go. But the ongoing drought had changed that. Even though he knew there would always be something, it was only now that the reality of feeling trapped had come upon him. He was sinking into red ink that would take a lifetime to pay off.

He slumped further down into his seat. A wave of exhaustion washed up behind these grim thoughts like a sucking tide. Being out with his mates, the adrenaline from all the attention winding him up like a frenetic toy, usually tired him out; but at the same time, it fired him up and distracted him from his worries, as well as distracting his mates from *their* worries. He leaned into the cold glass of the window and wiped his palm down the length of his face, coming back up to rest over his eyes again. It was all fun and games until you had to face going home.

★

Jodie kept her hands steady on the wheel, occasionally stealing a glance to her left. David was in one of his moods. The only thing that surprised her was the sharpness of the transition. He'd been like a bouncing bean all evening and she wondered if it had somehow been for the benefit of the new company and he'd now run out of puff. She was used to David going into blokey overdrive in the pub. She put it down to letting off some steam after a week of hard work, but there was more to it than that. And tonight had been a bit OTT, even for David. It was some tribal thing in him. Something about proving he belonged, that he really was like all the other men. But he wasn't. She knew it. And even though they'd only referred to it obliquely in conversation, she knew her mother knew it, too, which was sort of what she'd been saying to Martin earlier in the evening. It wasn't that he wasn't a good farmer. He approached the land like he approached everything else. With knowledge and dedication and sheer grunt work. No one worked harder, with the exception of her dad. *Well, that's where David gets it from, eh.* She turned to look at his dark head pressed to the glass and smiled.

They rumbled over the Mill Bridge, the reflectors lighting up like possum eyes in a tree. Her lips stayed tilted up at the edges as she stared out into the cold rectangle of light ahead, watching the lines zip under the car. She'd made some excuse to pop round during the school holidays, knowing David was on a break from uni. It had been late afternoon and she'd been surprised to find him in front of the telly. He'd made her sit down next to him on the couch. It'd been some movie with Elizabeth Taylor and Richard Burton in it. He'd started explaining it to her. Said it was Shakespeare. She was only in sixth class at the time, so it may as well have been in Russian. They'd watched it to the end. She'd been fascinated. She still remembered getting angry when Liz had let Richard place his foot on her hand…not her idea of a positive ending, but David had assured her there was a volume of information in Liz's eye that said all was not as it appeared. Of course she'd known that David was studying to be a teacher. Of course she could see he had a lot of books; he was always to be found reading one. But to hear him talk like that, getting all wound up about something so…*foreign*…to see how his eyes lit up…the only time she'd seen her father's face look anything like that was when he'd performed a Caesar on a dead cow and triumphantly extracted a living calf.

She glanced at him again, her mouth settling into a firmer line. Her recollection of that afternoon didn't end there. She was sitting on the couch drinking in everything David was telling her when suddenly the back door had slammed, and they heard the heavy tread of his father in the kitchen. She had a distinct memory of David stopping midsentence and his face undergoing a solar eclipse. She'd always been a bit scared of Mr Mulkerin. There was something about his abrupt manner that she couldn't quite put her finger on. He'd tramped into the room and had a go at David for wasting his bloody time, uni was no good for him, it was making him soft, blah blah blah. He made no allowance for Jodie's presence at all, saying awful things to David in front of her. She muttered an unheard excuse and goodbye and ran out to her bike, her face burning and the sound of Mr Mulkerin's griping in her ears.

The car juddered over David's cattle grid. He raised his head and seemed surprised at his surroundings. He rubbed his eyes and looked out into the glare of his own outside light as if it might mean something. "Sorry, mate," he mumbled. "Just tired. Thanks for driving." He gave her thigh a clumsy squeeze and stumbled out of the car.

Her gaze followed the sluggish swing of his shoulders as he climbed his front steps. He disappeared inside and an internal light came on. She stared at the front door for a long moment and then abruptly shook her head. She turned the car and as she gathered speed down the drive, she felt rather than saw the outside light extinguish behind her.

Chapter Six

There'd been a frost overnight, and there were still patches of white in the shadows as he walked around the western side of the house. The air was damp but sharp enough that he could feel it enter his lungs. A magpie hopped out from the shadows, its champagne warble bubbling out of its throat. He dropped the mattock, axe, and pick next to the tree stump behind the chook shed. He'd had a vague plan of going into the hardware store to get some things he needed and knock off some jobs festering on his to-do list. But he'd woken up feeling heavy and stagnant, in no mood to face other humans.

That old dullness in the gut sat like a smooth river stone. It had started building at the end of their night at the pub. Like a house with damp in the basement, the feeling rose into his chest and spread into his limbs, sapping his energy. He hadn't wanted breakfast but made himself eat it anyway. Then a strong cup of coffee. That was when he decided town was a bad idea. He had to fight this feeling from making it into his head. His solution was hard labour. As if it were possible to sweat it out.

He flexed his fingers around the pick handle, getting a feel for it in his palms as he slid his right hand experimentally up and down the smooth wood—felt the ridge of his scar catch. For a quarter of an hour, he lifted and swung and hacked at the ground around the roots of the stump. When he paused to lean on the handle, he became aware of the hard rise and fall of his chest and the path of chill damp between his shoulder blades. He inspected the chunks of clay set to rock, the matted grass roots, and the beetles panicking in the light. The tree's roots were more extensive than he thought. He used the axe to break them up, then applied the mattock to lifting out the chunks of burrowing wood. At the last he applied his shoulder to the mutilated mass until he heard the rewarding snap and crackle of it releasing its hold. An hour later he had a pile of rough firewood and a dip of loose earth.

All the while he'd been working, the chooks had been grazing at a distance, jerking and cocking their heads in his direction. As soon as he turned his back, they'd be into that disturbed ground like a woman rooting in a handbag.

He already wanted more coffee. Jumper leads for his flat battery. He brought his mug outside and sat on a crate beside the chook shed. His Rhode Island Reds were well into it. He sipped his drink while he watched them scratch and tear and defend their patches. He'd always found watching chickens soothing, even when he was a kid. Something about their moaning and clucking settled him; maybe it was what people meant when they spoke of meditating. Focusing on small things to block out the noise, the internal distress.

The late morning sun settled on his back and warmed his shirt. It reflected off the chickens, making their feathers shine like oiled cedar. He had spent a lot of time in those early years out here. When his mother was looking for him, which wasn't often, she'd come here first. Then Penelope had come along and the atmosphere in the house had become too close for him to bear. The smell of wee and talcum powder and mashed food, and of course the endless crying. He'd take himself off on long walks around the property, mainly up in the hills, sometimes with a book. Sometimes over to the Wilsons'. He'd found himself eating scones at Mrs Wilson's table more afternoons than he could recall.

He thought about those long walks now as he squinted at the distant hills. Perhaps he should head off and tire himself out. But he was afraid of the aloneness in his head. The thoughts that would fill his mind. That was when the nauseous fog spread and he allowed all the worst thoughts in—invited them, even—as if he had to make it as bad as it could possibly be before he could get any relief.

He flicked the dregs of his coffee away and went into the chook yard. Despite the lack of rain, there were still a few oranges on the trees and he thought, not for the first time, that he should juice them. He took his hat off and ducked into the dark interior of the shed. The foetid odour of chicken manure and sour-sweet straw clouded around his face like something solid. He peered into each box and placed any eggs he found in his hat. The last box had a chicken in it. She tolerated his hand as it burrowed under her downy pantaloons, the egg he found there blood-warm and smooth.

Back in the oppressive coolness of the house he made up his mind.

An hour later he was nearing the top of the low range directly behind the house. The walk had been jarring; the ground had no give. It was all exposed, packed earth, protruding rocks and determined tufts of grass. Once he broke through the tree line, he sensed a feeling of tightness, like the bush was holding itself in and withdrawing to its core until it was released by either fire or water. The shade harboured a deep cold, sharpening the fragrance of eucalypt and earth. Smells that brought back his younger self.

He laboured up the slope, picking his way over rocks and fallen branches, focusing on putting one foot in front of another and the sound of his harsh breathing. On the ridgeline he stood for a moment with his hands on his hips, recovering. Around to the right through the tree tops he could see the expanse of red that was the Wilsons' roof. He turned his back on it and headed eastward. The sun was now high in the sky and filtering through the canopy. In a place where some trees had fallen down, creating a view, he walked partly down the slope. The flatness of the Bruce valley was what made it so attractive as farmland—and so lacking in aesthetic interest.

On the hazy blue horizon beyond Bruce's red roofs, he could just make out irregular shapes that were the outskirts of Gibson. Immediately below was his own acreage. Pale-yellow handkerchiefs of land, some dotted with cattle, most empty. The house there, to the right, a chunky redoubt with the shed and a few small outbuildings. The fine thread of track sent out like a feeler to the Fullerton Road. But what he needed to look at required more weaving and manoeuvring through the trees; what he couldn't face close up could be viewed with objectivity from afar.

The broken edges appeared as he climbed up onto a large clump of rock. Walking out onto the ledge gave him a fuller view. It was as he suspected. The dam was all but dried up. All that wind last week would have accelerated the process, sucking the clay dry. A few cows stood in the middle around a small mirror. He really needed a closer look. From this distance it looked like he might have a few more weeks; closer inspection might tell a sadder story.

He took one last look, craning his neck to peer through the trees. He pressed his eyes shut for a moment, then looked around for a rock to sit on. It seemed he had two trains of thought to choose from, and both were bad. The memories associated with the dam were all tumbling into his mind and all he could replace them with were his worries about the farm. After what happened, he had only been there once during his father's time. He was with him looking for a cow that was close to calving and he had been unable to voice his fear or objections, knowing full well that his father had the right to more. His father had said nothing. It was almost like he was punishing him. Probably was. Probably? Definitely. His breathing had gone shallow, and he was feeling queasy and dizzy. The horror of fainting or being sick in front of his father was all that kept him focussed on putting one foot in front of the other up the bank. Then the expanse of water, the hoof-squelched clay around the edges, his mind going mad wondering *was it there? Or there?* A rivulet of sweat ran from his temple down his cheek.

David screwed his eyes shut and buried his face in his palm. After a while he pinched the bridge of his nose and opened his eyes. He was sweating now. More than his activity justified. So long ago and yet the memories were as sharp as they'd ever been. A crow let off a loud cawing close by. He looked up, glad of the distraction. His heart still pounded as he watched the bird trip up the trunk of a dead tree, higher and higher. Every now and then it paused to focus a beady eye on him. It switched from branch to branch, so lightly, so easily. Then it fluttered to a different tree altogether. David let out a disgusted sigh. "So bloody easy for you, isn't it."

★

After all his evening chores were done, he settled down in front of the telly with some cheese on toast. Usually, he'd get comfortable with a book, but he'd just been too mentally tired of late to face the effort. He resisted the temptation of getting into some beer. He flicked between his two options: the ABC and the local station. After receiving a nourishing dose of global conflict and the latest economic problems he tried to settle to some bland soap repeats, but instead he'd ended up staring at the flickering shadows on the ceiling with a growing sense of anxiety and frustration. He hadn't gone to the dam on the trip home. He'd convinced himself he'd do that tomorrow. Now the prospect was gnawing at his innards.

After he'd checked out the fencing on the other side of the ridgeline, he'd come down, all the while running calculations through his head of which cattle he would sell first and how much more hay he would need. Even if it were to rain next week, new feed wouldn't appear overnight. And one shower of rain would do nothing in any case. A storm would just wash away the topsoil. What was needed was two or three days of sustained showers. He decided to sell ten head at the next sale.

He levered himself off the couch and went into the office. Took a seat at his desk and swung himself around belligerently in his chair. Couldn't even get on the net and do some mindless surfing. God, he could have done with losing himself in some porn sites. Just some mindless relief. Then he saw the comics and mags he'd dumped on the shelves after his cleanup.

It was only a matter of ten or fifteen minutes before his thirteen-year-old self had reasserted itself and he was masturbating over the bulging tits of Wonder Woman. He sat for a while afterwards, his head thrown back on the chair staring at the ceiling, just breathing.

He rubbed his eyes with the heels of his hands and looked at the squares of window over his desk. Only his own desperate face stared out of the wet blackness. The television droned in the background, killing the silence. The tension release he'd felt had already evaporated. He was a boil ready to burst. He put the comics back on the shelf, trying not to meet the eyes of the horse. But they were there watching him, like one of those portraits in some B grade horror film. He reached for the album.

It creaked open, the bubbles in the aged plastic sheets crackling as he flattened it on the desk in front of him. There were the two envelopes. One was branded Kodak and contained one complete roll of film. The other was a more ancient envelope and contained a mix of photos of differing sizes and colour tints. It had been years since he'd looked at them, but he knew them all. He worked his way through the mixed ones first. Slowly flipping them over, peeling them apart. His breathing quickened and his chest was tight. Some baby photos, some of the whole family; several of them together with their identical cheeky grins, one dark head, one light. His shadow self. Back when he'd felt whole.

The Kodak envelope was the worst as it was the most recent, the last taken. His hands trembled as he flicked one after another behind the pack. Those eyes. That smile. He stuffed them back in the packet, unable to catch his breath. He stood and leaned one arm against the wall. He bowed his head and gasped as the old feelings of hatred and self-loathing invaded his head like a rampaging crowd, reliving it all, scene by ugly scene, the most damning playing over and over, himself the evil star.

As the pain sharpened to knife points in his chest, he began hitting his forehead against the wall. Desperate for the physical pain to blind the other, he continued faster and harder until he sank to the floor in a half swoon.

Chapter Seven

The pounding in his head had become so bad it was beginning to echo outside his head. He shielded his eyes with a hand and attempted to open them. He jerked up into a sitting position. "Hang on," he yelled. He whipped his jeans off the floor and dragged them on.

Out in the hall he came face-to-face with Martin peering through the screen door. His eyes were cheeky with amusement.

"I thought farmers rose early."

He squinted at his watch. Strewth. It was after lunch. "Christ, mate. I forgot."

Martin's smile faded as he stepped inside. He raised his hand to David's head as if to bless him. David shied away.

"Sorry…but that looks nasty. What have you done to yourself now?"

David raised his palm to his forehead, felt the egg, and winced. "Oh, you know. A drunken piss in the middle of the night. Ended up kissing the floor." He said this over his shoulder as he led the way to the kitchen.

"Hope you didn't use your tongue."

He snickered. "No, nothing French about it. Pure Glaswegian."

He felt Martin watching him from his seat at the table as he padded around in his bare feet, putting on a jug, pulling mugs out of the cupboard. When he grabbed the jar of coffee, Martin cleared his throat.

"Tea'll be fine for me, thanks."

David looked at the jar in his hand as if seeing it for the first time and laughed. "Ah."

"You've been to the good cafes in Sydney. How could you go back to that stuff?"

"Poor uni student, mate. Besides. I'm tough as."

Seated with his drink, David held the hot mug up to his cheek and closed his eyes.

"You must have really tied one on last night."

He opened his eyes and rubbed his stubble. "Yeah. Sorry. I normally make a bit more effort when I have company. Even get fully dressed."

"I've seen worse."

David swirled the last of his coffee around and frowned. It was bad enough having this clean-cut image stare back at him from the other side of the table, but that he had to be so cool and polite as well.

"You said you were at St Vincent's. Must have seen some horrible things."

"Yes."

David looked at the dark eyes in front of him and was unable to read them. He felt the urge to push. Get a reaction. "Like what?"

Martin frowned as he hunched over his mug and watched his long fingers wrap around it as if protecting it. "It doesn't really make for pleasant dinner time conversation."

"Go on. I'm curious."

"You want the gory details?" His voice rose. "You really want to hear about the half-severed limbs from car accidents? The stabbings? The drug overdoses?" A strange glimmer in Martin's eyes told him he had picked the wrong fight.

"Sorry, I shouldn't have—"

Martin sat up. Pushed his mug away from him. There was a long pause while he held David's nervous stare. "Let me tell you something. In case you hear it from someone else."

His insides shrank. "You don't have—"

"You become numb to a lot of it after a while. You have to, to survive. But the long shifts and adrenaline wear you down over a long period. Mistakes are made."

David wanted to speak. To stop him. *You don't owe me anything*, he wanted to say. But the intensity in Martin's eyes stopped him.

"It was two in the morning, in that party period before Christmas, when a young woman brought her four-year-old son in. Carried him. Screaming with stomach pain. Shrieked if anyone tried to touch him." Martin paused, looked down at his hands. The memory etched in the lines around his mouth. His chest rose and fell a few times before he continued. "The mother, who'd been drinking, said he'd woken in the night with it. Had given him Panadol. He was triaged at level two with abdominal pain. It was a bad night and a full fifteen minutes before I could get back to him. By then he was only whimpering, and his stomach was distended. There was blood on the bed."

David screwed his eyes shut.

"It was the woman's boyfriend." He spoke quietly, his white fingers were clutched tight in front of him, his head bowed over them. "He had major fistulas. We did everything we could, but he died, David. He died."

He took a ragged breath and continued. "Even after the damning police reports, the mother made a claim for negligence against the hospital. There was publicity and an inquiry which dragged on for months. It was bad enough having to constantly relive the suffering of that little boy but being publicly blamed for his death tipped me over the edge. I still have nightmares where I'm trying to stop his screaming, stop his enormous pain."

Martin wiped his eyes, focusing on the table in front of him. "Plenty of people have pain in their lives. It's how we deal with it that makes the difference." His mouth creased into a bitter smile. "I didn't deal with it very well. I wanted to quit, but they wouldn't let me. Sent me off for counselling. Six months later they assessed me as good to go and sent me here."

He looked up and met David's eye. "I'm sorry," he whispered. "I shouldn't—I hardly know you."

David frowned and shook his head, as if to shrug it off. His chair grated on the floor. He jabbed his thumb over his shoulder. Cleared his throat. "Gotta go…shower. Make yourself some more tea."

In the bathroom he pulled a foil sleeve out of a box. Stared at the white tablets sitting in his palm. Panadol. Jesus. He threw them back with some water. He stood there for some time, head bowed with hands braced on either side of the basin, a parade of horrible images running behind his eyes. Eventually he raised his chin and peered at his image in the mirror. He fingered the purple lump on his head—took in the red eyes, the matted hair and stubble. *You handsome bastard.*

He turned up the water as hot as he could stand and just stood there, wishing this time more than any other that he could afford more than five minutes. When he came out to the kitchen carrying his socks and boots, Martin was gone. Looking to see if his car was still there, he found him on the top step of the verandah. He went to push the screen door open but hesitated. Martin had his head bowed forward; his arms curved around something. Fang had weaselled in between his legs and was resting his jaw on Martin's knee.

The dog's eyes met his and he scrambled out of Martin's grasp, ready for action. David crouched down and rubbed the dog's face with both hands. "You faithless mutt," he said softly. "The minute my back's turned…" He sat down next to Martin.

"He's got a lovely temperament."

"A bit too lovely sometimes."

Martin watched them in silence.

David's pat had turned into an ad hoc inspection. "Been a few ticks around lately," he said, rubbing his thumbs in Fang's ears. He nudged him away and started pulling on his socks.

"I shouldn't have dumped on you like that. It was selfish. It just…it just links up with too many other thoughts and one thing leads to another and suddenly I'm there again."

"Forget it. You've been through a lot. I know how that feels."

"Do you?"

David held his eye with his lips set in a tight line.

Martin hesitated for a moment. "These things can follow you around."

They stood up together and David turned to face him.

"They can." He held out his hand and Martin took it. "But it won't be making up any conversation of mine."

Martin smiled and put his hands on his hips. "So, I'd better see about this computer of yours."

"Nah, there's no rush. Well, not for me. You gotta be somewhere?"

Martin shook his head.

David felt a tremor of relief. He might be able to face up to the nagging task at hand if he had Martin as a distraction.

"You don't wanna be stuck in the house at this time of day. I've gotta take a look at some things round the place. Wouldn't mind the company."

They walked over to the fence on the western boundary, the brittle grass crunching under their boots. There was no need to check the new fence, but it extended the walk and helped him prepare.

"Must be hard work, this." Martin patted the top of a post still yellow and red like a split peach in its raw newness and looked down the long line of posts to the main road.

"Bloody oath it is. And Dan made me work for it. He might look like an old guy, but you wouldn't want to underestimate him. Strong as, and can go all day without lunch. He's always been like that. There'll be something not right in my world when the day comes that I can outdo him in something on the farm."

"Jodie says he thinks of you as his second son."

"Well, son number one if it comes to getting me to help him out. Pete's a mining engineer. Works out at Tom Price earning a motza."

"Does Jodie want to inherit the place, do you think?"

They walked back north following the fence line. David jammed his hands in his pockets keeping his eyes on the ground in front of him. "I really don't know the answer to that. She's a fully qualified nurse, but she only does casual fill-in jobs. Why she'd want to stick around here when she's got a good career is beyond me."

Martin laughed.

"What's so funny?"

"She said the exact same thing about you."

David frowned and kicked at a tussock of grass. "Bloody different for me, isn't it."

"Explain it to me, David. Why is it you can't sell the farm and start a new life?"

"Because I have to…see it through. It's personal," he mumbled. "Can't explain it."

"Oka-ay then." Martin strode along in silence for a while although David could hear the ticking of his thoughts like a bomb about to go off.

"So. It sounds like you enjoyed teaching, but were you any good at it?"

David's head snapped up from watching the ground. "Yeah." He squared his shoulders back and shot a look at Martin. "Yeah, I *was. Actually.*"

Martin raised his eyebrows in response. "Measured by…?" The hint of a smile played around his mouth, annoying the crap out of David. That same mocking expression he'd seen on the day they'd met.

"Mea-sured by"—he drew out the syllables sarcastically—"the fact that my students enjoyed my classes. Once I got them going, they'd talk their heads off giving me their opinions on everything from what a knob Hamlet was to pulling apart the meaning of every word in *The Red Wheelbarrow*. They'd hang around after the bell and some would even follow me back to the staff room. Hung around like bad smells, some of them."

"Maybe they just got you talking to avoid doing any work. That's a common tactic. Or maybe they just thought you were a nice guy. The girls probably all had crushes on you."

David snorted a laugh. "I can't say about that. I think the marks did the final talking. I saw some amazing improvements in essay writing with some kids. Kids that were normally more interested in kicking a football around or chasing boys when they came to me. Most of the kids in my class had never seen a live play before. Each year I got to take them to something, and you should've seen some of their faces afterwards. It was like a whole world had opened up to them."

David was gazing ahead, recalling how good he'd always felt, counting them onto the bus to go home, hearing their excited chatter, seeing their lit-up faces. It was only when he turned to see Martin watching him that he realised he probably had a dopey look on his own face. He frowned and reached up to adjust his hat. "Yeah, well. It's not that hard. The need to hear and tell stories is in everyone. You just need to tap into it."

"Mmm." Martin nodded and smiled. "Simple really."

David paused and reached down to rip out some fireweed. He threw it away, shaking his head. "Doesn't matter how dry it is…"

"So instead of improving the potential of the next generation and giving yourself a thrill a minute you stay here alone banging your head against a wall—or the floor, sorry—watching the sand drop through the hourglass."

David glared at Martin. "Opinionated bastard, aren't you."

Martin smiled and shrugged. "Just calling it as I see it. The only thing I don't get is *why*. Unlike Jodie. It's obvious why she stays here."

David squinted up at him from under the rim of his hat.

"She stays here for you, you turkey."

David let out a gust of laughter. "That's the biggest load of—"

Martin raised his hands. "I'm not saying any more on the subject."

"Oh, come on. There's a ten-year age gap for Pete's sake. I'm an old guy to her. She's been like my little sister since she was born. More than Penelope ever was. And Dan and Mrs Wilson have been like parents to me. They still look out for me." David paused and smiled. "I guess Jodie is just becoming more like them. Thinks it's her job to worry about me, too, now. She's certainly getting her mother's bossy ways." He grinned and shook his head. He was teaching people Jodie's age and older when he was first out of uni. He'd never thought of his female students that way; there was too much else going on. But seriously: *How to ruin your teaching career in one easy lesson* by Humbert Humbert. Jodie was shoved together somewhere in his mind with those same sexless girls by virtue of her age…actually, no. Jodie was even further removed. That would just be too much like…like *incest*. He shuddered.

They walked on without speaking for a while, the only sounds their footsteps and the ambient burr of cicadas. David started to swerve them to the right as they approached the foot of the hills. Some branches in a nearby tree bounced around followed by a kookaburra letting off.

Martin shaded his eye and looked up through the trees. "Must be good hiking up there?"

"Yeah. Used to go up a lot when I was a kid. Is that what you do to keep in shape?"

"Walking's good. Some weights at the gym. Can't do anything too drastic with the asthma."

They'd passed the back of the house and had just finished legging it through a three-wire fence. David was still keeping his eyes on the ground. They were getting closer now and it felt like he was pushing through an invisible barrier, like trying to push the wrong ends of a magnet together. He was weak and pathetic dragging Martin out here, but he couldn't have done it otherwise.

"Here are some of your cows. And what's this up ahead? A dam?"

"Yeah," he said, looking in the opposite direction. "This is where the bad news starts."

"Water low?"

"Yeah. I need to see how low." Without meaning to, he started telling Martin about his plans for managing. Gabbling away like a condemned man being led to the scaffold, trying to stretch out time. They stood at the bottom edge of the dam looking towards where the rest of the cattle were, loitering under some trees. He was aware of droning on, sounding like those older guys at the saleyards, but he couldn't stop himself.

"And what if there's still no rain?"

"I have to rely on the kindness of my bank manager to keep me liquid, so to speak. We've had a few bad years in a row now."

Martin shook his head, speaking more to himself than David. "I don't know how you do it." He turned around and looked up the slope. "So, let's have a look."

David watched him lever himself up the steep bank until only his head and torso was visible as he walked around the edge, his towheaded cowlick blowing back in the breeze. David swallowed. He closed his eyes, his hand involuntarily covering them. So grown up now. Could've been. He could go now, drag him away—

"You coming?"

The pool of water in the middle was surrounded by jagged white lumps of clay dried to a tumble of building blocks where the cows had stumped through what had been mud. In his mind's eye it was always full and opaque, with a clay beach that resembled the Somme. Martin came up beside him. "How long will that last?"

"Coupla weeks."

"What about the creek?"

"Bone dry, mate."

"Then what?"

"I'll have to get tanks into the paddocks. Fire truck comes and fills them. Had to do it once before. Bloody expensive."

At another time Martin's questions may have irritated him, prodding him on a subject that he was sick to death of thinking about, but at this moment he was grateful. He hated being here and Martin's presence was stopping him from being sucked down. But then he caught him off guard.

"Was there more water when you were kids? Must've been great swimming here."

David turned on him. "Dams are *not* for swimming in!"

The acoustics of the water made his shouting reverberate. He stared at the opposite bank, his throat constricting. Had shocked himself. He could feel Martin watching him open-mouthed, waiting.

"They're—they're for livestock," he added lamely, breathing in through his nose, looking down at his boots. "Can't—can't muddy the water."

Martin's eyes narrowed. "What about yabbying? Isn't that what kids do on farms?"

"No. We didn't have yabbies either." He turned his back on Martin. "We can head back now." He half walked, half slid down the bank, aware that Martin was not behind him. Well, that was okay. He could catch up when he was good and ready.

Chapter Eight

By the time he'd got Martin set up in the office, the light was fading and he needed to feed the cattle. He'd left him there with a pile of manuals and CDs and his provider's phone number. As an afterthought, he'd come back in and stuck on some Bach cello suites. "To keep you calm," he'd called out.

Birds were gathering in the camphor laurel near the shed, their squawking and chirruping signalling the day's mash-up. He loaded the bales onto the ute tray, grateful for his ability to do it himself. Methodical repetitive tasks helped keep his head clear. His mood had lifted with the setting of the sun. It had been a long afternoon, but it would've been even longer and far more painful if Martin hadn't shown up. He couldn't have gone to the dam for starters. He felt a pang of shame for the way he'd snapped at him though. Martin had caught him on the raw with those innocent questions. He could have explained further maybe, but right there and then at the scene of the—no. All he could do was what he did. Run away.

He put the ute in gear. The prospect of Martin going home gave him an empty sensation in his gut. This was the grimmest part of his day, when the dark literally crept in, where he had to stare down the long empty evening alone to endure yet again the burning and gnawing inside his head. Sometimes he thought Prometheus had a better deal. Another night like last night was not a healthy prospect. He'd get two steaks out of the freezer when he got back.

He guided the ute without really seeing the road, stopping to open the gates like an automaton. His thoughts had returned to what he imagined a casualty ward would be like in crisis. Nurses and doctors hurrying around, in control of themselves, confident in their knowledge and experience. He imagined Martin, taller than the others, asking questions, issuing instructions, exuding an air of authority and quiet confidence. That cool exterior that made you feel like you were with a safe pair of hands. He'd been shaken by his revelation that morning. He'd never known a doctor or any other kind of emergency worker personally. He didn't count Jodie. She only joked about bedpans and rectal thermometers. And Charlie's biggest job of the week would be filling out paperwork. But here was someone who'd seen life teetering on the edge many times, had seen it topple over as he grabbed for it in midair. Whose inner core had been pierced by it.

He flung the biscuits of hay in the air and counted his stock. Next week he'd get Johnno's dad out here to pick up the ten for the midweek sale. He leaned against the back of the ute with his arms folded, enjoying the sound of the animals chewing. There were more than a few cows ready to drop their calves. He'd have to keep a close eye on them over the next while, especially that young heifer whose first time it was. Maybe he'd bring her up to the holding pen near the house…

Returning from the shed after feeding Fang, he quickened his step. He was looking forward to an evening of conversation. Jodie was right. Martin was a good talker. He might even flip the piano lid and impress him with the results of his recent practising. He tripped lightly up the front steps and levered his boots off. Delighted to hear Australian Crawl at full blast decrying carelessness.

He padded up to the doorway of the office where his grin fell from his face. Martin was leaning forward on the desk, its surface covered in shiny photos. He seemed to be examining a few in particular. The computer screen was covered in the blurry print of a scanned newspaper page. Martin looked up at the window and their eyes met in the reflection. Holding David's frozen stare, he slowly gathered up the pictures and slotted them back in the envelope. With a deliberate action, he folded the flap over and put it back with the other one on the side of the desk.

"Amazing what you can find on the net these days," he said, his voice low. "You'd left the photos here on the desk. I thought that was deliberate. I figured it was your way of telling me what you couldn't say. Then I got onto Trove and found this small column in the local paper about the time I guessed…" He waited to see if David wanted to look at what he'd found. When he made no move, Martin leaned down to the mouse and closed the page, replacing the soft grey newsprint with Google's sharp-edged primary colours. He looked back at David, uncertain. "I'm sorry if I got that wrong."

When David made no move, he stood and turned to face him, gesturing to the chair. David's mouth opened, but he was unable to speak. His mind was a confused jumble of angry accusations and defensive responses to questions that weren't being asked. They stood there, eyes locked, Martin's hand on the back of the chair, waiting, his expression one of calm sadness. It was the sadness that quelled his anger. The deep-set eyes that seemed to look at him differently, as if they recognised him, knew what was in his heart.

Something rose in his throat, but it wasn't intelligible. He coughed and tried again, gesturing towards the screen. "You—you got it to work." He sounded like a frog in a drainpipe.

Martin smiled, relief relaxing his features. "Yes. Give it a go."

He sat in his chair and clicked through a few pages. It was slow, but they came up. "Bloody genius," he murmured.

"More patience and persistence."

"You're a miracle worker. You'll stay for dinner? Nothing fancy. I'll sort you out for this properly another time."

He closed the computer down and pushed in the chair. Kept his hands gripped on the chair, willing them to stop shaking, as he waited for the screen to collapse into a white dot, the muted pop of its last breath. Waited longer.

"Tim died when I was nine."

His breath quickened. He couldn't remember the last time he'd spoken his brother's name aloud. A sacred word that now lived as a thought only.

The room was quiet, so he went on, almost talking to himself. "Everything shut down after that. I tiptoed around the house, scared stiff I'd make a noise, attract attention to myself. Then Penelope came along, and everything changed again. I didn't exist after that. I was a reminder of the time that was gone."

He looked up, still leaning heavily on the back of the chair. He turned to face Martin. His eyes were large and watchful, but there was something else. His silence seemed to absorb the pain and take it in without the need for comment or question. Slowly Martin nodded. "I know how that feels."

It was only then David realised he'd been holding his breath. He let out a soft sigh, his voice quiet. Waved a limp hand toward the door.

"Must be time for some food. You'll stay for tea?"

"Sure. If you want the company?"

"Yes," he said quietly. "That little trip today took it out of me. It's your turn to provide the light relief tonight." He smiled weakly.

He took a deep breath and followed Martin out, feeling a mixture of ache and relief as he turned his back on the room. But as Martin headed down the hall to the kitchen a twinge of uncertainty made him turn back and pull the office door closed.

David had provisioned them with a beer each and they sat quietly on the front step, leaning on their knees with the glare of the loungeroom light behind them. There was so little ambient sound they could hear the distant hum of their steaks defrosting in the microwave. Every now and then one of them would lift a bottle to his lips.

"Where's Fang?" Martin asked at one point, breaking a long silence.

"Ol' Romeo is in the cage in the shed. I have fielded a formal complaint from my neighbours, the Capulets." David turned and smiled briefly at him before taking another swig of his beer and continuing to stare down the dark driveway.

"Oh, I see." Martin laughed softly.

David swung his empty bottle to and fro between his knees. "I'm feeling a bit more myself now, thanks."

"I haven't done anything."

"Yes, you have. I needed the company. There's something about you…this will sound weird, but…"

Martin rested his chin on his shoulder, half angled towards David, and waited.

"You…it's like…you remind me of him."

"A seven-year-old? Thanks."

"No. No." David shook his head as if to clear it. "I mean…your company. It's like it would have been if he'd… something calming, filling a gap…this isn't coming out how I mean it. Forget it." He smacked the empty bottle with his hand.

"No, please. Go on."

"I'm not sure I can. I can't get my head around it."

"Then don't. Just take what is and don't complicate it."

David glanced sideways at him and drew a ragged breath. "You must think I'm a fruit loop. Is that why you stayed? To make sure I didn't do anything stupid?"

Martin laughed lightly as he angled his bottle above his head and finished off his drink. "No, that isn't why I'm here. If it makes you feel any better, I don't normally run around telling everyone what I told you today either. I'm not sure what triggered it exactly. It just vomited out. Felt right to tell you, somehow."

David gave him an appraising look and then turned to face the drive again. He brought up a hand to cup his chin. After a while he said, "Is it my imagination or are those crickets getting louder? Or maybe it's my stomach growling. Must be time to get those steaks on. Whaddya say?"

★

Martin opened and shut cupboards, doing a full inventory. David stood back, amused, while Martin added jars and cans and packets to two growing piles. In answer to his quirked eyebrow, Martin pointed at one pile. "Useless-crap-that-no-longer-resembles-food," and the other, "Keep."

"Right." David gathered up the first pile and nudged the lid off his bin. They made a satisfying crash in the bottom.

Martin gave him a rueful smile. "Not much of a cook, are you."

"No reason to be. It's not like the Queen gets out here very often." He handed Martin a bottle of beer and clinked it with his own.

"We should put on something interesting one night and get Jodie over here."

"Careful, mate. She might start fancying you."

Martin laughed.

David paused in raising his bottle to his lips. "Seriously. Do you like her? I could—"

"Please no, David. She's a great girl—fantastic company. But not my type."

David nodded and swigged at his beer as he watched him unfurl packets and sniff their contents. "So, what is your type?"

"Oh, um, not so into voluptuous. Leaner. But there's got to be something happening between the ears to really get me."

"Mmm. Some nights I reckon I could settle for double X chromosomes of any description. S'why I don't tend to drink much at the Black Rock. Could wake up next to anything."

"And I thought it was you chaperoning Jodie."

To David's amazement, Martin was able to salvage the ingredients to make an excellent peppercorn sauce. He also learned that night how to microwave potatoes before roasting them in the oven so that they were fluffy on the inside and crisp on the outside.

He wiped up his gravy with his last wedge of potato and sat back to savour his last mouthful. "That was just...stunning."

Martin leaned on the table with his chin in his hand, his dimples digging into his cheeks. "Just your usual meat and veg."

"Not *my* usual meat and veg, mate. Tell y'what. I'll clear out the spare room and you can move in for the rest of your time here."

"There's an offer too good to refuse."

"Yeah, I'm full of 'em. Actually, I tell you what. Would you like to come out to the sales next Wednesday? Might be a bit interesting for you. See what goes on around the place."

"I'll have to see what appointments I have."

While David scrubbed pans, Martin did a round of the kitchen, cleaning surfaces and brushing up crumbs, both of them singing along to The Radiators, which David had put on for the purpose.

"One more for the road?" David held up a beer. He'd been drinking two to Martin's one and was feeling pretty happy.

"No, I've had enough. Probably should think about making a move."

"You can't leave till I've serenaded you. I've been practising an' all." David led him into the living room where he turned off the stereo and gestured for him to take a seat in the armchair. He went over to the piano and swept out his imaginary tails.

"You sure you're sober enough to drive that thing?"

"Sure." He stretched out his interlocked fingers towards the photos. "I'm only just loosening up. I'm going to start with a little Mozart…"

Martin threw back his head and groaned. "Oh, come on. If this is your idea of seduction I can tell you now 'Twinkle Twinkle Little Star' won't get anyone's legs open."

"Combined with a bottle of vodka, mate, even 'Chopsticks' will do the trick, let me tell you. But if you're going to get fussy on me, I'll bring out the full Ludwig."

As the first dark chords of "Moonlight Sonata" resonated in the old piano, Martin laid his head back and smiled. "That's more like it." As David worked his way through the rising and falling throb of the treble hand, he snatched a glance over his shoulder. Martin was no longer smiling but had a small crease between his closed eyes. After the mezzo piano finish died out, David dropped his hands to his thighs and waited.

Martin let out a sigh. "That was wonderful. How can something so sad be so uplifting?"

David turned around. "Can't have been too good. Your knees are still together."

Martin's eyes sprang open and his face flushed pink. "I'm a bit coy. Give me an encore."

David ran through it again as well as a few other pieces he'd been trying out. He became so absorbed he didn't notice the lack of comment from the chair. When he finally turned around, he realised Martin was asleep.

He walked over, intending to give him a gentle shake, and stopped. Martin's head was thrown back and he had a slight tilt to his lips, his face softened and childlike. He felt an urge to lay a protective hand on Martin's forehead. David studied the girlish face for a moment longer, shook his head, and snorted.

"Come on, Princess Aurora. Time to get you out in the fresh air unless you want to sleep in the spare room." He leaned over and wobbled Martin's shoulder.

They stood out on the verandah as Martin shrugged on his jacket.

"Still a bit nippy, isn't it?"

"Yep, but you can feel summer's coming round the corner. If this drought doesn't break soon, we'll probably just bypass spring. Did I tell you I'm selling ten head at this sale coming up?"

"No. No, you didn't. Are you going to start managing your herd down with a view to…?"

"No, this is about buying hay. I'm not at the point of selling off the family silver yet."

"Right. Okay. It sounds like I'd better be there then."

David shrugged. "I asked you so you could have the experience, not so you could watch me squirm." He let out a grim burst of laughter. "I'll blend right in with all the other tragic faces there anyway. What a party it'll be. What was I thinking?"

Martin watched him for a moment as he adjusted his cuffs. "I'd answer you, but it's a hard thing to know what David Mulkerin is thinking. I'm working on it though." Martin gave him a lopsided smile.

David sighed and roosted his hands on his hips. "You're a better man than I am, Gunga Din."

Martin held out his hand. "I think it's been a good day," he said quietly.

David slapped him on the back as he turned to descend the steps. "Be seein' ya."

He stood on the verandah and watched Martin's red tail-lights bump down the drive until they disappeared round the pinch in the road. Next time they'd plan it a bit better. He'd fix up the spare room so Martin could have a wine and relax properly. He came back inside, toasty warm thanks to the bar heater, and sat back down at the piano. He was already looking forward to it.

Chapter Nine

Gibson had the advantage of more trees, the greenery making the place easier on the eye than Bruce with all its red roofs. The green didn't make it down to the ground, though, and the saleyards could be seen from a distance where a rust plume rose into the sharp blue sky.

Nev Johnson had come by the day before to help him round up his cows into the loading race. "Just the ten?" he'd asked as they leaned through the railings, watching the cows moan and shift around.

"Yeah. Buys me some time and more hay."

"Took a load for George Barry yesty, an' one for Ash Cooper. You wouldn't be selling in this market unless you had to."

David lowered his head and pushed his nose deeper into the arms folded on the rail in front of him. "No."

"Should've had some rain by now." Nev removed his foot from the bottom rail and took off his hat, ran his hand over his thin strands of hair before pushing his hat back on. "S'like playing poker. How long can you bluff it out, eh?"

"As long as the House lets you, I guess."

He walked from the car park towards the canteen, nodding at familiar faces that passed by. Martin had said he couldn't make it till after lunch, but he popped his head in anyway, just in case.

Trucks were still backing into the race and the air was full of whip cracks, whistles, and yarrs. This was the treble playing out over the groaning and screaming of cattle being pushed and jostled into the yards. David entered the western end. They were built like a maze and he often felt like he should come with a ball of twine. There were husbands and wives looking into the enclosures, either at their own cattle or ones they wished to buy, although he was pretty sure the main buyers at the moment were either city farmers with deep pockets or the abattoirs. If you could wear the cost and take the risk, you stood to make a lot of money. Or you could wipe yourself out.

The faces passing by began to look the same. Deep-etched lines in tanned skin. The squinting eyes clouded with grim determination, sometimes with a hint of black humour. It was a look he remembered well from his father, something men on the land seemed to have in common along with their hats and gnarled hands. He wondered if he was on the way to looking the same.

A crowd was gathered at the far end of the laneway he'd just turned into, and all faces were raised to the auctioneer standing on a walkway above the yards. He was flanked by men on either side, one scribbling in a notebook, the other with a long stick to prod the beasts. David stood at the back with his arms folded.

"Thought it was you, David. How ya holding up?"

He stepped back and held out his hand. "George. Good, mate. Y'self?"

"Awright. Wish I wasn't here as a seller though."

"Yeah. I hope there's some money left by the time they get to my lot."

"D'ya hear Sydney got a dump of rain last night? Drought's over now, apparently."

They followed the hats as they moved en masse round the corner to the next pen. The auctioneer was working hard for his money today. Squeezing a bid out of this crowd was like getting a starving person to vomit. It didn't take long for him to notice the bids that did eventuate kept coming from the same quarters.

"I hear Ash has got some in today."

"Yeah, saw him earlier. Said he barely got enough to pay the cartage and the fees."

At the end of the next row, George's cattle went under the hammer. He wiped his mouth and shook his head, his eyes telling the story.

"Mine'll be a while yet. Come and have a cuppa with me before you head off."

Walking up the ramp to the canteen, David caught a glimpse of a tall figure coming down the hill from the car park. George looked up at the same time. "Hmph. Here's one of them rich city buggers now. Too late for mine."

By the time they met in front of the canteen entrance, David had a huge grin on his face. "Where'd you get that hat, you bloody imposter."

Martin gave him a shy smile. The dubious look on George's face lightened, and he gave a quick nod as he grasped Martin's outstretched hand.

"George, meet our new doctor. Martin's filling in for Dr Jacobs while he's cruising around the Pacific."

When they joined the queue, Martin suggested they grab a table while he got the tea. Hats off and hair smoothed, they sat down among the wives and young children. George glanced over to the cash register. "The new doctor, eh. From Sydney, is he? I might go and see him about me back. Old Jacobs keeps tellin' me it's old age. Reckon this young fella'd be more in touch with what's going on with new treatments an' such. Sicka those boys tellin' me I'm past it."

David had been focused on pushing around the salt and pepper shakers. He stole a glance up at the older man. "Actually, George, I wanted to pick a bone with you. About those boys—"

"Ah David. Don't you start. In the middle of the night, the only people they're gonna hurt is each other."

He told George how they'd almost run Dan off the road.

"I dunno what you expect me to do about it," he said, his voice rising with an edge of panic. "They won't listen to me, or their mother, and I'm too old to thrash 'em. Charlie came round to give 'em an earful but not much else. They make all these promises, but the minute they get on the piss they're at it again. I dunno what to do."

Martin placed three Styrofoam cups on the table and sat down.

"If Mrs Wilson gets a hold of them, I reckon she'll thrash 'em for you."

"She's welcome to try." George slid a tea over and tore a packet of sugar, his face troubled. "P'raps I should get Ivy to invite her over for tea." He gave Martin an unhappy smile.

"George's boys have been causing a bit of trouble," he said in answer to Martin's look.

They yarned a bit longer about who was there and who wasn't, what was selling well and what wasn't, until David glanced up at the clock on the wall and then at Martin.

"We need to get ourselves down there shortly."

"Yeah, I better be on my way. Nice meetin' ya, doc. Thanks for the tea."

David could feel the looks Martin was getting as they entered the yards. Fortunately, on a sale day there were a lot of people wearing their fresh shirts and clean moleskins, so it wasn't so much his clothes that made him stand out as his height and his fresh face.

"Oh look, Steve. Here's Dr James."

A woman in jeans wearing a man's work shirt like a smock hopped down from a fence where she'd been getting a better view. Steve was inside the pen. The woman beamed up at Martin from under a mop of thick curls. "I wouldn't have expected to see you here…"

David hooked his thumbs in his belt loops and exchanged views on cattle prices with Steve with one eye on the animated face of his wife. Anyone'd think Martin was a rock star the way she was goggling at him.

They passed on down the lane and caught up to where the action was. Despite being early September, the afternoon had warmed up enough to create a strong atmosphere of sweat, cigarette smoke, dust, and animal hide, all shot through with the pungency of fresh cow manure.

After they'd watched another pen go under the hammer, Martin turned to him. "How much did you say a bale of hay cost? And the water?" David told him and he could see him doing the sums in his head. The sad frown that resulted told him his maths was pretty spot on.

"Well, that's that then," David said, as they walked away from the crowd. He'd finally been put out of his misery and they could leave. He'd got about as much and as little as everyone else with a few late bargain hunters making up for a thinning crowd. Barely enough to give him some contingency for a few more months, but it was something.

"What do you say to dinner in town? I still owe the IT guru and you won't find me so flush with cash again for a while."

"Why don't you come to me and let me cook something?"

"Save that for another time. I like to pay my debts. Come on." He slapped Martin on the back. "Let's get out of here before I slash my wrists."

"So be frank with me, David. What are you going to do?"

They both had their elbows resting on a red-and-white checked tablecloth as they scanned menus. David had given him the choice of Bruce's two restaurants and Martin had opted for Italian over Chinese. David rubbed his jaw. "Dunno. Think I might go for the funghi schnitzel." He looked up at Martin and grinned. "And a beer."

"David, I'm serious."

He let out an aggravated sigh. "Mate, my guts are constantly churning over it. Could you give me a break from it for just one evening?"

"I'm sorry. I'm just worried for you. I'd like to think you've got an exit strategy, not just sticking your head in the sand and crossing your fingers."

"Well, there's a lot of that goes on."

"I know. But you're smarter than that."

"It's not always about being smart. A lotta blokes have no choice."

"You're not one of those blokes, though, are you?"

The fraught stares across the table were broken by the waitress appearing with her pad poised. If she noticed any tension she covered up with sunny laughter.

As David watched her retreating back Martin leaned forward. "You could have a relatively easy time working anywhere you wanted, doing something you love, and yet you punish yourself with this life instead. It doesn't make sense."

"It doesn't make sense to *you*."

Martin sat back and poured them some water. He took a sip and put his glass back on the table. A beer and an orange juice were placed in front of them.

David held the cold wet bottle in his hand and stared at the label. Imagine selling off the farm. How could he? The thought of such a betrayal felt like hari-kari…but who would be there to cut off his head? He screwed his eyes shut to block it out. *Come* on, *you moping bastard. Think of something else for a change…*

Martin watched him as he drank off half his beer.

He wiped his mouth with the back of his hand. "You said to me once that you're the black sheep of the family. What's that about?"

"I didn't turn out quite as my parents hoped."

"What. They were hoping for a fucking astronaut?"

Martin's lips pressed together. "A man is more than just his job, David."

"You mean, what happened? Didn't they support you? It wasn't your fault."

"It's more complicated than that."

David's eyes narrowed as he took another mouthful of beer. "So how did you get on with your old man?"

"We'd have got on better if I'd played football. He thought I was a bit of a girlie-wuss."

"Yeah?" He let out a chuckle. "I used to get in trouble for staying inside reading. It wasn't like I didn't go out, but Dad didn't get it. You only stayed inside when it was dark or raining."

"You said you went round to help Dan a lot?"

"Yeah, that was…later on. Dad couldn't speak to me without criticising or carping and it got to the point where I gave up trying. Hard yakka at Dan's was like a holiday." He laughed and signalled the waitress, pointing to his empty glass.

"So, you take after your mum?"

"Yeah, she's the reader. Used to teach before she married Dad."

"Ah."

"Turned me into the sop I am today." He grinned.

Another frosted glass arrived, and their meals quickly followed. There was a pause as pepper and parmesan descended on their plates. It occurred to him as he took in the hot waft of tomato and cheese that the spotlight had yet again swivelled back to him.

"How about *your* mum?"

"She likes having a doctor for a son, although her big thing is the grandkids."

"You're an uncle, too, eh?"

"Mmm." He held up two fingers, his mouth full.

"My mum's the same."

They ate in silence, only pausing to make comments about their food or watch as a cake with sparklers arrived at a neighbouring table.

Out on the pavement they shook hands.

"Next week when you're in town I'd like to cook you dinner."

David rubbed the back of his neck, screwing his eyes up. "Mate, I'd love to, but I can't. You know I've got animals to feed before dark."

"A late lunch then? Surgery closes at three."

The boyish look of hope on Martin's face made him smile. "Okay, but nothing too gourmet"—he pronounced the t—"or you'll never get another invite to my place."

He did his shopping for the week and turned down the main street to run his last errand at the Co-op. A shed full of hay that would last until mid-November. Longer if he sold more stock. He winced when he signed the delivery slip. Prices had doubled since his last load. Murphy's Law dictated it would rain tomorrow after such an outlay.

He could only hope.

Chapter Ten

By the time daylight saving loomed on the horizon, they'd settled into a routine. Martin would come out on Friday evening with takeaway, and they'd watch a movie. Saturday they'd muck around on the farm together or go for a hike or drive. That night Martin would cook. Sometimes David would pop in for lunch midweek.

It was funny how quickly it had happened. It wasn't just that Martin's presence distracted him from his worries; he genuinely looked forward to the company. They shared a love of music and, it turned out, films, but the thing David liked most was that Martin was not afraid to challenge him and try to change his views on things. Only the other night, they'd had a vigorous discussion on the use of animals in scientific testing with Martin naturally taking the role of pragmatic rationalist and David the emotional humanist. Martin hadn't changed his mind, but he'd raised a few points that had made him more amenable to some ideas. And he'd never eaten better in his life.

Jodie had popped round one day to bring back some tools Dan had borrowed. Over a cup of tea, he happily listed the meals Martin had been making him. Caught up in the memories of so many exotic dishes he didn't notice Jodie's face until she spoke.

"Wow. You're getting spoilt. I'd be afraid to bring anything of mine round any more."

"Aw come on, Jodes. Don't give me that cat's bum mouth. You know you're the best baker around. Barring y'mum, of course. You should come round one Saturday. He'd love to show off a bit. And he really likes you."

"Yeah, well."

Pursuing his success in mollifying her, he said, "We haven't had a pub night for ages. You free Friday…next week?"

"I've been free every Friday! It's you who's been otherwise engaged. Mum said she saw you both walking down the street last week and you were as thick as thieves. Said you almost walked right past her."

"She's exaggerating. Did she tell you she invited us round for dinner? Martin's not the only one who likes showing off, eh." He winked. "Said he's never tried proper rhubarb crumble. Can you believe it?"

It was only after Jodie left that he stopped to think about it. It had been four weeks since they'd all three gone out together. No wonder she was pissed. The truth of it was, if he cared to admit it, he was just as happy not sharing Martin's company. He felt like he could be more himself when it was just the two of them; there was no worrying about being one of the boys, although he did have to be on his guard to a certain extent. Martin was good at throwing curly questions at him when he least expected it. But one day, if he'd had enough to drink, and Martin asked the right question, it was all going to come out. And if he started letting loose, there'd be no stopping.

★

Late Friday afternoon had come around yet again to find Jodie sitting at the table with the remains of an early dinner in front of her while she flicked through an old *Women's Weekly*.

Her mother came in from outside with a basket of washing straight from the line accompanied by a gust of Sunlight soap and spring warmth. She dumped the basket on a chair at the other end of the table and started to pull items out for folding and sorting. Jodie hadn't lifted her head from the magazine, but she felt her mother's eye upon her, which made her brace herself for the interrogation. She licked her finger to turn a page.

"What time's your shift start?"

She flicked an eye at the clock. "Six." She turned another page. Was it her imagination or was the snapping and shaking out of clothes getting louder? She pretended to keep reading, but all she could hear was flapping and smoothing and her mother's occasional huffy breath as she exerted herself. Finally, the cacophony stopped, and she realised this was worse. She stole a look at her mum who was standing at the end of the table with her hands on her hips looking at her.

"Jodie-girl—"

She pushed her chair out. "You wanna cuppa? I'll be heading off shortly."

Her mother's mouth set in a familiar determined line. "Yes, that would be nice. Your father's not due back till teatime."

She turned her back on her to put the kettle on, preparing all the defensive statements that had been running through her mind. By the time she set two mugs on the table there was a throbbing in her temple which did not bode well for an evening shift.

"Have you heard from Davey?"

"No, Mum, I haven't. Apart from dropping off those tools the other day. Nada, zip, donut hole." She held up her hand presenting a circle with her index finger and thumb. "Although I don't think I want to hear any more about all the fancy meals Doctor Martin James makes him. Seems to me they're setting up like a married couple."

"Oh, Jodie. Try and give him some slack. He's never really had a…buddy. A really close friend before. I know it's hard for you, but when I saw them together the other day and saw how lit up his face was…well. It brought a tear to my eye. It's like he's woken up somehow and become human."

Jodie glowered into her mug. "Well, he will get a wakeup call soon. People are starting to talk."

"Talk? What about for goodness' sake?"

"Oh, come *on*, Mother. Two men being chummy-wummy spending whole weekends together? What do you think they're saying?"

She looked up when her mother didn't respond and took in the hurt perplexed look on her face as she stroked her mug with her agitated fingertips.

"Anyone who knows David wouldn't believe talk like that."

"Okay, Mum." She was on a roll now and her Sherman tank was gaining momentum. "List me on your fingers the people who you think really know David? And I don't mean the plastic cut-out I used to drag to the pub."

There was a long silence as she fumed and drank the last of her tea. Finally, her mum spoke, and her voice was quiet.

"There are always people who want to sully and dirty things. You can't stop them. All I know is, I've never seen David so happy." She looked at Jodie. "I know that's hard for you to bear right now because it doesn't involve you, but if Martin can help David to become happy in *himself*, then that is going to overflow into his other relationships. You just have to be patient, girl. There's a lot of work to be done in that quarter." She placed her hand over her daughter's.

Jodie felt a pressure welling up in her throat, a convulsing that forced her lips shut. Then the tears started squeezing out. "Mum, it's n-not *fair*…" Hating herself for the tears but even more for sounding like a whiny kid on an American sitcom.

"Ah, Jodie-girl…" Her mother got up and sat in the chair next to her and put her arm around her head and pulled it to her shoulder.

"There'll be no later, Mum. Someone at the Black Rock'll b-beat him to a pulp before that ever happens."

Her mother pulled a tissue out of her pocket and put it into Jodie's hand. She felt the warmth of her mother's uneven breath in her hair.

She snorted and blew into the tissue. "And that's all without worrying what *Dad* will have to say about it."

"Your father would never believe anything bad about David…but I'll talk to him if it becomes necessary."

Her mother's lips pressed warmly on her forehead. Jodie lifted her face up and wiped it with her fingers.

"My suggestion to you, dear girl, would be to get some of your girlfriends together and go out to the pub without those boys and have some fun of your own making. You can't keep moping around waiting for David to come and pick up the pieces, because he won't, and you know it. He's not the only one who needs to work on making his own happy."

"But Mum—"

"You know I'm right." Her mother opened her eyes wide and nodded her head at her.

"Okay, *okay*." She pushed back her chair and sniffed. "I'm off to have fun at work. Sarah's on tonight too. I'll have a word."

Martin had brought out the ingredients for a beef korma. Under his instruction David chopped and diced and dug out the right pots and pans. He was already doing the washing up when Martin placed the lid on the Crock-Pot.

"We can do that later," he said, pouring some more red into his glass.

"Nah. Won't take long."

Martin leaned on the counter and sipped his wine. "And I thought I was the anal retentive in the kitchen."

"Ha. My mum ran a tight ship. You go and turn the telly on."

Martin had eyed him with overt scepticism when he'd suggested watching the cup match, but he'd come around when he suggested the cooking lesson. He was feeling quite chuffed with his negotiation skills.

The first forty minutes was a bloodbath. Martin watched the game in near silence, only interrupting David's yelling to clarify a rule now and then.

When the ads came on, David fell back into the lounge. "Are you kinda getting it?"

"I'm kinda getting that if I saw one of those guys coming at me in the street, I'd learn a whole new way of running."

"Yeah, they're big bastards all right. You shoulda seen Jonah Lomu when he used to play."

Back on the lounge for the second half they both sat forward over their bowls of curry.

"Aw. This is fucking fantastic," he said through a large mouthful.

"Something else to make when you're feeling wild and adventurous."

The Wallabies fought back in the second half, but it wasn't enough. David flicked off the screen and threw down the remote in disgust. "So apart from the result, what did you think?"

"I think I got more out of you enjoying it than the game itself. Must be fun watching it with a crowd at the pub."

"Too right. We'll go in for the last game. Jodie'd be up for that." He suddenly realised with a pang that the "this next Friday" he'd promised her had come and gone without comment. He'd really be in the bad books now. He'd call her up about the final tomorrow. He would.

The rest of the evening was pretty mellow. Martin put some piano concertos on low and they burrowed into opposite corners of the lounge chatting about nothing in particular.

Coming back from the loo around 1:00 a.m., he found Martin lying with his head back and his eyes closed. They opened when David's weight sank into the cushions. He blinked and squeezed the bridge of his nose. "Time for beddy-byes, I think."

David was just coming inside from dealing with the empties when he heard scrabbling around in the spare bedroom. "You all right in there?"

"Yep. Just left something in the car."

Ten minutes passed with the sound of car doors opening and closing. David came out into the darkened living room to look out at the area lit by the outside light. Martin's legs were sticking out from the back door of his car as he searched for something apparently under the seat. A while later he was at David's bedroom door.

"Sorry, I…I've…got to go…home."

Martin's eyes were large with worry. He was breathing through his mouth and his shoulders were pulling up to his ears with every breath.

"What's happened?"

"Puffer. Can't find. Home."

"You were fine a minute ago."

Martin braced an arm against the doorframe and dipped his head. "Gotta go."

"Take it easy, mate. I'll drive you."

He jammed his boots on and grabbed his keys. He ran down the front steps. He pulled open the door and looked behind him. Martin was still at the verandah taking one step at a time, his head bowed.

Jesus Christ.

He ran back and pulled Martin's arm over his shoulder. "Come on, mate, you'll be fine. Relax." But with his ear so close to Martin's cheek, he could hear the squeak of him trying to suck air into his lungs. Panic rose in his chest as his own breathing fell into the same shallow pattern.

He dropped him into the passenger seat and watched his head fall back, his Adam's apple straining against the skin of his throat.

The freezing air combined with fear was clearing his head. He tried not to think about how many beers he'd had. Thank god he'd left the wine to Martin.

Once they got off the dirt driveway, he wound down the window, needing the chill air to keep him alert. Then he put his foot down. There'd be no one on the road at this hour, but a stray roo could wipe them both out.

His own chest was heaving up and down in time with Martin's. The poor bugger was screwing up the material of his trousers with one hand, the other had a death grip on the dashboard. It was only then he remembered Martin saying the cold air helped to bring it on. Cursing himself, he wound up the window.

"It's all right, buddy. I'll get you there." His voice sounded like someone else's, low and calm. He wanted to reach out and squeeze his shoulder, but he didn't dare take his hand off the wheel again. They were doing one-thirty.

The Mill Bridge zipped rather than rumbled as they flew across it. Martin's head fell forward.

Jesus. Don't. *Don't.*

The speedo crept up to one-forty as Martin's head lolled around, the seat belt the only thing holding him up. David reached over and pushed him back in the seat.

It was like all his nightmares piling on top of him. Not being able to breathe. Drowning. Being sucked down, down, down.

The first streetlights were coming into view. In less than five minutes he was bolting up the brick path and savaging the lock with Martin's key. Kitchen table. No. Bathroom cabinet. No. He raced into the main bedroom. Bedside table. No. Top drawer. *Yes.*

Out at the car he held the inhaler up to Martin's mouth. "Come on, buddy, open up. *Please.*" He tried two puffs, but Martin couldn't inhale the spray. He started making choking sounds. *No! Not you.* He had to get him to the hospital. Should have gone straight there. Fucking idiot.

At first, he'd been grateful that the engine had covered the rapid, distressed squeaking. Now he realised there was something worse than hearing it. "Relax, buddy, relax. I'm going to get you to the hospital. They'll sort you out in no time. Stay *with* me. Martin, can you hear me?" The tremor in his voice threatened to push him over the edge. Frightened of what he might say, he started singing under his breath. The chorus of "Flame Trees" issued out in such a tremulous high-pitch wobble he stopped—his voice was breaking all over again.

He was running red lights now, squealing round corners. The tyres screamed as he burned to a stop in the circular drive behind the ambo out front. He leaped out of the ute bellowing like a madman.

"*Oxygen!* Get me some *oxygen!*"

Before he could slam his hands on the front desk people were bursting out of doors and running past him. He turned around, panting, waving his hands, trying to yell out instructions, but nothing could make it out of his constricted throat.

They had Martin out of the ute and onto a gurney in what seemed like seconds. There was shouting and pointing and great winds of antiseptic as forms in blue and white whipped passed him. Someone jammed a facemask on Martin, and another held a needle poised, waiting for another to tear up his sleeve.

As the gurney whisked Martin past him and through some swinging doors it felt like his intestines snagged on it and were being unwound and dragged through them along with the gurney. He staggered back inside, his knees on the point of collapse, found the men's. The responsibility shifting off his shoulders sapped him of his last ounce of resolve. His back against a wall, he slid down to the floor, his head on his knees, the choking sobs cutting his lungs to pieces.

David sat in a hard chair, almost in a trance, with his head leaning back against a wall in the recovery room. He sat bolt upright when he became aware of a nurse removing the nebuliser mask and in a moment of horrible disorientation, he thought it was because Martin was dead.

"It's okay," the nurse said, smiling at him. "The steroids have kicked in now. His breathing's back to normal. He's going to be fine."

He leaned over Martin then, propped up by a pile of pillows, and lowered his ear to his mouth. Still breathing. He stood up. The dark circles under his eyes made him look like a little boy. His cowlick was skewed and sticking up. He reached out his hand to smooth it, but it trembled so much he pulled it back.

He had never known fear like it. He had stood by helplessly as three people converged on Martin, the image of that big needle being thrust into his arm vivid in his mind's eye. He pulled up his chair and made himself comfortable on the bed-side. It was past three in the morning.

He woke to the pressure of a hand on his head. Fingers in his hair. He lifted his head off his arms to see Martin giving him a weak smile.

"You fucking, *fucking* bastard," David whispered.

The corners of Martin's mouth lifted a little higher. "I love you, too, mate." He let his hand slip from David's arm to the counterpane. "You look like shit."

"Is that right?"

They stared at each other in silence. It was Martin who broke it first.

"I'm sorry I put you through that, David. The last time was when I was a teenager."

"What the fuck happened? You were right one minute and dying the next."

"My asthma's been worse since I've been out here. I can't go anywhere without my inhaler. When I realised I didn't have it, I panicked."

"You brought it on yourself."

"Pretty much."

David's breath caught in his throat as he reached over to grab Martin by the hair. He ground his teeth together to stop the tears coming and gave Martin's head a shake. "If you do that to me again, I will kill you."

Dawn was breaking when he walked back down the brick path after dropping Martin back to his house. He drove home in a near stupor and when he got there, he collapsed into bed fully clothed.

After lunch when he was finally up and about, random memories and emotions kept intruding on his thoughts. When he thought about it too hard, he became short of breath, feeling a wave of panic return. Had to keep reminding himself that Martin was *alive*.

Kept thinking also of that vulnerable face among the pillows. What *was* it about this guy? He'd known him, what? A small handful of months and suddenly he felt like death at the prospect of losing him. He needed to get a grip. Martin was *not* Tim. He just wasn't. But all those feelings he imagined he would have had towards a younger brother were there. The shared intimate time; the in-jokes; the knowing; a sense that he needed to look after or protect Martin in some way, and a sense, more importantly, that Martin was close enough to trust with his deepest thoughts; his raw self. Well, maybe not quite that far. Still, it made the prospect of Martin's going back to Sydney at the end of the year something he thrust into the back cupboard of his mind. He'd deal with that when it became real. Too many other worries on his plate right now, anyway.

It wasn't until he was in the shed that evening, scooping dog pellets into Fang's dish, that he recalled how he found the puffer in the bedside drawer. Fear had blocked out everything but the essentials. Now he stood still, locked in place, staring at the shed wall, a clear picture before him of what else had been in the drawer.

A porn magazine. For gay men.

Chapter Eleven

When Mrs Wilson gave Martin a lift out to pick up his car, David made sure he was out on the property. He didn't drop in during the week and he spent the next few days dreading the ring of the phone. It was Friday morning by the time it did.

"I'm hearing a deathly silence. Is everything okay?"

"Yup. Busy is all."

"Ah." A pause. "Has your hay arrived?"

"Yep, yep. Shed's full now."

"Okay." Another pause. "David?"

"Still here."

"You don't want me to come out tonight, do you."

He exhaled a breath through his nose. "Yeah, I'm not really—"

"Tell me something, David. When you were looking for my puffer last weekend…do you want to tell me where you found it?"

David inhaled and exhaled a few times. He was desperate to hang up.

"David?"

"In your bedside drawer."

"I see."

Another long silence.

"Then we need to talk. I'll come out this evening."

"I don't—I don't want to talk about it. I'm still a bit…shocked."

This time Martin's response cut down the line with no delay. "When exactly would you want to talk about it then? When will you be a little less shocked? Or have you suddenly realised you've let someone get too close and this excuse for backing away is as good as any?"

"No…that's not it."

"I'm coming out this afternoon. And you'd better be there."

He opened his mouth to reply but the phone was already beeping.

He felt sick. He stomped around the house, walking into each room. His hands were surplus appendages flapping around annoying the hell out of him. He banged his fists together and stared out of the back sunroom. He needed to chop wood. Rip something apart. Break things. He went out to the garage behind the shed.

It was more of a workshop full of half-done jobs and junk. Boxes and skips full of shit that would be useful one day. He hated throwing things out; he was the classic hoarder. But now he was in a violent purging mood.

He spent the morning dragging things out into the light and piling them up. A lot of it was his dad's shit. Bales of rusted fencing wire, an old apparatus for churning butter, rotted hessian sacking everywhere he looked. The sharp sour smell of super phosphate. Bird shit and rat's nests. A few dead and desiccated creatures.

He was thirsty and his shoulders ached, but he pushed through, afraid to stop. He cleared the wooden slats on the walls that functioned as shelves, wiped off the layers of grit and spiderwebs. They needed a hose, but he didn't have that kind of water to spare. He fetched and carried and swept and wiped until the place was an empty shell and he was encrusted with filth. He walked around to the small tank on the other side of the building and wet his hands. The bleached shard of Sunlight soap took a while to lather, but it did the job. He cupped his hand under the tap and grabbed a few mouthfuls. As he wiped his mouth, he automatically tapped the ribbed exterior of the tank to find the level of the water.

Back out the front he surveyed the damage. In a parallel universe he'd have stumbled across something valuable. Something worth some cash. He grunted and shook his head. Even then he'd have to find someone with the money to pay for it. Good luck with that around here. He'd load it later. Take it to the tip. It was time for food.

He laid out six slices of bread on the cutting board and slathered them with marg. Dollops of chutney followed and then thick slabs of silverside. Flicking the telly on, he sat with the plate on his knees. He wolfed down the first sandwich with barely a chew. Coloured images were flickering in front of his eyes: blonde women chatting to each other about vacuum cleaners and juicers. It wasn't enough. The image that was now burnt onto his retinae kept intruding, blocking out everything else. He hadn't registered the title of the magazine, only that it was bold and red. It didn't matter really. It was the image that counted. A buffed-up man, naked, leaning back on a rock, his arm draped strategically over his groin. He'd tried to convince himself it might be a fitness magazine, but that futile hope had died pretty quickly. He knew what it was. What it meant.

He felt duped. Stupid. *Betrayed.* But there had been no obvious clues; yes, when he looked back in retrospect, but only because he now knew. Was everyone laughing at him? Did Jodie know? He thought of that cat's bum mouth again. Stalled at the third sandwich. Got up for some water. Stood skolling it at the sink as he looked at the camellia tree outside.

He braced himself on the edges of the sink and hung his head. He felt disgusted with himself, and yet he'd done nothing wrong. He let the thought that had been knocking and knocking come in. Did Martin…fancy him? The cringe rippled through his stomach. Had he been eyeing off his arse this whole time? He hated himself for even thinking it. There was nothing sleazy about Martin. If anything, he was a little too proper and nice. David was the sleazy one. Jodie would've pointed that out in a flash. Christ, people knew he stayed weekends. He stood up, rolling his eyes as if it would release them from his aching head. *I am exceedingly careful.* Everything Martin said was now coming back to him with a double meaning.

He looked at his watch. It had gone two. He had a few more hours. He needed to be busy when he showed up, not just waiting to be run over like a rabbit caught in the headlights.

★

It was dark by the time Martin's handbrake cranked in front of the house. No call, no nothing. David was furious. He should've gone out after all and serve him right.

Martin's expression was distant and professional. It could have been their first meeting all over again.

"May I come in?"

The stress of waiting had pushed David too far. As a result, he was now feeling thick-headed and emotional. Even so, he was sure he saw a mocking glint in Martin's eye, and it increased the feeling that he was going into combat unarmed.

Martin tossed his keys on the kitchen table but did not sit down. His eyes flickered over to the counter where a near-empty bottle of red stood. He pursed his lips.

David had been buoyed by anger and anxiety all afternoon, but his sails had now gone inexplicably slack. Words failed him. Now Martin was staring at him with that *bring-it-on* look he couldn't recall one line of the snappy dialogue he'd been rehearsing. Finally, at Martin's prompting expression, he stammered, "Does anyone else know?"

A look of contempt creased Martin's face. "Is that all that matters to you? What other people think?"

"It's all right for you. I have to live here after you've gone."

"Do you, David? Do you? But that's a different story, isn't it. Is this really about what other people think or is it about what you feel? Up until a few days ago you were enjoying our friendship as much as I was. Today you've got cold feet because you think I want to fuck you. Or that people might think we're fucking."

Hearing Martin baldly state what he'd been thinking took him aback.

"Of course, they'll think it. Everyone knows you've been staying weekends with me!"

"So, let's have it then. How does this change things?"

The anger in Martin's eyes made him look away. "I can't..."

"Can't what? See me any more? Can't summon the courage to have what you want in life? Can't stop running from everything like a coward?"

David balled his hands into fists at his side. "You don't know the half—"

"Damned right I don't. But it hasn't been for want of trying. You're a closed fucking book. A sea anemone. A cunt wrapped in three layers of chastity belts. And you have the nerve to stand there telling me you're worried about what people *think*."

Martin's hands were on his hips and he turned side on to him. He shook his head as if answering his own question and turned back to address him. "You're carrying a lot of pain around. I can see that. Oh yes, you've learned to cover it up with all your charm and banter, but if anyone tries to break through that...it's obvious why Jodie pussyfoots around you. I can see this is partly about Tim, but—"

"This is fucking nothing to do with Tim! It's about you being a...not straight with me. If you had any honesty or integrity, you would have told me upfront, but you—"

Martin slammed his palms on the table, his face flushed red. "My sexual preferences are none of your business, David, or anyone else's. I don't recall you confiding your own fantasies and fetishes upfront to me either."

"How am I supposed to trust you now?"

Martin stared at him, incredulous.

David's head was throbbing. This wasn't going as he'd expected. He pulled out a chair and slumped into it, fixing a belligerent stare on Martin.

Martin warily pulled out a chair and sat down also. He reached out and drummed his fingers on the table in the angry silence.

"Nellie and I had an interesting chat on the drive out the other day."

David gritted his teeth, a nerve beginning to pulse in his jaw.

"She's pleased you've found a friend. Said she understood when she saw us together." He looked at David and his head cocked to one side as if to taunt him. "Said I'm a grown-up version of Tim. Seeing us together reminds her of what could've been."

David was up and out of his chair before Martin could react. He grabbed him by the shirt front and dragged him up against the doorframe. Martin's body went limp, sensing what was coming.

"You've got no right," he roared, spittle flying out of his mouth. "If I hear you say his name one more time, I'll—"

"You'll what, David? Beat me up? Smash my teeth in?" Martin's voice was constricted by David's fists pressing in on his throat. "I'm used to people I care about hoeing into me. It's the sum total of my experience of paternal and fraternal love." Martin shifted, trying to avoid his hot breath. His nose was almost touching Martin's and he felt murderous.

Martin lifted a shaking hand and placed his palm at David's temple.

He shook him off and screwed his eyes shut. Ground out, "Don't."

Martin's voice was barely above a whisper. "David, what happened? Why do you hate yourself so much?"

He pulled him forward and smashed him back again. "You are so full of shit! You don't know anything." He pulled him forward again, but his grip weakened, and Martin raised his knee. He missed David's groin, but it was enough. He escaped into the living room almost doubled over. The next moment he was sprawled on the floor with David on top of him. They twisted and grabbed and rolled and in the fray his head hit the leg of the coffee table. Momentarily stunned, Martin was able to pin him down, their rasping breathing competing to be heard.

His head dropped back to the floor and he swallowed. He leered up at Martin, his chest heaving. "So, is this where you fuck me?"

"I think we have different ideas about foreplay, David."

"It's what you've been after, isn't it?" He sneered. "Come on, get your—"

He didn't see it coming. It was less a slap than an open-handed wallop. And before he could recover, he got a second one.

The shocked silence was broken by David letting out a long howl. He thrashed his head, pushed and bucked, trying to throw Martin off.

"Get off me, you fucking fucker. Get your hands off me."

"Not until…you tell me…what's going on here."

David looked up at him and whatever Martin saw made him flinch.

"He *drowned,* Martin, he fucking drowned! Is that what you want to hear? In that muddy hole of water." He drew a few ragged gasps, the next words choked out of him. "And we lost him…because of *me.*"

The fight in him collapsed and he was struggling to breathe, felt like he was choking. He could feel water running down the sides of his face. Martin released his grip on his shaking shoulders and moved away, allowing him to roll to one side. Still sobbing, he sat up. He brought his knees up and covered his face with his hands.

Martin went to the kitchen and returned with a damp tea towel. He handed it to him and sat down on the floor next to him, their backs to the lounge. They sat like that for a long time, the only sound David's heaving breath. Eventually he spoke, the words like they were being scraped out of him.

"We were alone in the house." He held the wet material up to his face as if to block out the memory. He continued, mumbling into the towel. "There was a cow in trouble. Couldn't get her calf out."

After a while he folded the wet towel and held it up to his forehead with the heel of his hand. "Tim was bugging the shit out of me. He was always pestering me when I wanted to read or just be alone. I told him to piss off and play outside."

He removed the towel and flung it on the floor in front of him. Both hands moved up to grab his hair, his eyes screwed shut.

"He was always—always wanting to go to the dam. Fascinated with water. All I wanted was to get rid of him. His whining voice. Him throwing things against my closed door. I didn't think about what he'd do. Didn't care." His shoulders crunched up sharply as more breathless sobs escaped him.

"It was around four when they got back, tired; covered in blood. They saved the calf, but the cow had to be shot, so Dad was in a fine mood. First thing Mum said was, 'Where's Tim?' Outside, I said. I heard her go out, her shout to Dad. There was a long period of nothing and then Dad came in and hauled me off my bed. 'Get out here and help us look for him. If he's at that dam I'll flay you alive.'"

His shoulders were shaking again, his breathing coming in shallow gasps.

The bottle of red was doing its work now. He looked at Martin with bleary unfocused eyes, tears dropping onto his shirt front. He continued, his voice small.

"I waited in my room, petrified. I knew it would only be a matter of time before they brought him back screaming and I would get the thrashing of my life. I listened for Dad's footsteps, not even game to go to the toilet. It felt like hours before I heard voices in the kitchen. More than voices. Keening and crying. The next thing I knew Mrs Wilson came into my room. I'll never forget the look on her face. Told me to pack some clothes. It was three weeks before I was allowed home." The racking sobs started again. "He never did flay me. Never. Should have—never touched me. Why didn't he, Martin? Why *didn't* he?"

Martin grabbed him and pulled his head under his chin, clasping his face with his hand, rocking him. "No, David, no."

"He died because of me. My little brother. Only seven! A little boy that I should have loved and protected. Never deserved him, I couldn't—"

"Shhh. No."

"They hated me. Everyone—" The words were catching in his throat and he broke out coughing.

"David, you were only a kid. No."

"No one could love me after that. No one. S'why everyone leaves me."

Martin's arms were around him, tight, gently swaying him. Then, with his face in Martin's shirt front, he got a heady whiff of his cologne and suddenly a shock wave of memory vibrated through his chest and he felt himself trembling, gasping, losing control of himself. "I l-lost Tim. And n-now…*now*…I'm going to lose…*you*."

"Oh *god*."

The rocking suddenly stopped, and he felt rather than heard Martin let out a long groan. "*David*…" Felt his lips in his hair. Softly moaning, "Okay, okay, I get it, I get it now, it's okay."

The last thing he recalled was Martin's grip tighten further and the return of the rocking motion that started to still his shaking. With it, an inexplicable feeling of safety started to pervade his sodden senses.

Chapter Twelve

He drifted out of sleep like a swimmer rising to the surface. His head felt heavy, and his eyes were glued up, but in his dream he'd been lying in the sun. And somehow the sun had got inside his chest. He smiled and shifted his face. Hair brushed across his nose. Then his body went rigid and his eyes popped open in the dark. *Shit.*

His right arm was underneath Martin's neck and there wasn't room for a sliver of paper between their fully clothed bodies. His heart started pounding as he wondered what to do. He swallowed hard as last night's events and emotions rose to the surface of his dulled mind. Martin was gay…*gay*! But right now, he couldn't process what that even meant. And last night. The cold fear and anguish began to creep into in his chest once more. But the strongest, most indelible memory was of Martin holding him and how that had felt. That sunshine in his chest, that warmth. That supreme comfort. A feeling he'd always craved, even if he always denied and stifled it. He'd felt safe. And yes; fuck you, fuck you, *Fuck. You!* He'd felt loved.

He lay there for a moment in silence, tears running down the side of his nose. Trying to recall how he'd felt only moments ago. That sun, that warmth. Couldn't he just give in to feeling good for a change? Allow himself to enjoy this fragile passing moment? Not lash and punish himself this once?

He wiped his face, grateful that Martin was deeply asleep. He shifted again slightly, testing things. He wiggled his toes. Good. No shoes. And his belt had been removed. He had a vague memory of throwing up in the toilet and being made to drink lots of water. Martin was curved away from him and his own body had curved with him. He took a deep breath and let it out gently. He was too comfortable to move. He allowed his face to fall back to where it had been, pressed up against the back of Martin's neck. He let the tip of his nose touch and inhaled the warmth.

His left arm was wrapped firmly around Martin's rib cage, his fingers tucked under, locking him in. There was a gentle expansion against his arm as Martin breathed and a feeling of tenderness welled up in his chest. He had become so keenly aware of that breath.

He trailed his closed lips where his nose had been, testing, smelling. He hesitated for a moment and then allowed his mouth to open. He pressed the warm wetness there, not moving. His eyes flew open, and he sucked in a sharp surprised breath through his nose. His body had begun to stir and tighten, and his breath was coming faster. Suddenly it just wasn't enough. He didn't even agonise over it. He turned off his scolding brain and tuned into the frequency in the lower half of his body. He moved his lips and gently sank his teeth in. Martin moaned in his sleep. David wasn't thinking about what might happen if he woke. He couldn't. His brain wasn't running the show any more.

He slid his top hand free and plucked at Martin's shirt. Loose. He sought out the bare flesh above his jeans. Soft downy hair, lean as. It was while his fingers traced through the snail trail up to his navel that Martin jerked slightly. David's heart drummed in the dark silence; surely Martin felt it thudding into his back. Martin's breathing had changed and his body had tensed, but he did not move.

David couldn't stop himself. He flattened his palm and wiped it firmly the width of Martin's abdomen, back again and then up to his chest, shifting his mouth to a location nearer Martin's ear. His lips felt the pull of Martin's Adam's apple as he swallowed. His hips were on their own insistent timetable doing a slow grind against Martin's rear. Martin lifted his elbow, and for a moment he thought he was going to be pushed away.

Martin wrestled his jeans open and a few shucking movements later, David's hand was guided to equipment that was not his own. He didn't have to be told what to do but he felt disembodied going through the familiar movements, as if he was wearing a strap-on. His right arm came up across Martin's throat, grasping his opposite shoulder, his grip hard and urgent. It was over quickly, Martin letting out a choked "ohh" followed quickly by David shuddering and whimpering into his shoulder.

He cupped his hand over Martin's groin and slept.

He opened his eyes and then screwed them shut against the glare. Jesus. Must be lunchtime. He lay on his back sprawled like a starfish. When he realised he was alone, a wave of relief hit him. Then he heard noises in the kitchen. *Shit.* A tremor of fear rippled up his body. What had they *done*? What had *he* done?

Jesus H Christ on a stick...he planted his hand firmly over his eyes trying to block it all out. Then he let his hand slide down over his mouth and he drew a few deep breaths through his nose as he stared at the ceiling. He'd got a hard-on from lying next to a man. Had his sexual deprivation (or was that degradation?) driven him to this new low level? The image on that magazine cover flashed through his mind and he groaned and rolled over, burying his face in the pillow. He felt sick.

Then he became aware of unfamiliar smells in his own pillow. God, what must *he* be thinking right now? *Maybe he's now got expectations this will happen again*...how to tell him...he didn't want to lose his friendship...but it couldn't work like this.

He propped his face up on his hands and stared at the headboard. He could now smell bacon and realised what all the banging around was. The fear of breakfast in bed was enough to get him vertical in a hurry. The front of his jeans had set like cardboard. He grabbed some clean clothes and did a quick cowboy walk to the shower. Fifteen minutes later, he was tentatively poking his head round the kitchen doorway. Martin was bent over a bowl employing some electronic gadget that had no place in his mother's kitchen.

The air was hazy with bacon fat. He ventured closer and looked into a saucepan of bubbling water where eggs were poaching. Martin still hadn't looked up when he peered over his shoulder at a whirring yellow mass. "Help yourself to some coffee; this'll be ready in two ticks."

He poured coffee for them both and sat at the table. Snatches of the night before were coming back to him and he began to wonder why Martin was still here. Why he hadn't smashed his head in with a brick and left. He could think of nothing to say as Martin handled popped toast, arranged bacon, slid out the eggs, poured on the hollandaise, and ground the pepper. All the while his long fingers moving with quick precision. Then it was under his nose. Like something you'd see in a cafe.

A nervous smile quivered on David's lips and his ingrained jokey habits got the better of him. "Are you like one of those guys you hear about that disappears after sex and turns into a pizza?" There. It was out there now. He held his breath.

There was a weighty pause as their eyes finally met. Martin's eyes crinkled in amusement and his voice was soft. "If I was going to disappear, mate, I'd hope to be replaced with something better than pizza."

They ate in silence, but all the while he was struggling with the push-me-pull-you emotions and arguments going on in his head and what to do about them. His self-preservation mode fighting with…with…what? His need for a shag? No. It wasn't that. No. It was his need for Martin him*self.* Just him. No one else. But this revelation breaking into his thoughts still didn't solve the problem of what to do or say right now. He knew he was going to fudge it, as usual. He just didn't have that kind of courage. By the time he nervously reached for the jam for his last piece of toast he saw Martin had finished and was now hunched over his coffee cup smiling at him. He smiled back and quickly dipped his head.

"Well, I need to know. Was that just a situational one-off?"

David's head snapped up, his mind screaming *Yes* only to be followed by a quietly resistant *No*. His mouth gaped like a landed fish. Being confronted with Martin in the flesh seemed to nullify and confuse some of his earlier thoughts. This wasn't just some random man. It was *Martin*. Finally, he spoke, like someone emerging from root canal surgery. "I…don't… know."

"Fuck off and give me some time to think about it?"

"No! *Please*." Something akin to fear had forced it out of him. Then, reassured by Martin's aura of calm, more quietly, "I don't want you to fuck off." He pushed his plate away and frowned at the window over the sink. They sat like that for some time, the quiet spinning out and out. He was miserably aware of a small bird twittering in the camellia tree nearby. He could see the top branches swaying, but the bird was hidden from view. When he finally turned back to face him, Martin's expression was steady and patient as if waiting for him to spell a difficult word. The gentle smile was his undoing; humour his only saviour.

"Sorry—I'm… You know I'm…right-handed."

Martin's eyes narrowed and he nodded. "Yes. I am aware of that."

He almost expected him to grab a pad and take some notes.

"But you clearly got some practise in when your hand was injured."

David's face split into a grin. "You bastard. You're lucky you kept your pants up. I was ready to—"

"I'm not into that."

"What? You don't…so you…"

He had that patient look on his face again. "Not all gay men are into penetration, despite what everyone thinks. I tried it once. It fucking hurt!" He laughed, almost to himself as he swirled the dregs in his coffee cup. His hand went to his throat and rubbed it. "Having said that, I didn't think I was into erotic asphyxiation either, but apparently there's a time and a place." He grinned and settled his chin on the heel of his hand. "I can only speak for the men in my own circle, but I think you'd be surprised to hear that the favourite activity is often kissing."

"Oh, come on." But then the memory of using his mouth on Martin's neck came back to him and that warmth started slithering back into his chest. He shifted in his seat. He was struggling in deep water now with no land in sight.

"So, what is it you do…with your…"

"Lovers?"

Dammit, he was enjoying this.

Martin shrugged and those dark-blue eyes stared him down. "I've been told I give a spectacular blow job."

David's mouth went dry. "Is that right," he croaked. A few more shallow breaths and he was on his feet, clearing his throat. "I'll um, be with you in a minute."

He leaned his left hand on the toilet cistern, dredging up long dead memories of what spectacular, or *any*, oral sex was like, while his other quickly dealt with his immediate problem. A quick grimace as he cleaned up and flushed the toilet. Sat down with his head in his hands. What the fuck was that? He stared through his spread fingers at the toilet door knowing it was the only thing between him and his house guest right now.

This was insane. He wasn't gay. He liked *women* for god's sake! Loved their breasts, full swaying hips…pretty hands. He always noticed those too. Suddenly thought of Martin's hands and groaned, reefing his fingers into his hair. Let himself think of other men at the Black Rock…considered them one by one. Each and every one repulsed him on any kind of erotic level; so, what was going on with *this* guy? He'd heard stories about homosexuality in the wars borne of desperation, fear, and pure need.

An image of Achilles and Patroclus suddenly popped into his head. His mouth twisted and he shook his head. *That* was different again. Certainly, you heard about shit going on in the prison system…but that was more about tribal domination and pecking orders…wasn't it? Could some men just turn this other side on and use it for the need at hand? He shook his head. It started him thinking of the nature versus nurture argument and he started to wonder if the seeds were in him from the start, dormant, unwatered. Is this what his father had seen? He shook his head, refusing to believe it.

It was true he hadn't been with a woman for an exceptionally long time. In fact, sad to recount, only one since he'd come home, and that was a serious mistake resulting from too much drink and an offer of a bed for the night when he hadn't had the benefit of Jodie's chaperoning. Of course, it got around. Jodie's sole reaction had been pursed lips and a stern, *so. Louise Fischer, eh.* She wasn't called The Fisher for nothing, and all he could do was joke it off like everything else. Fortunately, she'd married and left town some years ago now, although occasionally someone with a long memory would bring it up when they thought he was getting too uppity.

He refused to believe he was a closet gay, or bisexual even, for that matter. All he knew right now, at this moment, was that Martin had dovetailed into some missing part of him and he had to find some way of holding on to it, because losing it would hurt too much. He rubbed his face harshly and stood up.

He found a completely clean kitchen and Martin reading an old local paper at the table, an empty mug in front of him. He closed the paper and smiled at him when he sat down.

He smiled sheepishly. "Sorry, mate, you should have left the cleaning up for me."

"It's okay." Martin leaned his chin on his hand and gave him a searching look. "More importantly, are *you* okay?"

David let out a gusty sigh and leaned back on the back legs of his chair. Looked at his hands clasped in his lap. "I've been better. My head's a total mess right now."

"I can appreciate that."

David laughed. "That was your cue to say, how's that different from any other day?"

Martin smiled and said nothing.

David stared at his hands and sighed. "Ye-ep. Yep."

Martin pushed his chair out. "What say I leave you to it. I've got some jobs to do in town that would be good to get out of the way. I could always come back out this evening if you change your mind."

David had agreed, although he wasn't sure if he would change his mind. They stood facing each other with the driver's side door of Martin's car open between them.

"I see you've been busy." Martin gestured to the stacked-up piles behind the shed.

"Yeah. Time to flush out some dross."

"Find anything interesting?"

"Nup. All shite."

"Oh well. Better out than in, as they say."

David laughed. "You'd better go before this conversation starts to feel like psychoanalysis."

Martin still made no move to get in the car. He looked at David uncertainly. "You will call, won't you? I'll worry if I hear nothing."

"Sure. Sure." He felt bad now, as all he wanted to do was get rid of Martin and be alone.

He stood and watched as Martin's car raised a cloud of dust all the way to the main road, dimly aware of Fang's frustrated barking echoing in the shed.

Finally, he snapped to. "Right-o mate, all right. Freedom's coming; hold y'horses."

All afternoon his mind ran around in circles like a hamster in a cage. Nothing new resulted and he was beginning to feel like he was piling one rationalisation on top of another. He was getting sick of it. By the time the last rays of the sun were snuffing out he was feeling that cold creeping desolation again. After feeding the cows he sat with Fang for a while, giving him a bit of roughhouse and a tick-check. Gave him a quick hug before he grabbed him by the collar and scooted him into the cage.

"Just so you know I'm not turning into a complete sap," he said, as the dog barked at his retreating back.

By the time he'd completed the short walk to the house he'd decided. The phone rang twice before Martin answered.

"How goes it?"

"Okay. D'ya get your jobs done?"

"Yep. Just thinking about what movie I'll put on after dinner. You?"

"Mmm. I dunno." He was now feeling torn. Should he or shouldn't he?

"What's up?"

He let a few breaths go by before answering. "So, why don't you come out after you've eaten and we'll do a movie together. Stay over if you want. No funny business. Need to try and re-establish things, like."

He rang off the phone. "Weak as piss," he muttered.

Chapter Thirteen

After Martin left on Sunday, David went out to the ute and took a lot of the piled-up items back into the shed. He'd been over-zealous. There was some potential in some of those things yet.

He'd been relieved, again, when Martin had gone home. It was a good sign. He needed time to think, and he couldn't get his head around things with him there, as much as he wanted his cake and to eat it. It was like his presence confused a signal trying to get through. But it felt like his mind was going round and round in the same circles looking for a way out of the maze. The distance of a few days didn't seem to be delivering any more clarity.

There was no question that he enjoyed Martin's company. That was a given. But the events of Friday night and the early hours of Saturday morning had burned through some serious boundaries. He had felt for some time that Martin would be the catalyst for some kind of confession; a vomit that, once started, would continue until he was empty. But he had never for one moment anticipated the aftermath. Nor had he seen through his own deeper motives for wanting to expose his innards like that to Martin in the first place.

He was not gay—no debate necessary. He had never felt anything for the male form or any particular male, ever. Period. He was infatuated with breasts, for god's sake. But it was true he hadn't had his hands on any for an eon. That had to be part of the problem.

He let it all play out in his mind yet again. As soon as he got to the part where his mouth was full of Martin's neck he hardened. Then he forced himself to imagine it being someone else: Johnno maybe, or the guy on the magazine cover. He shuddered, a river of revulsion shivering down his spine. And yet, he had wanted to fuck Martin. What was going on with him? Nothing like it had ever crossed his mind till he'd been curled up behind him in the dark.

Even though there were now a few days between him and the rawness of Friday night, the memory of Martin's arms locked around him had him fighting back tears. He'd been in a vulnerable state, for sure, but there was no blaming Martin for taking advantage. There was even a vague unsettling memory of his begging him to stay.

He admitted it. It happened because of himself, and if he was honest, the thought of doing it again, or something similar, excited him. Excited and frightened at the same time. The intensity of the experience had shocked him. And his gun hadn't even left the holster.

After Martin returned on Saturday night, they'd simply fallen back into the pattern of doing the kinds of things they'd been doing together for weeks now. Everything seemed the same. But as Saturday night drew to a close, he became tense under the expectation that things were now different and Martin would be wanting more from him.

But Martin wasn't stupid, nor was he pushy. Sitting reading in their opposite corners of the couch he'd smiled at him over the top of his Patricia Cornwell and said, "You must be looking forward to having your bed to yourself tonight."

For a moment he hadn't known how to respond. The wave of relief was followed by an undercurrent of guilt. In the end he'd mumbled, "Yeah, I tend to spread out a bit."

That night he barely slept. Martin's smell was on the sheets and on the pillow. When he wasn't tossing and turning, he was self-abusing like wild fury, his face jammed into Martin's pillow. Twice he nearly went to the spare room, but fear stopped him.

At breakfast he was quietly pleased to see Martin looked less than his best.

"Mate, you look about as wasted as I feel."

Martin gave him a rueful look. "I jacked off twice in the night and I still couldn't sleep. You?"

David dipped his head and held up three fingers. They'd laughed like nervous schoolboys.

After breakfast they packed lunch materials and went hiking. On the ridgeline of the hill, they'd stopped to rest. Martin walked over to the edge of a rock shelf and sat down with his elbows resting on his knees. As David dropped his pack to the ground, he looked over at Martin's broad expanse of back and noticed how his fringe blew up in the breeze like a cocky's comb. There was no thinking about it. He walked over behind him and sat down, his knees on either side and his arms around his shoulders. Martin let out a sigh and relaxed back against him. Nothing was said and nothing more than that happened. But the heat had welled up in his chest again and he had been careful to keep his hands still and his mouth at a distance.

When Martin had thrown his bag in the back of his car he'd walked back to where David was standing and quickly leaned in for a kiss on the cheek.

"Lunch on Wednesday?"

David nodded, unable to speak.

"Good." He smiled. "See you then."

Now he was alone again trying to make sense of it all. He was beginning to hate his own company.

He was down with Fang that evening when he heard the car growling up the drive. He quickly shoved him in the cage and came outside. He was standing by the car door as Jodie opened it. She was wearing her uniform.

"You on the way in or back?" He never knew what her shifts were these days.

"Thanks for not being able to tell the difference." She gave him a sarcastic look. "Heading in. Dad asked me to return these spare parts he got off you the other day."

"Oh, no good?"

"No. He needs different sizes. I think his model is different to yours. He also said to tell you that Biddy's on the loose again, so you can let Fang out again. But he said you'd be summoned in the middle of the night to get him if he starts up again."

"Yeah, well, fair enough too." He went round to the boot and pulled out a box of drill bits and attachments. "Not sure what'll I'll do with him if he does though. Cross fingers, eh."

"I'm changing back to day shift soon, so yeah." She paused, watching him drop the box on the verandah and walk back to the car, looking like she wasn't yet ready to go. "So, what'd you boys get up to this weekend, then?"

"Oh. Just the usual stuff. He gives me a hand with a few things around the place and I pay him back with some dinner and a few beers. Nothin' too exciting."

"Mmm." She scanned her eyes around the property as if considering something. "David." She tapped her hand on top of the door.

"Yeah?"

"You aren't going to like what I'm about to say."

A spiky worm twisted in his gut. He folded his arms in front of him. "Go on."

"When I was at the pub on Friday—"

"You been going on your own, then?"

"People are asking after you, wondering where you've been. You and Fast Eddy get talked about in the same breath these days. Not all of it—"

"Well, they should keep their bad breath to themselves," he fired back at her, immediately angry when he heard his voice launch up an octave. His head was starting to pound. "Fuck, this place is full of gossips with nothin' better to do with their time!" He took his hat off and ran his hand through his hair, put his hat back on, avoiding Jodie's eyes the while, aware that she was staring at him. Decided some mock bravado might help. "Surely no one is accusing our neatly buttoned-up doctor of anything unseemly?"

"I've heard some of the nurses saying there's a reason why our Dr James isn't married."

"Oh, come on. He's only thirty-two for Christ's sake."

"I'm just telling you what I've heard. You're off in a little world of your own these days and I'd hate for you to get a rude shock. You need to show your face at the pub – not just talk about it. Might shut some people up." She glanced at his face, unable to see his expression in the shadow cast by his hat. "Anyway, I've said my bit. S'up to you what you do."

He watched her drive off, his thoughts whirling like a willy-willy full of dust and rubbish. Apart from all the confused things he was feeling, his fear of anyone knowing or even suspecting was very real. The thought of Dan or Mrs Wilson finding out made him sick with terror. Jodie liked Martin, or he thought she did, but he could still imagine the look of disgust on her face. The cool way she delivered her views just now a preamble to what was to come, perhaps. Fuck, he'd never be able to go to the saleyards again and some redneck would probably smash him to a pulp in the Black Rock car park, just to prove a point. All this could still happen long after Martin had gone back to his normal life in Sydney.

He caught himself thinking of Martin several times over the course of Monday, but this lessened over Tuesday. By Wednesday morning he'd come to a decision. He had too much at stake.

On the drive into town, he deliberately sought out his memories of a girl he'd been with at uni. Sonia her name was. Sonia Arciero. There'd been quite a few one- and double-night stands, at uni and later when he was working, but Sonia was the one who'd stuck around the longest. Where most of his sexual memories were. She had long black hair falling to the middle of her back and dark pools for eyes. He'd struck out in the breast department, but it hadn't mattered. Her skin had tasted of summer. He smiled as he recalled the lectures they'd missed, skiving back to her place while her flatmates were out. One time in particular he remembered was when the sun had been burning in through the window on him, his head between her legs. When she'd grabbed his hair, the scalding pull of it against his scalp had felt like a brand. He never figured out what went wrong. Everything seemed fine until one afternoon they'd argued. He couldn't even remember what started it; all he recalled was the term "emotionally constipated". What the hell did that mean when it was at home? He still didn't know. He'd thrown it in his mental too-hard basket long ago.

He became more aware of his surroundings as he pulled up for a red light. He was nearly there. As he pushed his trolley around the supermarket aisles, the queasy feeling he'd been trying to ignore rose like a flock of moths in his gut. His shopping and errands were over dismayingly fast and soon he was pulling up in front of the surgery. It was like he had a clenched fist in his chest.

The house door was ajar, and he walked in. In the kitchen Martin had a tea towel draped over his shoulder. He was leaning over a chopping board. The *tick-tick-tick* of the knife cut David's raw nerves.

"Hey." He turned and smiled. Then his smile disappeared. He slowly pulled at the tea towel and wiped his hands, his eyes not leaving David's. They stared at each other for a long moment until David found his voice.

"Martin, I—"

"No. I don't want to hear you say it. You're so obvious, David. So fucking transparent." He threw the tea towel into the sink, glaring at him. "You can't do it. What will people say? You're not gay. Blood rushed to your head. Am I getting close?" He turned and braced himself over the sink, his head lowered.

David stared at the expanse of back, the stooped shoulders rising and falling with his breathing, every line of his body spelling defeat. He had expected, no, he had *wanted* an argument. Anger would save him.

He tried again. "It's not like I—"

"So, we can't even be friends, is that what you want to say? Let's write the whole bloody thing off: baby, bathwater. That's it."

"You say that, but in a few months, you'll be gone. Back to Sydney. Back with your *lovers*."

"What do you—"

"Can't you see we lead different lives? There's no fucking point to this," he roared. His pulse jarred in his temple, each breath feeling like a knife. "I had nothing before you showed up and I'll be left with nothing when you're gone. You'll leave me."

David's voice cracked and he clamped his mouth shut, desperate for the anger to hold him together.

Martin stood up slowly and turned around, his eyes large. After an abyss of time, he walked over and stood in front of him, placed his hands on David's biceps, and nodded. Was silent for a moment.

"Now we're getting somewhere. I got that signal from you on Friday night, but to have you come out and say it seems like a big deal to me."

David let out an exhalation of frustration and reefed himself out of Martin's grasp. "I don't see how it fucking helps me either way. Once you're gone, we'll talk on the phone a bit every now and then, exchange a few emails maybe, and that will be it until your attention is diverted elsewhere. Assuming I haven't been done over with a cattle prodder at the back of the saleyards in the meantime." He turned back to face him. "They're already talking about us, you know."

Martin's face clouded over. "I see."

"*Do* you see though?"

Martin collapsed down onto the couch, extending his arms along the back on either side, his head flung back and his eyes closed.

David sat in the armchair opposite him. "So, you're taking the crucifixion option?"

Martin's head snapped up and he laughed grimly. "No. Just sick of narrow-minded shit. Why can't people just leave each other be?"

"That's what living in a small town is like. Your business becomes everyone's business. It's the negative side to having a 'community'. On that note, Jodie came and saw me after you left. She had a few pearls of wisdom to drop on me."

Martin looked up, his eyes suddenly wary.

"She says our absence from the pub has been duly noted and we need to show our faces. Stare down some of this fuckwit chatter."

"She said that?"

"Well, in so many words. Less the fuckwit bit. Although that's usually the subtextual reference to myself whenever she's imparting a piece of her mind. She also said there's some gossip being bandied around the hospital—"

Martin sighed. "I'm sorry, David. That was inevitable. There aren't Chinese walls between here and Sydney and I don't pretend to be anything other than I am—but I don't wear it on my sleeve either. My private life is my private life, but stuff still leaks out. People string little bits together and make up a necklace. I'm sorry it's impacting on you like this…on our friendship."

David was sitting with his hands tightly clasped between his knees. He looked up after a moment of thought. "Well, I think we should go to the pub for the rugby final like we said. Jodie's right. We need to get out and face this stuff down. You can't refute things if people can't say them to your face."

"You need to be careful, David. Don't go spoiling for a fight. You won't win, is my experience."

David ground the heel of his hand into his other palm. "Well, waiting for shit to hit me in the back isn't an option either. Better to die on your feet than live on your knees."

Martin smiled. "Midnight Oil?"

"Well done. Except I think Zapata said it first. What were you planning for lunch?"

Chapter Fourteen

So, he'd agreed, despite his misgivings—didn't feel there was a choice really. Jodie would've been on to him in a flash if he'd refused, and yet it gave him a feeling of disquiet. As if he would be appearing in public with a key piece of clothing missing.

"I'll have a drink with you guys, but I won't be staying for the match. I'm out for dinner with a friend."

He noticed that she took Martin's attendance for granted.

"You having your fancy nancy red, squire?" They were at the bar and David had pulled out his wallet.

"I'll get this round. I want to see what else they've got."

They found a stool for Jodie while they stood around a tall table in the room with the big screen. Kick-off was an hour away, but the room was already buzzing with activity.

Martin poured wine for Jodie. "So, what mischief have you been up to?"

She looked up at him, a wary smile on her face. "Oh, not much. Been taking on some extra shifts at work, so I've been a bit tired."

"You must be rolling in money then. Next round's on you, kiddo." David lifted his schooner to chink with her wineglass.

They bantered back and forth with each other and with random people coming up to chat and harass.

He looked at the clock on the wall. "We'd better get our orders in for dinner, mate." He turned towards the crowd at the bar, reaching back to place his hand on Martin's shoulder, leaving it to rest there just a fraction too long before hastily dropping it by his side. "The burgers here are pretty good?"

He strode over to the bar, mentally smacking himself in the head the whole way. *You dumb cunt.* Such a simple thing to do, but it spelt death if he didn't stay awake. He found himself scanning the room aggressively to see who might have seen or be looking back at their table. Thank god Jodie was with them.

He did his time queuing at the bar, delivering opinions about the upcoming game and exchanging nods with blokes standing around, paid for their order, and got himself a schooner. He flirted with the barmaid a bit longer and louder than he might have normally, wondering if he was being judged. He came back to stand beside Jodie, plonking down what looked like an alien spaceship on the table. He was chuckling. "There's a bloody Kiwi backpacker on the kitchen staff tonight, poor kid. She's on a hiding to nothing whether they win or lose."

"After the game we saw the other night, she might want to make a quick backdoor escape before the game's over."

"No. I've got a feeling in me water. We're—" David suddenly dropped his voice, a devilish glint in his eyes. "Hello. Here's trouble." He was looking over Martin's shoulder towards the front entrance.

Martin glanced behind him in the direction of a barrel-chested man with the face of a cherub approaching. He glanced at Jodie, who was now sitting up straight in her seat. The man ambled up, the flush in his cheeks seeming to increase with his proximity.

David stepped forward, his hand outstretched. "How's it going, mate?"

"Good, mate, good." The man stole a look at Jodie, a nervous smile on his full lips.

Before David could open his mouth again, she said, "Simon, I'd like you to meet Martin. The new doctor I was telling you about." Ignoring David, she turned to Martin. "Simon's taking me for dinner at that new restaurant in Gibson I mentioned to you, the one just down from the hospital."

Simon went over to a neighbouring table to grab a spare chair and David wasted no time leaning in. "You didn't tell me you had a date tonight," he hissed.

"I bloody did," she hissed back.

David mouthed, *but him?* as Simon hoisted himself up on his seat next to Jodie. They made small talk for a while, but all seemed relieved when the buzzer erupted in a flurry of farting and flashing lights. Simon got down from his stool and held out his hand to Jodie, who was focusing gamely on an elegant dismount.

David returned with their dinner and they took over the stools. He sat there staring at his burger for a moment, his expression one of wonderment. And here he was thinking she'd been working her fanny off all this time… *Jesus*, he rebuked himself, *not a good turn of phrase there…* Of course, she had to have a life, but this was the doughy guy she'd been running away from for *ages*. Why was he suddenly okay now? Or was it just without him around to protect her she'd given him a chance and found him…not so bad? He grimaced. Although the alternative of imagining her that desperate was worse. Finally, he looked up at Martin.

"Well, bugger me with a fish fork."

"I don't see why you're so surprised."

"You can't tell me you saw this coming?"

"Well, not exactly, but—"

"She told me he gives her the creeps."

Martin juggled his burger, strategising his first bite. "Clearly she's changed her mind then."

He shrugged. "Women, eh."

Martin had turned back to face her, her eyes still locked on his shoulder where David's hand had been. Her lips parted as her gaze shifted to David's departing back. She'd turned to Martin, her eyes challenging him.

Martin had returned her stare and sipped his wine. He placed his glass back on the table, smiled, and shrugged, his expression saying, *what do you want me to do about it?*

When she'd reached for the bottle and topped up their glasses, he'd said, "Planning a big night, are we?"

"Oh, no. Pretty low key." She'd been nervous about Simon arriving, and she was sure Martin had noticed her looking at the door one too many times. He had looked on the verge of asking the question when David had returned with the buzzer.

Before she had much time to think about it, Simon had shown up and whisked her away. Although not before David had cast judgement on her. Well, too bad. It didn't hurt for him to know she had other options. Of course, she wanted him to be jealous, but he was so self-absorbed she couldn't expect him to see what was going on right under his nose.

She sighed and made an effort to tune in to Simon's chat as they drove to the restaurant. Poor guy. He was always a bit nervy to start off with, talking his head off.

It was mainly due to Sarah that she was here now. He'd obviously found it easier to come up and chat with her in the company of a girlfriend without David around. Sarah had thought his keen interest in her sweet.

When he was at the bar buying both of them a drink, she said, "I mean, I'm not sure about his being your type, but why don't you give him a chance? You might have some fun and we might see a smile on your mush for a change. He seems like a gentleman. What have you got to lose?"

What indeed, she thought glumly, *except my self-respect*. But as it turned out they'd had some lovely meals together, and after his puppy dog excitement had settled down, she discovered he had a bit more class than she'd thought. He was quite the wine buff and, being a stock and station agent rather than a farmer, wasn't quite as emotionally weighed down as many others. Of course, he was impacted, but he wasn't having to work from morning till night like David and her father did for so little return. She had also smugly enjoyed David having to choke down his shock when he realised Simon wasn't there for a passing hello.

Simon was slowing down the car and with some relief she saw bright outdoor lights coming into view. Maybe now she could stop re-seeing David's hand resting on Martin's shoulder. It was very strange when he was so not given to intimate touching like that, unless of course, it was in jest. She just hoped no one else had seen it to lay their own interpretation on it and that he managed to keep his nose clean for the rest of the evening.

She had more important things on her mind now in any case, as she waited for Simon to walk around to her side of the car. It was date four and she was pretty sure she was going to get the hard word put on her at the end of it. In her current frame of mind, it was looking like she might just let herself go with the flow.

"Guess I might as well come in for a bit? Have a cuppa?"

"Sure. Stay if you want and I'll open a wine."

The evening had gone all right. He'd been nervous about losing the cover of Jodie's company, especially after that earlier slip-up, but once the game had got underway and they'd started yelling and hooting with everyone else, he'd been able to relax. And the Wallabies had squeaked home. Things were okay. Although his mind kept returning to the hand on the shoulder and Jodie's face. It had been so automatic, and he was kicking himself for it now. Little things like that could be his undoing.

Now, following Martin up the brick path, tension threaded up his neck and into his stomach.

Their conversation from Wednesday was still playing through his mind, as it had been on and off over the last few days. Martin had put it to him over lunch. If he sold the farm, he could come and stay with him in his flat—plenty of room—

but only until he sorted himself out, of course. He could pick up some supply teaching to start with, until he found his feet.

David had rejected the idea out of hand. Crazy talk. But his mind kept returning to it like a dog to a carcass.

He'd been able to put it in words to Martin, finally. "I can't leave here. I feel like I'd be leaving…him. He's here. In the house, out of it." He'd looked at him apologetically. "It's my penance."

Martin laid down his cutlery. He extended his hand and planted it firmly on David's chest. It was a while before he spoke. "Tim lives in here, David. You don't have to be out in the sticks to feel his presence. In your heart he will always be alive."

David had looked away, his eyes stinging.

"It's like I'd be giving up on something…"

"What? The constant punishment? The self-flagellation?"

David grunted. "You make me sound like a sick bastard."

Martin shrugged and went back to his lunch. "What's normal for one is kinky for another."

Of course, any moving in with him would have to be temporary. It was great that he was offering, as he couldn't eject his tenants at short notice and it would be expensive staying anywhere short term. Although with no heavy work and the way Martin cooked, he'd be the size of a house in a matter of weeks. And these weren't the only thoughts he'd been dwelling on. The possibilities opening up before him were driving him in other directions too. When he was with Martin there was an unfamiliar feeling of joy in his chest, a lightness in his head that must be like being on drugs. If it was, he was teetering dangerously, about to step off the edge of the cliff. And the more he felt it, the more intently he wanted to pursue it, push it. He was now allowing himself to imagine all kinds of things, and the imagining was making it real—something entirely possible, acceptable.

Martin's goodbye kiss had not been the anxious peck of Wednesday. But David still hadn't known how to react when his lips had lingered and soft breath had feathered his ear. The urge to break the moment had been strong and he had to quell the desire to fidget by jamming his hands in his pockets.

"I haven't been able to make myself change the sheets," he said.

Martin pulled back to give him a look that combined distaste and amusement. He put on a camp lisp. "That's dis*gust*ing."

The shock of hearing him speak like that had him choking back a laugh.

So, the bare fact remained. Lust was beginning to shut down his ability to think rationally. To think at all. Mrs Palmer and her five daughters were all very well, but he wanted contact, warmth, a response. And it was there for the asking.

All his conflicted thoughts were playing a push-pull game under his skin and in his mind as he lay back in the sofa cradling his wineglass in his open hand. Martin had put on a Sarah Vaughan CD and David had thrown his head back in luxurious recognition when "Summertime" came on. He smiled, his eyes closed. "You know I'm a disaster when I start drinking wine. Anyone'd think you were planning to take advantage of me."

When no answer came, he opened his eyes. Martin's eyebrows flickered up and down as he swirled his wine around, the lamplight creating a sparkling shimmer in his glass. "I don't know, David." His voice seemed to have taken on a silky smoothness or maybe he was just imagining things. But he wasn't imagining the cheeky tilt at the corner of Martin's mouth. "That doesn't sound like a particularly smart strategy to me."

Even with the wine softening everything, he was intensely aware of every move Martin made. It was like watching a film where he was doomed to be a passive observer. A feeling of despair began to wrap its fingers around him.

He awoke to a hand ruffling his hair. Martin was standing behind the lounge, gently extracting the wineglass from his hand. "You're done in, lad. Time for bed."

David rubbed his face and stood up. It was only now he wondered where he'd be sleeping. It was too late to make up a bed now, surely. Something began to unwind in his chest, like leaves unfurling to the light.

He stood at the end of the table as Martin rinsed their glasses. He looked down at his hand tracing patterns on the table, felt Martin turn around and lean on the sink. He watched David for a moment and then came over to stand in front of him.

"You'll have to help me, David. I don't know what you want."

There was a cool intake of breath as he glanced up at him, but his gaze quickly dropped to Martin's shirt front, his hand continuing its movement on the table.

"I, um—" He reached up and grabbed a loose handful of Martin's shirt.

Martin inclined his head forward. "What's up?"

"Can we—" He tilted his head back but it was too slight for Martin to notice.

"Can we what?" he asked softly.

David let out a gust of air. "Stop being a bastard."

"I'm not going to risk second-guessing you, David. Spell it out."

David's shoulders bounced up and down in frustration, his eyes rising only as high as Martin's mouth. His voice was an anguished whisper.

"I want to…" His breath caught in his throat and he tried again. "I wanna…I wanna do…stuff to you."

The mouth in front of him trembled into a smile. "You can do whatever you like, my friend." There was a hesitant pause and the smile wavered. "Within reason."

David raised his eyes abruptly to Martin's and grinned.

"I can be reasonable."

He watched as Martin moved around the kitchen switching lights off and then walked ahead of him to the bedroom. Despite his heart being in his mouth as they walked down the hall, he still had the off-putting thought that this was where old Dr Jacobs and his wife slept and where they—urrgh. *No.* No, *not good.*

Martin hadn't turned on the light and there was just enough dim ambient light to see shadows and forms. He found him standing at the foot of the bed. There was less than a foot of space between them, but his skin crackled with electricity.

There was a long pause when only their breathing could be heard, and he realised Martin's was as sporadic as his own.

A murmur came to him in the dark. "So…this *stuff*…?"

Martin must have moved slightly as he got a sudden nose full of his cologne, a sweet smell of the sea: salt and wind and waves. He felt again that rush of sun in his chest and took a deep breath. He reached out in the dark and anchored his hand on Martin's belt buckle. With his other hand he started tugging at his shirt, pulling it free, remembering how that had felt the first time he did it. His knuckles grazed bare stomach and Martin jerked away and gasped.

"You know I don't know what the hell I'm doing here," he whispered.

"Shhh. You're d-doing just *fine*."

The quaver in Martin's voice fired his purpose and he quickly undid his buttons, reefing his shirt open. He pulled him forward so he could smell his skin, open his mouth and taste the base of his neck. Noted with excitement the bursting pulse there.

"Come and lay down."

He ran his palm smoothly over Martin's chest, moving down until he hit that downy trail of hair underneath his navel, where his hand stalled. He leaned down and replaced it with his mouth.

The body underneath him heaved. "Christ, you'll make me come in my pants."

David laughed softly. "Well, we can't have that now."

Quickly the pants were shed and hit the floor and David's brain was racing, realising what he was doing, or about to do.

Maybe it was a bridge too far…maybe he couldn't…but while his analytical brain was in overdrive trying to jam both feet on the brakes, his body had just steamed ahead as if the next steps were obvious and natural.

It wasn't all smooth sailing. He made a few clunky moves, and it was strange encountering the kinds of smells he associated more with himself than any woman he'd ever been with. It also wasn't long before his jaw was aching, giving him a whole new perspective. It was all quicker than it seemed, though, as Martin's body was rampant underneath him and soon let out a final convulsive shudder. He felt a surge of power thinking that this was the neat buttoned-up doctor who had everything under control whose sobbing breathing he could now hear.

He crawled up the bed to be level with Martin's face. "Well, that was something different."

He heard a breathy laugh, then a hard swallow, as Martin tried to gain some control.

"Has it been a while?"

"Yes…and no. It's different with someone you…really like." Martin rolled onto his side and David felt his own belt buckle being grabbed. "I can't be the only relieved soul in this bed."

"Ohhh, you'd better be careful." An animal groan escaped his lips when Martin's fingers slipped under the material of his jocks. "Highly combustible…you'll lose an—"

He gripped Martin's hair and his brain liquified. "Spectacular" just didn't cut it.

Chapter Fifteen

Living like an ascetic for more than five years had been worse for him than he'd realised. If Martin had been surprised at the sudden level of demand he'd been subjected to, he made no comment—in fact he'd seemed chuffed. But by Sunday afternoon he was almost begging to leave, saying he needed to get some sleep before his week started.

And David had his own work to catch up on. Some cows had dropped their calves during the week and one of them wasn't doing so well. Martin thought that he should give it till Monday before calling the vet and he'd been easily convinced, dreading the expense. He also had to organise his next delivery of water, and already hay supplies were on his mind again. If it didn't rain by the end of November, chances were it wouldn't all summer. And then there would be the double hazard of fire. It was coming at him from all angles and if he didn't keep moving, he'd be frozen with worry.

He drove the ute around, feeding animals and checking things. He was in a daze from lack of sleep and a surfeit of sex. It made him feel hollow knowing the house would be empty when he returned—he told himself it would be good to have his whole bed back and actually use it to get some sleep, but in just two nights, dozing with Martin's naked body curled into him had become like breathing. He despised himself for behaving like a hormonal teenager, when Martin seemed so together and mature, but he'd settle down. It was just the novelty.

It wasn't until he was fixing himself some beans on toast for dinner that he realised he'd neglected to strip the bed. In the commercial break of a show he was watching, he pulled out some fresh sheets and walked into the fug that was his bedroom. *Whoa.* He went straight to the window and wrenched it open. He couldn't wipe the grin off his face as he yanked at the sheets. Oh well, it wasn't a shrine. There'd be plenty more where that came from. Then he stopped mid yank. Or there would be until December anyway. Trying to make himself think any further down the road than that, on top of all his other worries, just made his head hurt.

On Wednesday he signed several large cheques. With each squiggle of his name, he felt his overdraft ratchet up like a physical thing in counterweight to his sinking heart. He was skating close to his limit and Ethan would soon be on the blower asking him to come in for a "chat". He was desperate to get to Martin's where he could put it all out of his mind for a while. Their time together was quickly becoming a brief oasis of relief from it all, which partly explained his frenetic need, but he always had to come home to reality in the end.

An hour or so later he was lying back on the lounge observing Martin search the floor for his shirt buttons. Since he'd barrelled through the door there hadn't been a word exchanged. But now he frowned and sniffed the air. "Is something burning?"

Martin leaped up and ran to the kitchen. "That would be lunch. I hope you like your pizza cremated."

As they crunched their way through Martin's ex-gourmet pizzas David described his morning activities.

"Jesus, David, this can't go on."

He stared at the remains of a crust between his fingers. "I know it can't. I'm gunna...I'm gunna have to see Ethan next week."

"And what? Ask for a bigger overdraft?"

"Putting the place on the market isn't going to stop the bills rolling in."

"Selling off your cattle would kill some of your immediate expenses and give you some cash."

"Yeah, I know." He picked up the charred crusts on his plate and began snapping them between his fingers.

"I know this is tough for you." Martin placed his hand on David's, halting his mess-making. "But it's better for you to sell under your own terms than have the bank do it for you." He dipped his head trying to get David to look at him. "Isn't it?"

He breathed out gustily through his nose, his mouth set in a grim line. His answer, when it came, was barely above a murmur. "Yeah. It is."

He helped Martin clear up and they sat down for a last drink before he left. They discussed their plans for the weekend and the fact that they would be over at the Wilsons' for dinner on Saturday night. He already had a bit of a story ready about how Martin was helping him get onto a few old fusty jobs; those extra nice-to-haves you never got around to. He wouldn't have to overexplain that to Dan. He wasn't altogether comfortable about undergoing Mrs Wilson's close scrutiny, but just had to have faith that he could bluff and tumble his way through things as usual.

"You're going to be treated to a proper rhubarb crumble, I'm told."

"I'm looking forward to it, after all your raving."

"Not sure if Jodie'll be there, now she's got a bit of a diversion going on."

Martin suppressed a smile. "You don't sound altogether happy about it. Is that the big brother coming out in you?"

He gave him a despairing look. "I guess it is. I just think she could do better, y'know? He's a bit bloody old for her, doncha reckon?"

"He can't be older than you?"

"Same age, give or take. That's my point. That's about ten years' difference—she's just a youngster. Plus, she's got everything going for her—why waste it on *him*? I don't know what's suddenly got into her. Clock ticking d'ya think? She could do better, that's all." He sniffed and wiped his cuff across his mouth. "Anyway," he said gruffly. "S'her business, I guess."

Chapter Sixteen

"I'm so glad you could come, Martin. It's such a pleasure to have you here." Mrs Wilson took the bottle of Penfolds he held out and she passed it back to David. "I'll let you deal with this." She winked at Martin. "We're not big drinkers in this house, but Jodie will enjoy sharing it with you."

Jodie was yet to appear; her shift only ended at six.

"She's been putting in the hours lately?" David watched Mrs Wilson carefully.

"Ye-es. But you know she's been seeing that Simon Kelly. It's not all been work."

David folded his arms. "And what do you think about that, anyway?"

"Oh, he's nice enough. Dan likes him."

Dan roused, hearing his name. "Yeah, he's okay."

"You don't sound convinced."

"Heavens, David. It's not like she's about to marry him. Having a man falling over himself to impress her won't do her any harm." She sent an exasperated glance in Martin's direction who grinned back at her.

He drummed his fingers on the back of a chair. Not the reassurance he'd been looking for, but then what *had* he wanted them to say exactly? Something to show they were on his side? Which was…?

A dog barking outside interrupted his mooching and Dan turned his head. "Here's Jodie-girl now."

She appeared in the doorway in her uniform and soft shoes, some loose strands of hair escaped from her bun, framing her face.

"You're just in time for some red." David held up his glass.

Ignoring him she said, "I don't think I'll be joining you, Mum. I'm absolutely knackered."

David put his glass down and walked towards her. "Aw, come on. There's gonna be rhubarb crumble?"

"I've had it before," she said dryly.

"But we haven't seen you for ages." He made a clumsy lunge and wrapped his arms around her. Jodie went rigid and her expression resembled a dog's when they realise they've been caught for a bath.

"For god's sake," she snapped, pulling away from him.

Mrs Wilson pursed her lips and turned back to stirring something on the stove. "Go and freshen up, Miss Cranky-pants, and see how you feel then. You can grace us with your presence for a short while, can't you?"

Martin sipped his wine, an amused twinkle in his eyes. He walked over and sat next to Dan at the table. David soon came up to lean on the back of a chair facing them.

"Martin's been giving me some cooking lessons, Dan. I can make a pretty mean beef curry now."

Dan's eyes lit up. "Curry, eh? Nell won't make me curry."

"You know I don't like spicy food." She rolled her eyes. "You poor put-upon man."

"You'll have to sneak over one night, and we'll have a boy's night."

"Every night's a boy's night at your place these days, isn't it?"

Jodie had returned, her face pink and her hair falling on her shoulders.

"We behave ourselves all right."

Jodie raised her eyebrows, pretending to read the label on the wine bottle. Martin took it off her and poured her a glass.

"I think you'll like this one," he said. "It's softer than that one we had the other night."

"You've spoilt her, mate. I haven't seen her drink a Tooheys New since you've been here."

Jodie opened her mouth, a sharp retort obviously on her lips, but she stopped herself. Instead, she politely clinked glasses with Martin and sipped her wine.

There was a pause in the conversation while David looked around at them all. He cleared his throat, looking into his glass. "Well, while I've got you all here, I'd ah, like to make a little announcement."

Jodie put her glass down looking like she'd just seen a rat crawl over David's shoulder.

David addressed himself to Dan. "I'm going to put the farm on the market."

There was a pause while Dan took this information in and then he closed his eyes and nodded.

"Oh, Davey, I'm so sorry. Well, no, I'm not completely sorry, but…" Mrs Wilson had come over to grab his arm and look up into his face.

Still watching Dan, and unable to keep a pleading tone out of his voice, he said, "I—I've got to. While I've still got a chance of getting a price higher than my overdraft."

"It's a bastard life in the bad times, Davey. Even in the good times there's no money in small farms any more. Get out while you can." Dan's voice was dull and there was sadness in his eyes. "I'm just sorry I can't make you an offer."

David let out a grim laugh. "At least Penelope will be pleased. She might get some money at last."

Jodie had been looking from her father to her mother, open-mouthed, saying nothing. When she finally spoke, she was looking narrowly at Martin. "But what will you do?"

Martin stared into his wineglass, aware that David was also now looking at him.

"Go back to teaching. Martin has offered to put me up until I can get set up; I'll have to give my tenants the proper notice. Then I'll be back in Maroubra."

His eyes flicked from Dan to Mrs Wilson and back again. His stomach felt loaded with the finality of it. It hadn't seemed real until now, just shooting the breeze with Martin and dreaming, but now he could see the impact of it on these faces that he loved.

Mrs Wilson sighed heavily. "It's the best thing for you, Davey, but it will be hard not having you nearby."

"Anyway." He stood back from the chair and sighed. "That's what Martin's been helping me out with every weekend, clearing and tidying up for a sale. Next step will be some building repairs and cans of paint."

Dan had meanwhile scraped out his chair and disappeared out the back.

David reached around Mrs Wilson's shoulders and gave her a side hug. Her eyes shone with tears. She laughed apologetically at Martin. "He's like my own son. I'm allowed to cry." She bustled over to the Kleenex box.

Dan re-entered the room with something large and dusty in his hands. Cobwebs trailed over the tablecloth as he set it down.

"Oh, Dan. Not on my clean table!"

Unperturbed, he said, "I think it's time to crack this open, Nell. That place has been in Mulkerin hands for three generations now. It's the end of an era."

"Fair crack of the whip, Dan, it's not sold yet. D'ya wanna wait?"

"Nuh. Now's as good a time as any, while we're all here together."

Martin leaned forward, squinting at the label, half eaten away.

"Dad, that'll be rotten by now."

"I've had it laid at the bottom of the stone shed. It'll be worth a sip, I reckon."

"Grandfather Port?" Martin scraped some grime away with his thumb, trying to see more. "How long have you had this?"

"Wedding present." He smirked at his wife.

"Are you serious?"

Nellie laughed. "I told you we weren't drinkers."

Soon Dan was carving the roast at one end of the table while his wife walked around wielding tongs and roast vegetables. Then David's favourite part: the passing round of the gravy. The next while was given over to the clinking of cutlery on plates and conversation was stymied by bulging cheeks and laughter. There was a moment there, when he paused to pick up his beer, that he looked around at this unrelated group of people who were more family than family. Felt a sharp dig in his heart to know this experience that he'd come to take for granted, to rely on, would be hard to come by if he moved away.

He glanced over at Martin who was laughing behind a napkin held up to his lips, Dan boggle-eyed, explaining something with jerky hand movements at full stretch. He wanted more than anything to bring Martin into this warm circle, could see how easily he fit it. But of course, that was only until they found out, then it would all fall down like a pack of cards. He'd be out in the wilderness, ostracised. He wiped his mouth, unable to bear the thought. Why did finally getting the love he needed have to mean giving up everything else he'd ever loved? He must have been staring into his plate for too long as he suddenly got a sharp jab in the ribs.

"Big changes. Made your mind up pretty quickly, didn't you?" Jodie's tone wasn't friendly. A quick glance showed eyes full of anger and hurt.

He leaned into her, angling his face behind her head, keeping his voice low. "We can talk more about this later."

She sniffed and pushed her chair out, taking up his plate and hers and collecting the others before taking them over to the sink and scraping the meagre remains into the dog's bowl.

Dinner was soon over with Martin exclaiming suitably over dessert and having to accept seconds as a result.

Mrs Wilson was beaming under his praise. "We need to get you *eating*, Martin. You're so thin."

Then the crystal glasses came out of the display cabinet. Mrs Wilson gave them a whisk with a tea towel and placed them in a line on the table. "You do the honours, Martin. It looks like a doctor's steady hand might be required."

He looked at the five glasses. "So, you're all having some? This isn't going to end with you dancing on the table, is it, Nellie?"

Nellie blushed and waved her hand. "It'll more likely end up with Dan snoring."

Dan seemed to be having second thoughts. He looked at Martin from under his bushy brows. "It might be bloody rubbish…"

Martin was standing up so he could ease the cork out as gently as possible. "Yes, it might be. But it might also be the most fabulous thing you've drunk in your life. That's the fun, isn't it?"

"Well, that's promising." Martin held up the cork, which had emerged in one piece. He sniffed it and passed it to David, who did the same, looking at Martin for guidance.

Martin poured five glasses, the liquid a dingy brown. David was first to take a mouthful.

He smacked his lips. "Smooth as."

The others took wary sips, waiting for Martin to finish swirling his mouthful.

"Hmm. I think you've caught it just in time, Dan. Like dark molasses."

Dan visibly relaxed and took an eager mouthful.

Martin held his glass up to the light, scrutinising the colour. "Even if you could find it to buy, a bottle like this would cost you several hundred dollars."

Dan made a noise like a suppressed sneeze. "Bloody hell! And I've gone and wasted it on you lot!"

It was getting late, and Martin was deep in conversation with Mrs Wilson in front of the fire while Dan, in the armchair opposite, had his head flung back snoring. Nothing had been seen of Jodie since the washing-up had been finalised. He got up to go to the loo—still the old outdoor dunny for these guys, one thing he was glad his father had taken care of even if it did mean being extra careful with your grey water. It was easily managed when it was just him. He was just washing his hands at the outside laundry tub when the screen door shut and Jodie came to stand beside him.

He shook the droplets off his hands and grabbed the hand towel on the hook. She was leaning up against the other tub, arms folded, looking at him belligerently.

He watched her for a moment, placed the towel back on the hook and sighed. "Jodie, I'm sorry. What do you want me to say?"

"I want to know why years of toughing it out has suddenly collapsed in a heap now Martin James has turned up. What's going on?"

David's lips jammed shut, and he breathed in a harsh breath through his nose.

"I tell you what's up. The price of hay has doubled in the last few months, I've got calving cows worth almost nothing, and I've got rates due soon and an overdraft up to my wahzoo. An overdraft that may not even be paid off even if I do sell the farm. It could rain tomorrow, and my situation wouldn't be very much different. My back's about fucking broken, Jodie, that's what."

"Do you think it's any easier for Dad?"

"I can't make decisions for your dad. I can only make them for me."

"But why *now*? What's he been saying to you?"

Anger rose in David's throat and he did his best to swallow it down. "I told you why just now. All Martin has done, if you want to blame him for something, and clearly you do, is to point out that I have realistic alternatives to financial suicide and killing myself."

Jodie winced. "You could keep the farm and teach here. Sydney's a long way away."

"How do you reckon your dad'd go getting a full-time job while he kept the farm running full tilt?"

"Dad's got Mum…and me. Same way you could have—"

"No, Jodie. Apart from all the other things I could say to that, I would not drag someone else down this gurgler with me. No."

He looked at her for a long moment. "So. Is there anything else you want to blame on Martin before I go back inside?"

She stuck her chin out with a mutinous look on her face. "Not yet. But there will be."

Chapter Seventeen

On Sunday they made arrangements for the cows that had calved. With Fang doing most of the legwork, they separated the new mothers and calves from the rest and herded them up to a smaller paddock closer to the house. The paddock had an adjoining enclosure where the cows could be bailed up for milking. The calf David had been worried about had recovered and was frisking around behind his mother. After lunch they returned with David carrying a bucket of hot water and a stool he'd grabbed from the shed.

One by one, they bailed each cow up. David leaned under and cleaned the udders with the water and a cloth. As his fingers worked their rhythmic way down alternate teats and sharp sprays of milk rang in the bottom of the metal bucket, he looked up at Martin, his eyes twinkling in the shade of his hat brim. "I don't s'pose you have a lot of tit experience. Do you wanna give it a try?"

Martin's mouth quirked to the side. "No, I'll let you get on with it."

When David had satisfied himself that each cow had a good supply of milk, they took the bucket back to the house, but not before Fang had been given a splash in his dish.

Martin scalded the containers and David poured the frothing milk through a sieve.

"Mum'd make us custards and junkets galore when it was calving time. She even did a fancy blancmange once."

Martin gave him an indulgent smile. "You've got plenty of eggs. We'll do a baked custard."

While they were digging out possible receptacles, Martin flicked through an old cookbook he'd found in a drawer on an earlier occasion. "Good old Mrs Beeton. How about we try a cake as well?"

David had decided that AC/DC was appropriate musical accompaniment to baking, which had earned him a bemused look from Martin. When "You Shook Me All Night Long" was blasting and David was doing his best Angus Wilson impression, Martin came in and turned the sound down.

"Mate, this cake will be as flat as your singing if you keep bouncing the floor like that."

Later, while the coffee was brewing on the stove, Martin made some icing for the butter cake that was cooling on the rack. David had finished cleaning up and was folding the tea towel over the rail. He stood and watched Martin paste the icing on the cake with precise movements. "You're quite the housewife, aren't you?"

Martin glanced up and smiled. "I can see that's a real problem for you."

"Yeah, well it's going to be." He patted his stomach.

Martin stood up and raised an eyebrow at him. He handed him the rubber spatula, still slathered in icing. "Planning on sticking with me for a while, then?"

David nodded as his tongue wrapped around the spatula. "You have to stop looking after me so well. I'll be like that mould infestation you can never get rid of."

Martin regarded him for a moment before turning away. "When you're finished deep-throating that spatula you can pour us some coffee, yeah?" David saluted his back before giving him a filthy grin.

With afternoon tea done, they were in the shed getting ready to feed the cows before Martin went home. The stacks of hay bales were getting low and there was a build-up of loose hay and chaff on the ground that hadn't been cleared away from the previous load. "Should really get and clean that up or I'll have rats up to my Khyber Pass."

"Can do it now, if you like." David watched Martin as he prepared to grab a bale. Suddenly he lowered his shoulder and tackled him side on, hearing the breath forced from his body. Martin crashed into a hay bale and rolled into the loose hay on the ground. He struggled between David's crushing weight and the prickly hay until he was at last face up, panting into David's grinning face. "Can't let you go back to Sydney without saying you've had a roll in the hay."

Martin let his head fall back. "You're such a *boy*."

David's grin faded into an expression of contrition. "Aw, Princess." He brought his hand up and gently pressed his thumb into Martin's cheek, which was bleeding from a scratch. "Lucky it wasn't a scrap of fencing wire." He leaned down and licked the wound.

Under his ministrations he felt Martin go still except for the rise and fall of his chest. "You Wannabe Wallaby. There are other ways to show affection, you know."

"Mmm. There are." He reached down to pull Martin's shirt from his trousers.

Martin halted the progress of his hand looking at him intently. "What I really want is for you to kiss me."

David's eyes widened.

"Kissing's really—that's something you do with girls. Besides," he leered, "I might get carried away, and then I'd want to fuck you."

Martin turned his head away. "That's just bullshit."

David rolled off him and lay on his back, staring at the crossbeams under the galvanised iron of the roof. He raised a hand and ran it through his hair.

"It's funny. You won't kiss me but you're happy to jam your—"

"It's just too…close, all right?"

Martin rolled over till he blocked David's view of the roof. "Too *close*? David, I know what a passing physical encounter is, and I know what having a lover feels like. Am I getting this completely wrong or is this just a holiday fuck for you until you find an available woman? It's time you were honest with me. I'm becoming seriously invested here."

An available woman? The thought hadn't occurred to him. The intensity of his encounters with Martin had driven any thoughts of women from his mind.

He frowned, shaking his head in wonder.

A dart of pain crossed Martin's features. "What's that mean?"

"This is serious," he whispered.

Martin's face relaxed and he brought his palm up and placed it over David's forehead. "You'd better mean that, because I'm in *love* with you."

David could hardly think what the words meant. All he could see was the look in Martin's eyes, knowing he could never let go of the feelings he gave him. Before he realised what was happening Martin's open mouth was on his. He tensed at the sensation, at Martin holding his head down. But he soon gave in; they were swimming, their mouths like water, their tongues like fishes. He heard a sob, not sure if it had come from Martin or himself. The kiss eventually ended but his grip on Martin hadn't and they continued to lie squashed in the hay. Slowly he became aware of the prickles through his shirt and the itches. He also noticed the wheezing in Martin's lungs.

"You got your puffer on you?"

"Yeah." He rolled away and dug into his pocket.

"Shit, and I thought you were happy—"

Something over Martin's shoulder had caught David's eye.

"What?"

David started easing himself up, his eyes locked on something. When he spoke, his voice was low and calm. "Roll slowly towards me, buddy. That's it. Don't make any sudden moves. Now get over and stand near the ute."

Martin looked behind him when he stood up. "*What?*"

"Snake. Big brown. Keep an eye on it while I get the gun."

"You're leaving me here with a fucking snake?"

David went over to where the dog had been lying at the entrance to the shed. He grabbed him by the collar and dragged him over to Martin. "Stick him in the ute."

"*Jesus Christ!*" Martin had located the snake. At a height of only two bales, its fat stomach was looped over the edge of the top bale, less than a metre above where their heads had been a moment before.

Martin was still frozen to the spot when he heard the screen door slam and David was running towards the shed, shotgun in hand. In the doorway he stopped to load two cartridges. As soon as Fang saw the gun he started barking and pawing at the window.

"Looks like he's got a belly full of rat, so he won't be going anywhere fast." He raised the gun, ready to take aim when a scratching, slithering sound erupted on the far side of the ute. The window on the driver's side was down five inches, enough for Fang to squeeze out. Now he was baying at the snake.

"Bastard of a dog. Get out of it! Grab him will you, f'fuck's sake!"

The snake had reared up and was spitting at Fang. Before Martin could call him, the explosion ripped through the air. Fang leaped back, yelping at the noise, a shard of snake tail flying in the air. The snake dropped off the bales into the loose hay. Fang darted past David's legs, bumping him as he fired again, and a cloud of chaff rose in the air.

The now-furious snake uncurled its remaining metre and a half and slithered towards Martin, who had his back to the ute. His heel sought the wheel behind him, and he levered his arse up onto the tray. He was half aware of David running to the wall behind him.

"He's going under the ute."

Fang was already growling on the other side, his head low. David ran back with the axe. One swinging blow and a metre of snake spat back, contorting in spastic movements.

"Thank god for that—"

"Stay where you are. There's still the head." David was at the back of the ute looking underneath, trying to see what was going on.

"Fang! You dumb cunt, getaway *outta* there!"

There was a snarl and the sound of scrabbling paws. A high-pitched yip split the air.

"Noooo."

Fang crawled out from behind the ute towards his master, dragging his back legs, a spot of blood visible under his jaw. He whimpered and licked David's hand.

"No." David's voice had gone thin. "You stupid dog. You stupid fucking dog." He gathered him up, ready to put him in the cab.

Martin put his hand on David's arm. "Let me have a look." He lifted the dog's jaw, inspected the wound. "You won't make it. The bite's too close to his heart."

David screwed his eyes shut and angled his face to the roof. "Not my dog," he whispered.

"Just make him comfortable. It's all you can do."

Fang was already panting, foam gathering around his lips.

David laid him in the straw, kissing the dog's head. "It's not all I can do. I can't let him suffer." He ran back to the house.

In the short time it took for David to return with his rifle, the dog's tongue had become blue and swollen and his breathing was laboured and irregular.

The shot, when it came, scattered the birds in the camphor laurel for the third time that afternoon. But this shot was cleaner and sharper. And followed by silence.

Chapter Eighteen

The surgery door was still open, so she walked in. Mrs Campbell looked up from the reception desk.

"Hello, can I help you?"

Jodie waved her hand. "No, I—it's a personal errand. Here to see Martin when he's free."

"He's just with his last patient now." She smiled and went back to flicking through her magazine. Jodie sat at the far end of the room where she was out of the line of sight from the door. She clutched her sweaty car keys and waited. Her churning stomach made her feel five years old again as she sat next to her mum waiting for her tetanus shot. Not much had changed since then. The same old fish tank still whirred and churned at the end of the room. Probably the same slime growing up the side of the tank too. Same faded prints on the wall. Same classic FM floating in the background. Martin had not put his personal stamp on anything.

The door opened and laughter tinkled into the room. It was Sally Munro. Even with the loose work shirt, Jodie could see she was getting on. Skinny as a stick everywhere else though. But Steve had always gone for thin girls, even back in high school. Sally's little boy rushed out into the room, apparently demonstrating something for the doctor. Martin came out and crouched down to the boy's level, his large hand giving the little shoulder a squeeze. Jodie's brow puckered; she looked away.

Martin saw his patient out of the door and came back for a few words with Mrs Campbell, who was already packing up. She called out "cheerio," and in a flash of rings, was gone. Flicking through some papers Mrs Campbell had handed him, Martin walked back into his office.

Jodie stood and walked to the centre of the room. She hesitated. The anger she had nurtured for weeks was fragmenting in the face of nerves. She clutched her keys tighter and walked to the surgery doorway.

Martin was leaning back in his chair side-on to the desk, absorbed in the contents of a letter. She was about to manufacture a cough when he threw down the paper and turned to his computer screen. Startled, he pulled his hands away from the keyboard.

"I didn't hear you come in?" His look of surprised pleasure faded when he saw the expression on her face. "What's wrong?"

Jodie stood in front of his desk throwing her keys from one hand to the other.

"Sit down."

She shook her head, still not speaking. It was as if she was waiting for the starter's gun.

Martin gave a resigned sigh and placed his palms on the desk in front of him.

"I've come to see you—"

Her voice shook so much she stopped and swallowed. Her eyes were darting all around the room, unable to register anything. She took a breath and tried again. Her eyes screwed up and she spoke in a hiss.

"*What* are you doing with David?"

Martin regarded her, his gaze level. "You'd better be more specific."

"Jenny at the hospital. Knows other nurses in Sydney. She told me about you."

"And what did that entail?"

"That you're—" Jodie's breath caught in her throat, her chest rising and falling. Then it erupted with her plunging forward, planting her hands on his desk, the keys smashing into the wood. "You're as gay as a row of holiday accommodation! A poof! And here you are chasing after David, trying to seduce him. It's disgusting! You going out there spending all that time, staying overnight. What do you think people will say? He probably doesn't even realise. He can be so…so…*dumb*."

Martin's palms had not moved from their place on the desk, and he remained as he was, steadily meeting her accusing stare, waiting for her to finish. "I see."

"You don't fucking *see*." She slammed her keys into the carpet. "You don't know how damaged he is. How vulnerable to…" Her hands flew up to cover her nose and mouth, her eyes screwed shut. Her gasping sobs whistling through her fingers. She slumped into the chair in front of his desk.

Martin's voice was hesitant but gentle. "David's talked to me about a lot of things. He's found it helpful—"

Jodie looked up sharply, her eyes wide and angry. "What things?"

"What happened to Tim. What happened…what he went through afterwards."

"He told you about that?"

Martin drew his fingers up and rubbed them against his thumbs. "Yes. And many other things. He has a lot of…issues bottled up."

Tears ran down Jodie's face and her voice was throaty when she spoke, the words coming out in pulses. "I have been *scraping* away…at his cave door with a spoon…for longer than I can remember and you just—you just *come along* with your *little stick* of dynamite…"

"Jodie, he loves you more—"

"Loves me! I'm just a *mate*." She spat the word out.

"Isn't it possible to have deep love for your friends?"

"He'll never love me like *that*."

"So why have you waited?"

Jodie's eyes flared and her lips pressed together as if keeping something from blurting out. A tense moment passed, and she seemed to gain control.

"How can I—I *can't*—"

Her shoulders shook as she sobbed and Martin looked on in silence. Eventually she wiped her face down, pinched the snot from her nose.

"When I found out about you it all made sense. I can see how you weaselled your way into his trust." Her eyes narrowed, her voice barely above a whisper. "Has he fucked you?"

Martin's face puckered in distaste. "Perhaps you should ask David that."

"And now you've brainwashed him into selling up. What else are you making him do?"

Martin's eyes glittered. "What you're saying is ludicrous and you know it. You of all people know the price David has paid to keep that place going. You'd like him to stay until the bank forces him off? Is that what you want?"

"He could get some teaching work until the drought breaks. There are alternatives to cutting and running."

"Yes, he could wait until the situation crushes him completely. I suppose that's when you planned on swooping in to pick up the pieces."

Jodie gasped, the heat rushing into her cheeks. "How dare you. What I want is for you to stay away from him! Keep your filthy hands off him. I could make life so difficult for you—"

"You would do that to David?"

Jodie's mouth opened but no sound came out.

Martin closed his eyes briefly as if to collect his thoughts. When he opened them, he spoke softly, and his face was compassionate. "I can't and I won't stay away from him, Jodie. He needs me. You can either accept that fact or hate me for it. It's up to you."

Jodie stared at him for a long moment. Slowly she stood up. She wiped her cheeks and squared her shoulders. When she spoke, her voice sounded dead. "So, what do you plan on doing then? Living in Sydney like a couple of fags? Mum and Dad'll be horrified." She leaned over and picked up her keys. She walked to the door and turned, her chin stuck out in defiance. "David is *not* gay."

A small smile quivered Martin's lips. "No, I'd say that's a fair assessment. But there's something you need to be very clear on." His voice softened even further. "He's in love with me, Jodie."

She spun around unable to speak, unable to breathe, blindly searching for the exit.

Chapter Nineteen

Martin had called him on Thursday night with a change of plans. He was leaving for Sydney after lunch the next day. There were some issues he needed to sort out with his next job. And something about lunch with his accountant. David couldn't remember the rest. It all added up to Martin not being around. The reasons didn't matter.

He drove to the Black Rock. Played pool, caught up with the lads. Someone asked him where Fast Eddy was, but other than that no one commented. Johnno had jabbed him in the ribs when he beat him at a game of pool. "Gettin' a bit rusty ol' son."

He stood watching the next game with a schooner in his hand. Johnno came to stand beside him while his opponent leaned over the table. "So, where's Jodes? Haven't seen much of her lately?"

David grunted and gulped some beer. "She's been seeing someone."

"No shit?"

"Yeah. Gibbo man's been wining and dining her."

"Ma-ate." Johnno shook his head, smiling. "Had to happen sometime."

David left early. Something was out of alignment, and he just wanted to be alone. Well, no, that wasn't what he wanted, but it was the next alternative. He felt all loose inside, like the leash that had been holding him firm had just been doled out a few more feet. Of course, he could use the time to get the place tidied up and ready for sale. He worked more efficiently without Martin around. He stared out into his high beams, the broken white lines zipping past the ute.

Thinking of the work he had to do, his mind came to rest on his little brood of calves. The new lives that he wouldn't be able to see through to fruition. Those gangly little legs, their satiny coats. Their necks stretched through the fence bawling, their eyes rolling, when their mothers were bailed up for milking. His mouth set in a grim smile. That was him all right. A lost bleating calf waiting for his source of nourishment to be given back to him. How piss-weak he was. He shook his head as if to rid himself of the self-loathing that was creeping up the back of his neck.

It would be good, some time out. Good for both of them. Then he recalled Martin saying he'd be staying with an old friend, catching up with others for dinner. His stomach turned over. Would any of them be exes? Would Martin...no. *I am exceedingly careful.* And he'd said he loved him. But what did that mean?

He snapped to when his headlights lit up his front gate. He'd driven the whole trip on automatic. Martin had given him a contact number but promised to call Saturday night. The temptation to call hit him hard in the stomach when he walked in the front door, but he couldn't. Martin'd be out enjoying himself. Having a sophisticated time with his doctor buddies...or those nurses who couldn't keep their hands off him.

His mouth crooked at how sly Martin had been answering those early questions. Or worse, some male voice would answer the phone and he'd spend the night in a sweat of imaginings. He stood in the kitchen, his hands clasped on top of his head. When he opened his eyes, he saw Martin's supply of red on the bench top and he groaned. To get drunk or wank himself senseless, that was the question.

In the end he decided to do both.

It was past eleven when Martin called. David ran to the phone like a schoolgirl and then checked himself and did a lap around the living room before he picked up. Something perverse in him strained to sound uninterested as Martin told him about the restaurants he'd been to and whom he'd caught up with. There was a pause on the line as Martin waited for David to offer some conversation of his own.

"You don't sound happy."

"I'll be happy when you're home."

"You *have* missed me then." The triumphant tone put a sheepish smile on David's face.

"I've done nothing but talk about you since I've been here. My friends can't wait to meet you."

David was quiet, disconcerted; a vision of his future social life before him.

"I was clear on one thing though. I told them if you ever get sick of me, they can forget it. I'm a one-off."

"Ha. Yeah?"

A pause. "Am I wrong?"

"You're very bloody wrong."

David grinned into the stunned silence for a moment.

"I'll never get sick of you."

Somehow David stopped himself from storming into town Monday morning before surgery hours commenced. He chuckled to himself imagining what Martin would've done if he'd booked the first time slot. Then he stopped laughing, imagining all the things that Martin might've done. He was there dead on three parked a long way down the street but still close enough that he didn't dare get out of the ute till he saw Mrs Campbell leave and whizz off in her ancient Morris Minor.

The door opened and whatever Martin was going to say was forced out of his lungs in a loud gust. David slammed him up against the wall, pinning him groin to groin, pulling his head down with both hands. After a desperate interchange of lips and teeth David tore his mouth away, his hand savaging Martin's belt. "Open up. Now."

Later, calmer, they lay quietly on Martin's still-made bed. Martin lay on his back with David's face hidden in his neck.

"If I'd known I was going to encounter a force majeure, I'd've taken out appropriate insurance."

David grunted. "You came pretty close to getting force majeure'd, I'm telling you."

The quiet stretched out as Martin threaded his fingers through David's springy hair.

"It's an issue for you, isn't it."

David bit into his neck. "You know it is."

Martin pulled away so he could face him. "Is this some primitive thing about putting your stamp on me? Claiming ownership? Because I can tell you, David, you will never own me."

"It's not about that." But even behind the hurt frown he'd allowed to wrinkle his brow he felt a twinge of something like guilt. He wanted nothing left undone between them. It was unexplored territory constantly teasing him, beckoning. He wanted it all. "I just want to be as close to you as possible. I don't know. It feels like a barrier between us. If you really do love me—"

"For fuck's sake, David. Not that old chestnut. Give me strength! You're like a dog wanting to piss on a tree."

"Please don't make this ugly."

Martin let out an annoyed sigh. "I'm sorry." He raised his palm to his forehead and closed his eyes. A moment later, in a softer voice he apologised a second time.

David had moved in on his neck again, glancing down to see if this was getting him anywhere. His hand slid down over Martin's stomach. "Would you at least try with me? Just once?"

A negative sound came from Martin's throat.

"I've been doing some research."

Martin's eyes flew open, his pleasant focus broken. "Research?"

"Mmm." David's mouth glided away from his neck as he slid his thigh over Martin's legs. "I could gentle you into it. I'd be a picture of control—" He lifted his face up and grinned. "—and aim."

Concentration was becoming tenuous as David's teeth gently sank into his stomach. Martin let out a breathy laugh and threw his head back. He swallowed. "I'll...I'll think about it."

Chapter Twenty

"Don't just stand there, Dan, come in."

In the kitchen Dan put a container down on the table. He looked over to where Martin was occupied pouring drinks.

"G'day, doc. Hope y'like apple pie." He looked down at the container, tapping its lid absently with his stubby fingers. He glanced up at David.

"Sorry to hear about your dog, son. He was a good 'un."

David handed him an orange juice. "Yeah. I'm gutted about it. I keep looking for him, and the ute reeks of him—makes me wanna cry every time I get in it." He shook his head ruefully as he took another swig of his beer. "I still remember seeing him in the litter wobbling around on his bandy little legs. I knew he was the one, and I was right. Best dog you could have." He let out a gusty breath. "But I guess it's for the best. You can't have a cattle dog in Sydney."

Dan nodded and gave his arm a pat.

"Doesn't stop some people," said Martin.

"That's just wrong. They're too smart, anyway. Cause no end of trouble. You need a dumb dog in the city." David grinned at Dan. "And a dumb dog's not worth having."

"Y'got that right." Dan drained his glass. "So, what's that smell makin' me dribble like an old man?"

"Lamb rogan josh." Martin lifted the lid on the pot and beckoned him over.

He leaned over and inhaled. "Blimey." He looked at David with wide eyes. "I can see why y'keep him round. Y'need to marry this bloke."

David's mouth fell open and Martin quickly interceded. "Actually, this is David's handiwork, pretty much. I reckon you could throw it together yourself. It's not that hard."

Dan shook his head and gave David a knowing look. "As if Nell would let me do anything in her kitchen. I'm lucky I'm allowed to eat in there."

"Well, you don't want to set any precedents. You might find yourself strapped up in an apron before you knew it."

Soon Martin and Dan were seated in the living room, dinner trays on their knees, watching David fiddle with the old VHS player.

"Dad taped these off the telly, but they should still be okay. We can fast forward through the ads."

Martin had groaned when he found out he would have to endure not one but two westerns.

"Just be grateful I don't have any John Wayne. They're his favourite."

Dan was astounded at Martin. "Never seen *Shane* or *Cat Ballou*! They're classics, lad. Wait'll y'see Jane Fonda. Sweetest little piece of—y'know, before she went all funny with that exercise stuff."

Halfway through *Shane,* Martin reached over to prod David in the leg. They both smiled at Dan, legs crossed at the ankles, arms folded, keeling to one side. "Should I offer to drive him home?"

"Nah. He'll be right as rain when he wakes up."

After a lot of hand shaking and back slapping, he walked Dan down to his car. He came back to stand with Martin on the verandah and they watched the red taillights disappear round the bend. A riffle of sadness threaded through the air as he became aware of the non-barking silence. He made no effort to move, and Martin slung his arm over his shoulders.

"He really enjoyed himself, didn't he?"

"Yeah? If I'd known I'd've had him round sooner. I'll just have to hope I haven't put the girls' noses out of joint. Jesus." David shook his head in wonder. "I nearly bloody choked when he said I should marry you."

Martin gave him a squeeze. "I know it scares the shit out of you, them knowing, but I have a feeling Nellie and Dan might surprise you."

David turned to him. "There's no bleeding way—"

"I'm not telling you what to do. All I'm saying is, if they found out by accident or gradually figured it out for themselves, I don't think it would be the horror-fest you're imagining."

He shook his head.

"They love you, David. And where there's real love, there's acceptance."

He continued to stare out into the dark, his jaw set. "It's not that simple."

Martin reached up and tugged on his earlobe.

"Sometimes it is."

★

Martin's words were still eating at him later when they were sat on the sofa with their last drinks for the evening. The latest Tim Winton, bought for him by Martin on his trip, lay open on his lap, still on the page he'd opened it at.

"So, tell me about the acceptance in your family."

Martin turned from the television to look at him. He turned back and grabbed the controller and switched off the noise.

"Mum accepts me, but it's complicated."

A memory came vividly tumbling back into his mind. "What was that you said…something about the men in your family beating you up? What's that about? I'm sorry I've never asked you before." He shot a quick look at Martin. "Assuming you want to talk about it, that is."

Martin rubbed his forehead with his palm and leaned back into the arm of the sofa, folding his arms over his chest. "Not one of my favourite topics. I said to you where there is real love there is acceptance. I stand by that. My brother is an arsehole, to be frank. And because of…things, I don't get to see much of his kids. Nothing of them, actually. His wife toes the line. I get second-hand news through Mum. It's very sad."

"Shit, I'm sorry."

"Don't be. My mother loves me. She's the one who counts."

"Tell me about your mum."

"Oh, she's an Eastern Suburbs Lady." His mouth tilted up at one end. "A bit of a lady-who-lunches. She's beautiful. She's elegant—"

"Like you, Princess." Smiling, he poked him in the arm.

"Yeah," he laughed. "Thanks. And the man she married kept her squashed under his thumb. He's been dead for years but now she lets my brother carry on the job. I wish she had some backbone, but she's just not been brought up that way. Too giving."

"I look forward to meeting her. What will she think of you taking up with a rough yokel like me though?"

Martin eased himself up out of the corner of the lounge and leaned towards him. He playfully grabbed him by the ear and steered his face towards his. "She'll see how I look at you and she'll know."

He dipped his head and spent a long time plundering David's mouth.

David shifted his weight so Martin was more lying next to him.

"What will she know?"

"That you're the rough, real, yokelly thing."

Chapter Twenty-One

It was not yet December, but it had been summer for a good month already. Dry heat rising from the ground, hot air rattling under the eaves and gutters. The sky a washed-out blue, the sun leaching the remaining colour out of the landscape, rendering the distant hills a faded lavender.

David shovelled some cow manure into a plastic crate. He carried it up to the house and distributed it over the base of some plants he had on life support. One of them was a stunted looking tree that had been at the back of the house since he was a kid. His mother's tree. Yesterday-today-and-tomorrow, she called it. In the good years, its leaves had been glossy green, its flowers an abundant cloud of purple, mauve, and white. This was the season for its flowers, and he noticed a few charred buds.

His morning had been taken up with the real estate agent. David had expected old Tom Standish, but he'd sent his son, Owen, who'd been a few years behind him at school. He'd come out in his crisp shirt and trousers, clipboard in hand. David had taken him for a run around the paddocks, down along the creek. Then they'd walked around the house, finishing at the kitchen table where Owen had spread out his paperwork. David leaned on his hand, his face grimly resigned.

"There can't be many interested buyers at the moment."

Owen glanced up. "Oh, there're some. Asian, mainly. Looking for bargains. The patient money."

David chewed his lip. That would go down a treat with Dan. Christ, maybe *he'd* end up selling to them in the end as well. But then he smiled. No, he'd never sell. It would be Nellie or the kids who would have that pleasant job.

And so, it was done. He agreed to the terms. Signed the papers. Felt empty and cheap as he watched Owen drive off in a cloud of dust. And no Fang to see him off. The pain pricked at his heart. That was when he'd headed to the cow yard. Shovelling shit was all he felt up to.

He waited till quarter past three and called Martin.

"It's done."

"Ah. Do you think you'll get a fair price?"

"Gotta find a buyer first."

"Whatever happens, David, you can stay with me for as long as it takes. You don't have to sell to the first vulture that swoops in. Once you've got some cashflow, you'll have room to manoeuvre."

The line was quiet.

"I'll help you fix that guttering up on the weekend, and we'll get that painting done. It'll make a big difference." He paused, his voice soft. "Babe, it'll all work out. I'll be with you every step of the way."

David's throat constricted. "Yep."

"David?"

He forced himself to swallow. Took a breath. "Yep?"

"I'll never leave you, okay?"

★

The weekends were spent removing old paint and painting on fresh while the weekdays ground on, the hard work broken up by a visit to town on the Wednesday.

"I'm becoming a bloody hardware expert," David said, throwing the paper down on the kitchen table.

Martin picked it up, reading the ad David had jabbed his finger at.

"Reads okay. And it'll be in the *Sydney Morning Herald* on Saturday as well, yeah?"

"Yeah. These ads cost a flaming fortune."

"Hmm." Martin folded the paper and put it away. "So have you heard from Jodie lately?"

David looked up. "No. No time for me, these days. I hope he's showing her a good time." He grimaced. "Makes me feel ill imagining him touching her. Clumsy oaf."

"You've had her to yourself for too long, David. She has her own life."

"Yeah, I *know*, but…"

Martin smiled. Slid a plate of sandwiches in front of him. "Besides, you said yourself it's what's inside that moves you. The outside is what you get used to."

"Yeah, but I was talking about—"

"It's no different, David."

He sighed. Took a large contemplative bite. "I guess."

"I might have a bit of drama over the weekend."

David raised his eyebrows, his jaw working a mouthful of ham and salad.

"Sally Munro is getting close to time. A bit overdue, actually. If she doesn't go by the weekend, she'll be induced on Monday."

David wiped his mouth. "You're not a baby specialist."

"No, but I promised her I'd be there. She had trouble with her first and they live a fair way out, as you know. She's worried she's going to get caught."

"Ah well. Mum had me in the ambulance, screaming in at seventy mile an hour."

"What, her, or the ambulance?"

"Both, I reckon. I came in at ten pound she said."

"Crikey."

"You wouldn't know it when I was growing up. I was a weed. Tim was the chunky one. He'd've been the farmer."

"You can't know that."

"He was the one used to tag along with Dad everywhere. S'why he never forgave me."

"Presupposing how life will turn out leads to disillusionment all round, David. Anything could have happened. No one has a crystal ball. Easy to blame you for his disappointment."

David looked up from his hands stretched out in front of him. "I rang Mum the other night. Told her about the sale."

"Yeah?"

"She's relieved, I think. Says she'll be glad to have me closer in Sydney."

"From what you've told me, it sounds like your mum gets you more than you realise."

"Maybe. When she has time."

Martin slid a hand over David's. "You can be pretty prickly, you know. It took me a while to figure out how to approach you without getting stabbed."

"Is that right." A small smile puckered David's lips.

"Poor Jodie's still trying to figure it out."

"She's used to me. Anyway, she's spending her time more fruitfully now." He watched Martin's hand on his. "So, you did fancy me early on, then."

Martin grinned. "Sure. In the time it took to stitch your hand I'd ripped your shirt off maybe fifty times. I was desperate to lick you."

"Hum." David cleared his throat. Looked at his watch, and then at Martin. "Oh my." He was up and heading towards Martin's bedroom, pulling his shirt tails out as he went. "Is it *that* time already?"

He raced in to pick up the phone, thinking it would be Martin.

"Hello, Davey. Everything all right?"

His whole body slumped into anti-climax. "Yes, everything's good here. Did Dan go in for that test today?"

"Yes, he went into the hospital after breakfast. It'll only take half an hour if that specialist's on time. Said he'd pick up some feed on the way home. I was wondering if I could get you to do a little job for me. I need you to have a look at that chicken coop. Dan thinks it's fine after he fixed it before, but something's had another go at it last night and I don't want to ask him again."

David laughed. "Sure. He doesn't have to know. I've got some spare offcuts I'll bring around."

"That would be lovely, dear. And I'm about to put some scones on."

"You beauty."

The fix to the chicken coop took very little time and he found himself agreeing with Dan that it wasn't that big a deal, not that he would have dreamed of contradicting the lady of the house. More time for eating scones, is what that meant. He took his seat at the table and watched while Mrs Wilson set the teapot on a trivet between them next to a fragrant mountain of scones.

"There's some of my marmalade there or some bought strawberry if you'd prefer," she said as she pulled up her chair.

"Always go the homemade, I say." David grinned at her. As he helped himself and slathered his scone halves with butter and marmalade, he became aware Mrs Wilson wasn't even pouring herself a tea. He began stealing glances at her between movements. Finally, he laid down his knife and picked up the teapot. "Shall I be mother?"

"Please." He watched her out of the corner of his eye as she placed a scone on her plate but made no move to do anything to it.

He stirred his tea and deliberately met her eye. "I'm waiting." He laid down his spoon and lifted his mug for a sip. "Either you've got bad news or I'm here to get a piece of your mind over something."

Mrs Wilson pressed her lips together and stared ahead of her into the lounge room. She sighed and looked back at him. "I'm sorry, Davey. I need to talk to you about a letter we received."

He watched her steadily over the top of his mug as he took another sip. "Go on."

She reached into her apron pocket and pulled out a thick square of paper that unfolded many times to be a piece of lined foolscap. From where he sat he could see large capital letters scrawled in blue biro. His hand shook slightly as he lowered his tea to the table.

"Before I show you this there's something I want to say, Davey." She reached over and placed her hand on his. "You know that you are as good as a son to Dan and me. Better, sometimes." She smiled at him. "And…and I want you to be very clear, that nothing will ever change that fact and how we feel about you."

David let out a breath and extended a shaking hand. "You'd better pass it here." He tried to swallow as he read, but there was a blockage in his throat.

"I'm sorry, Davey, it's so ugly. I don't know who could possibly have written such a thing."

He took it all in at a glance: the words "pervert", "poof", "not welcome", and at the bottom, "away from our children" and even, "Sydney diseases". His eyes were bulging and he was unable to blink. When he finally managed to speak, he sounded like he was choking on his rising panic. "Has Dan seen this?"

"No."

"Are you going to show it to him?"

"No."

He made another attempt to swallow and heard his throat crackle. "He can't…he can't know about this. *Please.*"

Mrs Wilson still had her hand on his and he flipped his hand over underneath hers and grabbed it firmly. "I'll die if he finds out."

Mrs Wilson brought her other hand to cover his and smiled at him. Speaking softly, she said, "No, you won't."

"What do you mean? How will I be able to look him in the eye ever again? He'll be ashamed of me. Disgusted! He'll—"

"Davey, now you listen to me." She shook their hands up and down between them for emphasis. "I won't let Dan see this filthy letter, but I will have to talk to him so he isn't caught off guard by some horrible kid yelling at him from across the street in town. You owe him that much."

David let out a long groan. "He won't understand! How could he?"

"He will understand the same thing I have come to understand over these last weeks, watching and observing on my own account, Davey. That meeting Martin has changed you. You're like a shrivelled up little plant that finally got some water. Do you think we haven't both spent nights worrying about that lonely little boy living next door? And now about his closed and isolated existence? Of course, we would love for you to find the right girl and have some children of your own. Every parent wants that. But we just want you to be happy, son, and that's something we've rarely *ever* seen…until now."

He was fighting back tears. "Mrs Wilson…I'm not…I'm *not* gay."

Mrs Wilson frowned. "So, you *are* just friends, then?"

"No…yes, I mean…I'm not attracted to men…I… bloody hell."

"Davey, I don't need to know the gory details of my children's sex lives. No doubt what Pete gets up to would shock my hair to grey, and *he* likes women."

A little laugh escaped David's lips as he raised the back of his hand to wipe his nose. "Okay, okay. But does it make sense to you that I fell for what's inside…that…the outside just kinda came along for the ride?"

Mrs Wilson smiled. "Yes, dear, it does. Do you think I fell in love with Dan for his handsome looks?" Now they were both laughing. It was David who sobered first.

"I'm still worried about you telling him though. That he'll look at me differently."

"I won't tell him any more than he needs to know. It will be all right, Davey, you'll see. Dan's already passed judgement on Martin, in any case."

"Oh?"

"Yes," she put on a gruff voice, "'that doctor's a good bloke.'"

"Well, that's something." He picked up his tea again and tossed it off in a few gulps. He was frowning as he set the mug down and wrapped his fingers around it. "I'm worried about who dropped off that little packet of poison though. Sending it to me would be one thing, but to send it to you was malicious and nasty."

"Some people have nothing better to do with their time, Davey. You can't let that worry you. They're usually all talk."

"But I do, Mrs Wilson. And what if they aren't just all talk? Martin's at risk too."

"I don't know what to tell you, Davey, except keep your heads down and don't attract attention to yourselves—you'll be gone soon in any case. You're both smart boys. You'll figure something out."

The first of December had come and gone. David's inner tension was rising with the heat. He kept telling himself it was about having the farm up for sale, but that was only part of the story. Dr Jacobs would be back on the job after Christmas. Despite the promises and the plans, David could not suppress the itching pain every time they parted. His own neediness disgusted him. If he wasn't careful, he'd turn Martin off. He was pathetic.

On Friday night he drove in and they went for a pub meal and some pool. He'd been pleased when they spied Jodie. She was at a table with her back to them, but he recognised the girlfriend who was looking at them over her shoulder. She leaned in to say something to Jodie, but Jodie didn't look around.

"Mind if we join you, ladies? Back on the Tooheys New already, eh?" David winked at Jodie.

With a tight smile Jodie introduced her friend Sarah, a fellow nurse.

Martin gave Sarah a charming smile. "Didn't recognise you out of uniform."

"Mum says you boys have been renovating up a storm."

"Just some painting and repairs. Only what I can afford." David directed this at Sarah, who was casting conspiratorial looks at Jodie over the rim of her drink. She gave him a return glance in acknowledgement. "Which isn't much, even with slave labour."

Sarah addressed Martin. "I see Sally Munro's booked in for Monday. Poor thing being pregnant in this heat. She must be desperate to get it over."

"It'll all be in the distant past when she gets a first look at her new baby."

David looked around the room. "You giving your man a break tonight?"

Jodie grunted. "Yes. I've worn him down to a frazzle."

Sarah snickered.

David's mouth set in a line. "Geez, Jodie. Y'too feisty for that wally. Y'need a real man who can keep up with you."

"He's man enough." She cast a look at Martin, who held her eye.

★

"S'okay," he whispered. "Easee…"

"*David*—"

"Shhh." A barely breathed whisper. "Stay with me. Stay with me."

A groan halfway between frustration and anguish erupted from Martin's throat.

"No?"

The only response was stertorous breathing.

Infinitesimal movements. He shifted and reached for Martin's hand. Martin cried out again and he froze.

"Stop?"

His hand was squeezed tight. The answer a long time coming.

"Nooo."

"Sweetheart."

David was leaning back on Martin's kitchen bench, chewing a piece of toast, when Martin finally made an appearance.

David's cheeks bulged in an evil grin as Martin walked gingerly towards the table. Martin glowered at him.

"You are a vile seducer."

"Is that a not-so-nice way of saying I know how to get what I want?"

Martin eased himself down onto a chair and winced.

Trying not to laugh, David snorted like a pig. "Come on, it was hardly a one-way street."

Martin stared straight ahead, ignoring him. "Fix me a slice of toast, house boy. I want the peanut butter thick. *Really* thick." He turned to glare at David. "Then I'm going to mash it into that smug mug of yours until you choke."

Recovering himself, David reached for the bread. He raised his eyebrows as he inspected both sides of a slice.

"Okay. I'll try anything once."

★

The morning was overcast and sultry. On the drive out there were spits on the windshield. Enough to turn the dust on the ute to mud. Such was David's faith in the weather he was hanging out the laundry he'd done at Martin's when Martin arrived.

"What about that rain on the way out?"

David spoke through the pegs in his mouth. "Nothing to get excited about. Just enough to grease up the roads and make them dangerous."

"They've been predicting rain all week. A cool front coming in."

"Yeah, well; we'll see."

Martin leaned over and pulled a shirt from the basket. He hung it and looked over at David. "Seriously though. You wouldn't change your plans if it rained?"

About to grab another item from the basket, David stopped and stood up. Gave Martin a long look. A realisation dawning on him that hadn't been there before. "No, Princess," he said quietly. "It's a done deal."

As they worked through the afternoon, purple clouds piled up over the hills behind the Wilsons'. There was a metallic smell in the air.

Around seven in the evening, a grumble of thunder rolled in the distance. It was too hot and sticky to lie on the couch. After dinner David set up two cane chairs on the front verandah, where they drank chilled beer and watched shards of lightning flash above black ramparts of hills.

"The tension's killing me."

David shrugged. "It could go on like this all night and nothing come of it. Biggest cock tease there is."

David wasn't sure if he'd been asleep when the sound woke him. Thought he was dreaming. "Moonlight Sonata" rendered by a canary…or something. Awake now. Shoved Martin. "S'ya phone."

He was still groggy when Martin leaned over to kiss him on the mouth. "Gotta go. Steve's called the ambulance. I'm going to meet them in there."

David grunted and rolled over.

Again, he was woken. This time by a harsh spraying sound. Jesus. His eyes bulged in the dark. "Holy shit." He leaped up, ran out to the verandah, naked. Let the pulsing air push at him, the water splash and tumble from the overflowing gutters. He grabbed a post and leaned his head out into it, holding his mouth open. Gulping lungs full of air, loving the clean sweet taste. There was nothing like it. Nothing. Closed his eyes in extreme pleasure.

"Dammit, y'bastard. Why aren't you here with me?"

Jodie stood for a moment with the glow from the reception area behind her, rendering the rain in its range a curtain of vibrating tinsel. She pulled her cardigan up over her head and made a run for her car. She patted the dashboard as she did her seatbelt up. "Long time since you've had such a good wash, eh, Bessie?"

As she left the last of the streetlights behind her she began craning her neck forward in an effort to see. She'd forgotten what it was like to drive in wet weather. Normally she would have the radio on for company, but she was feeling the need to concentrate, so it was just her and the *thump-thump-thump* of the windshield wipers and the peppering rain. After a while the rain eased, and she was able to dial the wipers back to intermittent. She was just approaching the Mill Bridge, groping for the radio switch, when a dark shape seemed to rise up from the road. She braked and jerked the wheel, heard her tyres scream, felt the car slide in the wet.

In the quiet that followed her heart thudded in her throat, constricting her breath. She looked up and saw she was facing the guardrail on the right side of the bridge. Further down she could see a ragged tear and a loose piece flailing out in midair. She gripped the steering wheel. *Please don't let it be anyone I know.*

She started the car again and brought it over to the left side of the road. Put her hazard lights on and opened her glove box. She grabbed the torch and got out. She had a St John Ambulance kit in the boot.

A quick survey told her there were two vehicles smashed on the bridge. She peered over the guard rail and flashed her torch around. Her stomach lurched when it caught the back end of a third projecting from the creek bank. She swallowed and dialled 000 on her mobile.

It was only as she approached the two vehicles, facing each other off in silence, that she recognised the Audi.

No.

She wrestled with the door to get it open. Couldn't. Had to use a loose piece of metal to clear the edges of shattered windshield out of the way. She crawled up on the bonnet and felt her hand around the neck of the familiar fair head resting on the wheel. Felt his pulse. It was faint, but it was there.

★

It was still raining when he woke around dawn. The light filtering through the window soft and grey. He snuggled further under the covers. Had pulled a blanket up during the night. Supposed Sally had her baby by now. He smiled. Double celebration for them.

He was just drifting off into sleep again when he heard the car engine. Jerked out of bed, peered through the lace curtain. Back already? No. Dan's Toyota Hilux. Shit. He yanked on a pair of jeans. Was ploughing his hands into shirt sleeves when the knock came. Stopped short in the hall. It wasn't Dan.

David's hands froze on the buttons as he stared at Mrs Wilson. A cold bolt of fear plunged into his chest.

He'd seen that face before.

Chapter Twenty-Two

He stared out into the rain, his joy in it gone. The taste of vomit was still in his mouth, burning the back of his throat. His mind was stuck in a repeating motion like the wipers pulsing back and forth. *Martin, accident, hospital. Martin, accident, hospital.* There had been Mrs Wilson's guiding hand on his arm, pushing him into the passenger seat. The déjà vu sending his mind reeling.

Mrs Wilson applied the brakes as they approached the Mill Bridge. Police in yellow raincoats and luminous vests stood around heavy vehicles and tow trucks. Broken glass like ice.

David slammed his fists on top of the glove compartment. "I will kill those stupid fuckers."

Mrs Wilson kept her eyes on the road, her hands steady at ten and two. "Richard Barry's already dead," she whispered.

Tears streamed down David's face unheeded, his breath coming in fast gasps.

Mrs Wilson took the turn for the hospital, glancing at David. "You need to prepare yourself for the worst, Davey."

She pulled up in the car park, the rain pouring on the roof like nails. David turned to face her, and his lips barely moved as she reached over and gripped his arm.

"If I lose him, too, it's all over."

David burst out of the lift and ran towards the reception desk. Hardly noticed George and Ivy Barry huddled together near the water cooler.

"Martin James. Where is he?"

The two girls behind the desk looked at each other and one picked up the phone. David cracked his knuckles hard on the desk, oblivious to the pain, until Mrs Wilson pressed her hand on his arm to make him stop.

A door down the corridor opened and they both turned. It was Jodie, her eyes red, her hands pinching and squeezing each other in front of her.

David ran towards her and grabbed her shoulders. Started shaking her. "Where is he?"

She burst into tears, her eyes pleading. "Sweetheart, he's gone."

He didn't hear it. Couldn't have heard it. But her face…

Someone let out a guttural howl. "*No!* He said he'd *never*—"

"Four o'clock this morning. There was nothing they could do."

His knees threatened to give way, making him shake her even harder. "Nooo. No. Where is he? I have to see him. Now. *Now.* Where is he?"

Strong arms grabbed him from behind and frogmarched him to a small room. He struggled and yelled, his arms pulled back in a vice-like grip. The grip stayed tight even after the needle punctured his skin; it only loosened when he stopped hyperventilating.

Outside in the foyer, Jodie stood by as her mother spoke into a pay phone. She had just issued her husband with a set of instructions. She listened for a moment and then looked a question at her daughter as she held up two fingers. Jodie nodded. "Yes. Make sure you get both of them."

"I'm not overreacting, Dan. And if I am, I'll answer for it. Just get round there and do as I say."

His head was thick and heavy. He was distantly aware of Jodie holding his hand in both of hers as he stared at the ceiling. He could only take in fragments of what she was saying. Martin on the bridge. Stephen and Richard Barry hooning. Between twelve and one. Nowhere for him to go. Flipped and pinned. Richard catapulted from his vehicle off the bridge.

Jodie's sweaty hands clutched his as she whispered. "It was a few hours before the accident was discovered. By then it was raining. When they found Martin, he was blue. Hardly breathing. Pinned from the waist down. He didn't appear to be badly injured—"

David rolled his head from side to side, his breathing ratcheting up again. "Couldn't get it. Couldn't reach—"

"I was here when they came in. They tried everything, David, honestly, they did. He'd been starved of oxygen too long."

David screwed his eyes up and pulled her hands up to his mouth, kissing them. "Please, darlin', *please*. I have to be with him. For god's sake."

Jodie bit her lip and left the room.

He was shown into an anteroom adjoining the theatre. The door closed behind him and he approached the gurney. He stood there for a long moment, unable to believe his happiness was lifeless beneath that green covering. Knew when he lifted the sheet it would all become real. No longer deniable. He reached out and staggered back at the sight of Martin's pearlescent face. Throat locked. Shaking, willing himself to some kind of control. Stroked Martin's hair. Kissed his forehead. Held his face, pressed their mouths together. It wasn't enough. Nothing was ever enough. He eased himself onto the gurney and threaded his arm under Martin's neck. Hooked his leg over and braced his arms around him tight, his face pressed hard in his neck.

Chapter Twenty-Three

It was late afternoon when Mrs Wilson drove them home. The rain had eased to a thin mizzle, the air heavy with wet. The bridge was clear when they passed over it, as if nothing had happened.

They travelled in weighty silence. Unspoken thoughts like taut threads between them. When Mrs Wilson drove past David's gate, his eyes asked the question.

"You're staying with us tonight."

"No."

All he wanted to do was go home and wrap himself up in the bed—their bed—that smelled of him. No more people jarring and bouncing around him.

"Yes," she said in that old familiar voice that brooked no argument.

His breath came faster, his voice hoarse. "Nellie. Turn the car around."

She stopped in front of her own gate, the engine still running. The dots of rain erased by the intermittent wipers. She stared straight ahead as a tear rolled down her cheek. David reached over and took her hand. Pressed it. His voice heavy with gentleness and finality.

"Take me home, Nellie. Please."

In front of his house, she spoke again. Her voice decided. "Jodie's getting her sleep at Sarah's." She turned to face him. "Her shift ended at two last night. She was the one who found them, Davey. Drove back with the ambulances." Her eyes flickered over David's face, considering. "I'll send her over this evening."

"Please don't—"

"Son, I'm not asking your permission."

He walked around the house, touching things, looking for any mark Martin had left. Found his kitchenware, his coffee. In the bathroom he clutched his toothbrush to his chest, then gently placed it in the cabinet. His bottle of Acqua Di. He doused the front of his shirt in it, inhaled deeply, and closed his eyes.

His work boots were out the back, lined up next to David's; those he left untouched. Some shirts hung in the wardrobe, some Calvin Kleins in the bedside drawer. Also in that drawer was some lube and the spare puffer David had insisted upon. The sight of it caused a thrill of pain imagining its brother enclosed in the glove box of the car, beyond Martin's grasping fingers.

He pulled the blind across and slowly peeled off his clothes. His focus on Martin's side of the bed, images of him curled in sleep or on his back, naked, with his dimpled come-hither look.

He slipped under the top sheet and slid his hands over the bottom one, feeling for the crusted patches of semen on Martin's side. Wanting to gouge the memory of the smell and taste into his mind, so it could be there on call when he was a watery-eyed old man.

He lined up the spare pillows in the hollow made by Martin's body and wrapped himself around them. Buried his face in Martin's pillow, wishing there was someone to hold it over his face and put an end to his pain.

The glow of headlights made him unglue his eyes. Red numbers burned in the grey dark: 6.51. Went to get dressed and thought *fuck it*. Pulled on Martin's dressing gown hanging on the back of the door. Stood still for a moment to absorb the comfort.

Gentle rain was still falling, and he watched from the shadows as Jodie stamped her feet and put down her umbrella. Somewhere water *tick-tick-ticked* and a gentle gurgle flowed down the pipes to his tanks. Without a word he held the door open for her.

In the kitchen he sat at the table, wrapped tight in the soft navy material. Jodie's face was drawn and pale, her mouth a small crease. She laid plates on the table and put the food in the microwave. It hit him that he hadn't eaten since the meal with Martin the previous night.

He looked into the bowl placed in front of him, the rich fumes of beef stroganoff clouding his face. Jodie picked up her fork and paused to look at him.

Whispered, "You have to eat, David."

He did eat; tasted nothing. Watched as Jodie cleared up. She folded the tea towel on the rack, eyeing him nervously. "Mum said I'm to stay tonight."

His palm resting on the table in front of him turned into a fist. "You are not staying here."

Her voice trembled. "Mum said on fear of death I was not to show my face at home tonight."

David glowered at her. "Well, you'll just have to screw up your courage, girl, because you're not wanted. Tell them I chased you off the property with the stock whip. Just go."

"David…" Her voice pleading. "What will you do?"

"Wallow in my own shit!" He stood up.

Her eyes round with fear. "Mum said—"

"Don't make me get that whip out, Jodie."

Head down, flicking tears from her face, she darted past him and out of the door.

When the sound of the Falcon's engine faded, he returned to the kitchen. There were three items of Martin's that he had no wish to preserve. He opened one and drank straight from the bottle. Now the serious part of the evening could begin.

The rain returned in earnest around midnight. David was halfway through the third bottle but he was still lucid enough to realise it was roughly twenty-four hours since that fateful phone call. He wondered about the baby. A life for a life.

He sat on the sofa, hunched over the bottle sitting on the floor between his feet. His mind was a kaleidoscope of memories flickering and changing shape, recalled from this angle and that. Every caress, every laugh. Every suck, every last lick and fleshy mouthful. Lying on the gurney that afternoon, the utter madness of tearing Martin's heart out for keeping had flashed through his mind. Or for devouring whole. Have him inside forever, a part, never apart.

The alcohol was wearing away at his mind, making things swim and sway, but the pain was alive in his brain. Eating and corroding. In his chest and in his gut.

He replayed the events at the hospital in his mind over and over. His feelings for Martin on public display, now all over town. Astonished that he no longer cared. No longer needed to know what happened tomorrow. Where there was no Martin, there was nothing. He was a dead man.

He'd buried his dog out behind the chook shed. Felt a pang not knowing what would happen to Martin. A family plot somewhere, perhaps. If it had been up to him, it would be cremation, ashes scattered off the top of the hill behind the house. But he didn't have that right. The hospital had done all the necessary informing; made all the requested arrangements.

The rain pounded the roof in waves. There wouldn't be a thimbleful of topsoil left on the place when it was done. He finished off the last of Martin's wine, feeling the vibration of the pouring water as he upended the bottle to his lips. The dam would be filling up. Put his face in his hands. Tim…Fang… Martin. He couldn't hold on to a goddamned thing. Everything slipped through his fingers.

The round of pictures and memories was swirling faster in his head and the pain was becoming excruciating. And there was nothing to put an end to it. He stopped pulling at his hair and raised his face. He tried to focus on the wall above the front door. Frowned. Refocused. What the fuck. The gun rack was empty.

He burst out with a horrible laugh. Shades of blackness intruded on his vision, the wine pulling him down now. He tottered up from the lounge and threw off the dressing gown. Banged his leg on the coffee table and lurched out to the front verandah. Reached out to the verandah post and crashed his forehead into it; heard the roof rattle. The bile rose in his throat as his body thrust forward to vomit his stomach's contents on the ground.

He wiped his mouth and staggered down the front steps, felt the rain sting like hail. Embraced the cold and the pain of the gravel biting into the soles of his feet. Held his arms out and skidded on thin grass. Around the back of the house, his eyes adjusted to the dark shadows, the sheet waves of water. One foot in front of the other, the grass mulching underfoot. Water running through his hair in rivulets down his face, cleansing the tears and stinging eyes. Through the hair on his chest, any air movement chilling his nipples.

Another skid, his face in the mud. He struggled up onto his knees, crawled, head hanging down. Tasted blood. Vomited again. Staggered to his feet. A large shadow looming ahead. He half trotted half pitched toward it. Fell to his knees and clambered up the darkness. Smelt the wet earth and clay. Wanting to be part of it, sink into it.

The high pitch of water spraying on water. Deep breaths sucking in rain, making him cough. His feet squelched in oozing clay, sank up to his ankle. One foot in front of the other. Being sucked further and further down.

"Oh, Tim." He beat his chest with his fist, his face collapsed in anguish. He fell to his knees with a splash, pitched forward onto his chest and rolled over, the water lapping over his ears. Choked and cried, his mouth full of grit. Pressed his fists into his eyes to somehow block out the falling rain. Began beating his forehead. "Princess. Please. Can't…do it. Can't."

Chapter Twenty-Four

"Mum, he's gone! I've looked everywhere."

She was verging on hysteria. She'd run around the house, the sheds and other outbuildings, fearing the unspeakable. Then she'd jumped in David's ute and driven around for half an hour.

"He's only as far as he can walk in this rain. There're the hills up the back, the creek, the main road…" There was a pause. She could almost hear her mother's mind clicking over. Just hearing her business-like voice helped her slow her breathing. But when she spoke again, she sounded less confident. "Did you say you checked the dam?"

She hadn't. She also hadn't mentioned the trail of vomit that was still evident out the front.

After an extended silence, her mother's voice had lost its steadiness. "Jodie-girl, that's where he'll be. Wait for us to come round."

"*No.*" She gripped the phone in terror. "Mum, no. Everything'll be fine! I'll go and get him. I'll call you when we're back." She slammed down the receiver, noticing for the first time the dressing gown strewn across the floor.

Drunk. Out in the cold beating rain, god knows how long. She raided David's linen cupboard and pulled out a pile of towels and a blanket. Gritting her teeth, she filled the electric jug and switched it on, ready for when they came back. *God damn you, David Mulkerin. If you think you can just…* She couldn't even complete the thought.

Pulling up at the base of the dam, she now saw the skid marks that had escaped her first panicked inspection. Her mum was right. Jodie gripped the steering wheel and let her forehead fall to press against it, letting the tears come. The last twenty-four hours had already taken a severe toll on her, but now the gods were really twisting the knife.

She raised her head and stared in misery at the mist of droplets on the windscreen. She wasn't any use to anyone like this. She looked up at the rearview mirror and saw her tired red eyes glare back at her. "You are pathetic." She needed to get her Big Girl Pants on. She took a deep breath and thumped the steering wheel with her two closed fists. She needed to get angry, get her adrenaline pumping. "I swear to god, David-you-bastard, if you are alive, I will smack you from here to kingdom come for doing this to me."

She jumped out of the ute, her sneakers squelching in the tufts of grass and mud. A fine rain was falling but her T-shirt was already damp with sweat. She clambered up the slope, not wanting to get to the top. On the edge of the water, she looked around, her first reaction one of relief, until she saw something sticking out of the water closer to the far side.

"David!"

Half of his face and a shoulder, the rest of him submerged in the cloudy soup. She ran around the perimeter as close as she could get, and then splashed into the water. Her foot skidded on the slimy bottom and she nearly lost her balance. Was forced to move carefully, feel her way. She wanted to scream. Was his mouth above the water? Nearly upon him, she was sending waves over his shoulder. She lifted his head, pressing her fingers into his neck and her ear to his mouth. Breathing. Just. His skin was like a jelly straight out of the freezer. She hooked her hands under his shoulders and heaved. Angled up on the bank, she held him by the hair and slapped his blue face.

"David, wake up. Wake *up*." She rubbed his cheeks, cursing herself for not bringing a thermos of tea. Her distress was increased by the memory of Martin's blue face, little more than a day ago, and her continued efforts to blow air into his seized lungs until help arrived.

But David was breathing. Now she was worried about hypothermia and how she was going to get him back to the house. She couldn't leave him like this. She ran to the ute and got a towel. After clearing the worst rocks and lumps, huffing and blowing, she dragged David onto it. Then she dragged him on the towel to the edge of the bank and from there slid him down.

She was considering whether to wrap him up in the towels and blanket before racing off for help when he stirred, his head lolling back and forth, his teeth beginning to chatter.

"M-m-m-m. *Urrr*—"

It took twenty minutes of holding him against her, rubbing him with the towels, trying to get enough circulation going for him to move. She was used to moving heavy patients, but not from ground level. He had cuts and grazes everywhere and the towels were now bloody. Through adrenaline and brute force, she got him into the passenger seat, refusing to worry about his extremities banging on everything. Once in the cab she tucked the blanket around him and turned on the heat.

Back at the house she let the engine run as she took his hands in hers and rubbed them. Small spots of colour were returning to his cheeks, but he was a mess. There was a gash on his forehead and blood mixed with mud streaked his face. Now the worst had passed she relaxed enough to allow the tears to come. She pressed her palm to his cold cheek.

He was alive.

A smile trembled on her lips. She could kill him later.

She ran a lukewarm bath and helped him into it. Ratting through the cupboard under the sink, she found a box of Epsom Salts, set like a brick. She cracked it on the side of the bath and let a chunk fall in. As David's colour returned, she turned on the hot tap.

He gestured at the tap, mumbling some kind of protest.

"For god's sake, David, there's plenty of water, use it."

Steam filled the room. The hair on his legs and chest ran vertically on his white skin. His dark neck and forearms blared out in contrast. All the while he didn't speak. He hunched in sullen silence as she dropped some shampoo on his head and rubbed it in. Massaged his head and neck. Made him lie back to rinse. A fug of thwarted intent between them.

Now her heartbeat had slowed and she wasn't in crisis mode, the details of the situation began to present themselves with more clarity. This wasn't some anonymous patient. It was the man she had loved and lusted after for most of her conscious life.

She'd bathed more men than she could count and directed many a penis into a plastic urinal, but now with the naked body of her fantasies under her gaze, she felt awkward. Almost couldn't look. But of course, she looked. And after all the fevered imaginings, he was just normal sized, normal looking. Shrunken and caked in mud, a thread of weed in his pubic hair.

She brought in a chair and sat next to the bath watching him soak, her hands on her knees. Gathering herself together, she spoke with firmness.

"Well, I can easily confiscate the stock whip, David, but whatever else you threaten me with now will be useless. I'm not going anywhere after that little caper."

His eyes flicked up at her and back down to the water in front of him.

"My guns, now my stock whip," he muttered into his chest. "Don't forget the knives and forks."

"No need. I've got a nice little straitjacket for you out the back."

He glowered at her from under his brows, but she was relieved to see a glint in his eye.

She wiped him down as he leaned a hand on her shoulder. He said nothing as she rubbed the towel in his pubic hair and patted his privates dry. She quietly enjoyed the last touches of his naked skin she may ever get. Got him to sit down on the chair while she dabbed at him with Savlon. When she was done, she held out the dressing gown. He took it from her, a hint of the old twinkle in his eye.

"Hardly need it now, eh. But I guess you've seen worse."

"It's no reason for you to parade around the house naked. I have some aesthetic standards."

"Not when you've been porking—"

"Can it, will you! It's getting really bloody tired."

Seeing his contrite face, she pursed her lips. "Go and lie on the couch and I'll make us some Milo."

Jodie sat at the opposite end of the couch, with him silently hating her for being in Martin's spot and being so profoundly not Martin.

He snuck a look at her over his mug. He was caught between angry resentment and thinking what a little trooper she was. When he started coming to, the horror that he was still alive seeped into his brain, quickly followed by an awareness of extreme cold and pain. When he realised who it was pulling and grabbing at him, cursing and grunting, something in him had been amused. And relieved that it wasn't anyone else.

After the Milo he was hungry, so she made cheese on toast. He put the empty plate on the floor, lay down on the couch, and closed his eyes, comforted by the domestic noises coming from the kitchen. He had a piston banging away at the inside of his forehead, but the Panadol Jodie had given him was beginning to kick in. His core temperature had returned to normal; he was clean, although stinging and aching everywhere, and he had some food in his stomach. The only thing he was missing was the weight of a long lean body to lie back against him. The emptiness came on him in a rush and a sob rose in his throat. He choked it down and wiped the hot tears with the heel of his hand. But the hollow ache in his gut remained.

So many times he'd watched Martin perform the simple act of returning from the kitchen or the bathroom to ease back down onto the couch into his arms, not realising that every time it filled him up, kept him buoyant. Now he was empty, sinking, clutching at space.

When Jodie came to take his plate away, he was curled on the couch crushing a pillow to his chest, eyes screwed shut, fighting tears.

Tears spilled down her own cheeks as she felt the impossibility of absorbing his pain. She eased her weight onto the edge of the lounge in front of him; caressed his cheek.

"Sweetheart," she whispered, "I'm so sorry."

When she leaned over and kissed his forehead, he erupted in shuddering sobs. Quickly she lay down beside him and gathered his head under her chin, his agonised cries clawing at her heart. There was only one thing she could do.

She held him, and she held him, and she held him.

Chapter Twenty-Five

Jodie let the book drop to her lap when he entered the living room. She was about to make room for him, but he lifted her feet up and placed them on his lap. He let his head fall back against the back of the lounge.

"How'd you sleep?"

"Like shit." He turned his head towards her. "How about you?"

"Not so great. I don't see how Martin put up with that bed."

David looked at her for a moment, took in the I-shouldn't-have-said-that look on her face. One corner of his mouth lifted slightly. "I should have thought it was pretty obvious by now that he didn't."

Jodie's eyes darted down to her book. Watched her fingers smooth the cover. She let out a stilted breath. Nodded. When she looked up at him her smile was pure bravado.

"So, you've decided you're gay now?"

He frowned and turned his head back towards the front window. The absence of rain created a dull emptiness around them that teased at his nerve ends. He stroked Jodie's feet for a moment. When he spoke it was almost to himself.

"I never consciously decided *anything*. My feelings for Martin don't fit into some box with a label on it. All I can tell you is that I loved him. He had a man's body. I learned to love what he had. Does that make sense?"

He gave her a look of sad appeal. Then he let out a bitter laugh, threw his head back. "I loved him. Jesus. Now he's gone, I can say it." His mouth crumpled and he quickly covered it with his hand. His shoulders heaved silently. He pinched between his eyes, trying to control himself.

"Ah, Jodie," in a ragged whisper. "He said it so often. But I could never say it back. Like I was playing some kind of game or making some point of principle. Holding onto myself. Saving it for a special occasion, for Christ's sake." He wiped his face. "Now he'll never know that I loved him more than anything."

Jodie reached over and pulled his hand into her lap. Spoke quietly, deliberately. "He knew, David. Of course, he knew."

"What makes you so sure?"

"Because we had an argument about it."

She told him about her visit to his surgery. How she had abused and threatened him.

"Oh, Jodie-girl." He sighed, his face serious. "He never said a word about it. Only ever said nice things about you. Always."

Now she was crying, struggling to speak. "I'm sorry, David. I'm so sorry. But I was angry…and—and jealous. But he knew exactly how I felt. He understood me right from the start."

David gave her a look of pity and reached out to stroke her cheek with the backs of his fingers, but she pulled away.

"And then—and then, when I was leaving, he said, 'This isn't some fly-by-night thing, Jodie. He's in love with me.'"

David swallowed, his eyes locked on her face, hungry for any more words she could give him. When no more came, he nodded, pressed his eyes closed.

Jodie put his hand back in his lap and swung her feet to the floor. "They say you can't choose who you love, David. But you were lucky enough to choose someone who loved you back." She stood up. "Some people never experience that at all."

She turned quickly and headed towards the kitchen. "I'll make us some tea."

Ten minutes later, he was taking a hot drink from her hands. He gave the contents a tentative blow.

"Oh shit."

Jodie paused in bringing her mug to her lips, a look of enquiry on her face.

"I need to go in and clear Martin's stuff."

"Mrs Jacobs—"

"No." He got up from the table, wiping his mouth. "*I* have to do it."

Driving helped clear his head. His elbow crooked out of the open window, he breathed in the clean rain-fresh air. The sweetest smell on earth. The dark bitumen was smeared with pasted caramel mud, the purple hills draped in threads of mist. His eyes feasted on the wet solid colours that had so recently been painted on. In a few weeks there would be green.

There was a sign on the surgery door redirecting patients to the hospital until Dr Jacobs' return. He fingered the key on his key ring. Didn't want to give it up.

He walked into the hall, steeling himself. Knew he could never see Dr Jacobs as his doctor ever again. In the kitchen he stood there dazed, looking at the empty table where they had shared so many meals, forgetting what he'd come in there for. Remembering, he ducked out to the laundry and grabbed a handful of plastic shopping bags.

There wasn't a lot, and what was Martin's was pretty obvious. He wrapped the cord around the coffee grinder, wedging it next to the pot. In the laundry was a case of wine, still with three bottles remaining. He hesitated, thinking he'd leave them for Dr Jacobs, that he should never touch the stuff ever again, but thought better of it and placed the box on the kitchen table with the other things.

In the bathroom he shed tears over all the personal items. Even the half-used foil of Panadol took on meaning for him. It was ridiculous to keep such detritus, but he bundled it all up anyway, unable to make such decisions.

Martin's suitcase resided in the bottom of the wardrobe. He flipped it open and pulled open the drawers of the tallboy. It took a long time to pack as he felt the compulsive need to fondle almost every item. Gently removing each shirt from its hanger, he folded each one and laid it carefully down. None of Martin's clothes would fit him—he was too broad in the shoulders, too thick in the waist—but the shoes were a possibility. He smiled at the shiny brown leather covered in a whirl of pinholes. Perhaps a little too natty for him, but they might do in a pinch. He could see Martin rolling his eyes at him now.

He'd never seen Martin wear a tie, so felt no attachment to the selection he found. He held some of them up and was surprised at their reserved colours. Maybe Dan would like one. He'd ask Jodie.

The suitcase packed, he finally turned his attention to the bedside drawer. Handkerchiefs, puffer, some more lube, and the magazine. He sat back against the pillows and made himself comfortable. Only half focused on the turning pages, he was deep in recalling a night he'd stayed over. Martin was in the shower and he'd fished it out to have a proper look; see what the attraction was, whether his ideas had changed. They hadn't. He flicked through the pages of oiled thighs and shaved skin, the Latino complexions and black cocks, almost with relief. Martin came in rubbing his wet hair with a towel. When he saw the magazine, he paused and grinned.

David waved his hand at the open pages. "Does this turn you on?"

He smiled. "Some."

"Which one does it for you, then?" Hearing the petulance in his own voice.

"Hmm." He leaned over David, giving him a heady nose full of clean body. Flicked the pages. "This one." He tapped a page. A pale body from the waist down with a black head of hair in the way. Kind of in the way.

David glanced at it, pretending to be dismissive. "That's nothing we can't do."

"Yes, but you're not here every night, are you."

"I would be if I could."

He looked for that picture now. It was part of a series. It only dawned on him now. A blond man, almost a boy, with a tanned, built man. Not exactly, but close enough if viewed through half closed eyes. He propped the magazine up on a pillow and undid his jeans.

Later, with the bedsheets rolling around in the washing machine, he sat down to a lunch of tomato and avocado sandwich with a stub of cucumber to munch on at the end.

He thought he was done when he packed Martin's CDs. All but one. He couldn't resist putting on the Sarah Vaughan. It was then he realised he'd forgotten the surgery.

Feeling like he was trespassing, he poked his head into the office. Memories raining down on him. He rubbed his right palm, felt the thick ridge crossing the fleshy part below the thumb. Happiness welling up at the thought that he would have this mark forever. He looked around the room, at the books on the shelf, the posters of bodies with exposed veins and muscles, immunisation promotions, the stethoscope hanging from a hook on the wall; stupidly thinking, *he was a doctor*. He sat in the chair behind the desk and looked around. He was about to stand up when he spied the black notebook next to the keyboard. David's heart sank as he flicked through the pages of names and addresses. People who knew Martin, people who had known him far longer than David; people who didn't know he was gone. He dropped the little book into his chest pocket, its weight feeling like lead.

Days passed; he didn't know how many. Jodie and he rubbed along in companionable silence, routine conversations over dinner, watching movies together in the evenings. She'd accepted a few day shifts and he tried to get back to the jobs that needed doing. But he kept putting them off. Knew he'd keep looking around for Martin, seeing the work they'd already done or half done together.

Once, Owen brought out someone to see the property. He almost didn't care anymore. Just wanted everything to be over.

One evening after dinner he sat down with Martin's address book and went through it. It was hard to tell if some of the entries were professional contacts or friends. He knew that Maureen and Ken James were his parents. The only other James couple listed were Brian and Thelma; Brian must be his brother. He wouldn't be ringing any of them. The only other name he recognised was that of Pamela Wells, the friend it turned out he'd stayed with when he went to Sydney. He went into the office and dialled the number.

A deep voice answered.

"G'day. David Mulkerin here. I'm after Pamela."

"Oh, thank *god*. *David*. I'm so glad you called. I've been going out of my mind! I didn't know how to contact you."

They talked for over an hour. The first ten minutes were the worst, reliving the horror of that day, although he spared her some of the worst details. Spared himself. Friends who still worked at St Vincent's had let her know. She had been mown down by the news but was powerless to do anything.

"There was no way I was phoning *them* up," she said, meaning his family. "I was almost at a point of hiring a private detective to find you. Dipstick never mentioned your last name."

A small smile crept over his lips. "He said he told you all about me."

A smoker's laugh issued down the phone. "Oh, sure. Everything down to your dick measurements, but not your last name."

Jesus. And he would soon be meeting this woman. She'd already threatened him with violence if he didn't come down to Sydney soon. As they began swapping Martin stories and he became more comfortable with her deep voice and throaty laugh, he realised it was exactly what he needed. To be with people who knew and loved Martin, who would be happy to talk about him endlessly, keeping him alive.

He felt empty when he put down the receiver. The warmth coming down the line from Pamela had enlivened him, made him hungry for whatever she could give him. Yes, he would visit. He'd organise things and get back to her in a few days. He'd head down in a week or so.

The next day the decision was taken out of his hands.

Jodie had dumped the mail on the table when she got home from work and dashed to the bathroom to have a quick shower. David made them a curry for tea and was laying the table when he heard the pipes crank up.

While he was waiting, he went through the envelopes. Bills mostly. Then a cream-coloured envelope. Navy embossed business name with a bunch of surnames in it. Bloody marketing material. He was still reading the letter when Jodie returned, tying her hair up in a ponytail.

"What's up?"

Without a word, he handed her the two pieces of paper he'd been flipping between.

He watched her intelligent eyes zip back and forth like a typewriter carriage. After flicking over the page, she allowed the hand holding the letter to drop. "Oh David. He must have left you something."

David leaned on the table, holding his head in his hands. "He must have seen his solicitor on that last trip. He never said a thing to me. Bloody cagey bugger."

Jodie gently placed the letter on the table in front of him. "It says this Friday. That gives you three days to get your pooh in a pile. You'll stay with this Pamela person?" She reached out and squeezed his shoulder. He lifted his head from his hands.

"I don't think I can face his family, Jodie. Fuck. They'll all be there. Staring at me across a table thinking who the fuck are *you*."

She stood beside him as he gave her an imploring look—raised her fingers and touched his hair, smiling. "You can face them down, David. It's you that he loved."

Chapter Twenty-Six

"The longer I can hold on after this rain, the better prices I'll get."

Dan agreed.

David shifted the receiver to his other ear. "I've ordered a bit more feed. Enough to see me through to January. I'll see you right. You can have my little Jersey and her calf—I'd hate to sell her."

"Don't go worrying about that, son. Just do what you have to do."

He felt better after the call. Apart from visits from potential buyers, the only urgent thing was keeping the cattle fed. Knowing Dan would run an experienced eye over the place and keep things ticking over helped him relax. Meant he could stay longer. Being in the house facing all the memories every day was not helping him. And Jodie could get back to her normal life with a clear conscience.

While Jodie watched her favourite soaps, he pottered around in the bedroom. He dug out an old suitcase and cleared the junk out of it. Threw a few things in. Wondered briefly whether he should take Martin's clothes back to Sydney.

Decided against it. He was still faffing around when Jodie popped her head in to say goodnight.

"You've got three days to sort that out."

"I know. But my mind's going a hundred miles an hour. Gotta do something."

It was after midnight when he crawled into bed, his mind still jumping like a frog on a barbeque plate.

It was pitch black, his screams still echoing in his head. Arms held tight around him.

"It's okay," she whispered, "it's okay."

Crying and shuddering into her shoulder, drenching her T-shirt. He'd been running and running. Knowing that Martin was just ahead of him, if only he could run faster. Then the ground had given way and he'd collapsed into deep water…saw Martin sinking below his feet…had reached him only to have his head jerk back and have Tim's lifeless eyes stare at him.

After what seemed like an hour he'd calmed down, but he was still holding Jodie in a death grip.

"Shhh, you'll be okay now. You need to get some sleep."

He groaned. "Don't leave me, Jodie. Please."

He felt his way back from the bathroom. When he eased into bed, he realised that Jodie had rolled over. He spooned up behind her feeling an ache of déjà vu.

Compared to Martin, Jodie felt like a plush toy. So many folds to hold onto, sink his fingers in. So much hair. And nothing where he wanted it. When she'd cuddled up to him his hand had automatically slipped down to cup her groin. When his hand fell on flat pubic bone the desolation had hit him in the gut.

Now he reached down and lifted a generous buttock and wedged his penis in the tight fold of flesh and underpants.

Jodie stirred, grumbling. "What the hell are you doing?"

"Just getting comfortable."

He gathered her hair up in a rope and twisted it away from her neck. Buried his nose against her and fell asleep.

Woke again; thought he'd had a wet dream, only to find himself engulfed. Jodie's sporadic breathing.

"Baby, no—" But could no sooner stop her than a tidal wave. His mind spinning out of control. He held on tight and let himself go.

He'd been up for an hour, his packed suitcase now standing by the door. He finished dunking his teabag and dropped it in the bin. Went out in the damp morning air and sat on the front step. The soft yellow behind the hills made their edges stand out hard and black. He clasped his hands around his mug, not drinking.

It was wrong, what happened, but there was no stopping it and there was no changing it. He felt ill. Had committed a crime against her; against himself. All the memories of his one time with Martin flooded him. There had been none of the sharp intimacy and special care he had taken with his lover; it had been all blind rage and want. He shut his eyes and wiped his hand over them, trying to obliterate the memory. Thought he had called Martin's name; wasn't sure. The only saving grace was he hadn't tried to back-door her.

Except for that one time, Martin's climaxes were always quiet gasping affairs. Not like him, a dog straining at the leash until it snapped. A brief smile flashed on his lips and was gone. He was surprised to learn Jodie had a rowdy dog of her own.

But it was no good. All he'd done was add to his pain and self-hate. And now she would hate him too.

The sun was now sending spears into his vision, blocking out everything in the far and middle distance. He sprayed the dregs of his tea on the ground. The ground that was now peppered with green.

He rinsed his mug and took the wine and a few other items out to the ute. He'd got online early and bought his ticket. Had to be at the airport by twelve. Had rung a dozy Pamela, apologised, and said there'd been a change of plan.

"Mmph. Okay. Meet you under the clock at Central. What time?"

He told her. "How will I recognise you?"

A chuckle bubbled down the line. "Aw, bless. Did he not tell you? Honey, I'm the size of a house…with granny flat. You can't miss me."

He ran lightly up the front steps, only his suitcase to go. Stopped in his tracks, his breath catching in his throat. She was there. Standing in the bedroom doorway, her face *War and Peace*.

Hours passed, or perhaps only a moment, as they stared at each other. Her eyes dropped from his face to the bag in his hand. "How long?"

"Don't know," he whispered.

Big breath through her nose. Trying not to cry.

He wanted to rush over, squeeze her hard. Knew it was the wrong thing to do. Shook his head, his face creased with sadness. When he managed to speak, his voice sounded unnaturally high.

"I—I've got nothing to give you." His chest rose and fell, each breath giving him pain. "I'm stone empty, girl. You know it."

Her mouth clamped shut and she nodded. A little too hard.

He opened his mouth, wanting to say more; thought better of it. Adjusted his grip on the bag in his hand. Gave her a brief nod and walked out of the door.

Chapter Twenty-Seven

"Holy flaming good morning."

That was all he heard before being crushed by pendulous arms. On approach, taking in the expanse of black skirt, the short rose-pink hair, and the heavily blacked eyes, Jodie's voice echoed in his head: *you can't choose who you love.*

Released at last, his lungs sucked in a spicy aroma of cigarette smoke and perfume. Staring speechless into her pale-green eyes at the same level as his, he had the unnerving feeling that he'd known her all his life. She flashed him a set of perfect white teeth, the stretch of her lips revealing a stud in the bottom one.

"Can't remember the last time I got to squeeze something so pretty. Come on, I'm in a naughty park."

Her presence beside him as they made their way out into the open air made him feel weighted to the ground. He watched, mesmerised, as the granny flat flicked saucily from side to side and expanded as she bent over to close the boot over his suitcase. He surprised himself by thinking, *sexy as.*

Once they were strapped in, she commenced backing out, turning and checking mirrors. "Martin said you're a one-pot screamer on the wine, so I need to drop by a bottle shop and pick up some beer. Wasn't game to choose, myself."

He let out an exasperated sigh. "If he was here, I'd fucking kill him for his big mouth."

She grinned into her rearview mirror. "Hon, you're safe with me."

It was then, watching her unobserved, that he realised all her beauty was in her mouth. Those even teeth, the shapely lips; the stud the final adornment.

"Or we could do spirits. I have vodka back at the flat."

The traffic of Broadway closed around them. The heat and the fumes. He'd forgotten how narrow the lanes were. More cars than he'd seen in a month of Sundays. They crawled up towards the university and peeled off toward Newtown. Looking past Pamela to the green, he could see people lolling around on the grass, the pool in the background.

"God, it's been a long time," he said.

Pamela's flat was the top level of a small terrace in a leafy street a few back from the main drag. With her hidden in the tiny kitchen, he jammed his hands into his pockets and looked around the small living room. In the corner beside the shaded verandah was an ornate fireplace, a large Andy Warhol of Marilyn Monroe above it, dominating the space. Adjacent, there was a low shelf stacked with art books, the TV sat on top. A CD rack, full of jazz, blues, and soul stood beside that. She called out could he put one on.

With Billie Holiday crooning away, they sat in shabby old armchairs on the verandah and clinked their vodka and oranges.

"To happier times," he said, and took a sip.

"I don't know." She kicked off her shoes and put her thick ankles up on a milk crate, exposing a tattoo of angel's wings. "I'm feeling pretty stoked right now, imagining Martin tramping around heaven in a snit, cursing that I'm here with you all to myself."

He looked over at her as she stared out over her drink at nothing. "Our Martins seem quite different," he murmured.

She turned to him as if she just realised he was there. Dug her hand into the nut bowl. "Oh, you've got to remember I've known him his whole life; it colours how I see him. We were kids together. We were six when we first met. In Mrs Marshall's class at Bellevue Hill public. It was his first day." She put her drink down and licked her lips, still facing out to the foliage of the plain tree, the filtered afternoon light giving her complexion a pale-green tint.

"You know what kids are like. They smell difference and weakness ten mile away. I found some third formers roughing him up behind the sports shed, his sandwiches stamped into the dirt. I launched in there like…well, I've always been big for my age." She turned and winked at him. "He stuck to me like glue after that. And I liked him. He was quirky and clever. Unusual." She pulled a packet of cigarettes off a side table, glancing at him. "Hope you don't mind?"

He shook his head. Watched as she lit up and blew smoke towards the roof.

"Martin hated me smoking. His asthma, you know." She paused, gathering her thoughts. "Anyway, by the time we got to high school, the tables had turned. Puberty was not kind to me, I'm telling *you*, Sonny Jim. The biggest boobs you've ever seen and pimples galore. Turned out I had a thyroid problem, but that's another story. Beau Brummell, on the other hand, had somehow become popular overnight. Girls had discovered him. Everyone wanted a piece of him." She sat for a moment, puffing on her cigarette, deep in memory.

She reached over to an ashtray and stubbed out her butt. Her voice was husky when she finally continued. "He would only accept invites if I was able to come too. If not, he politely refused. I found my feet by about year eleven, but I wouldn't have got that far without him." She flicked away a fat tear. "He's always been my champion."

David was quiet for a while, absorbing this. "So, he was into girls back then?"

"Oh sure. He loved girls. There were a few botched attempts at sleeping with some of them, but nothing stuck really. Meanwhile I was stewing in my own jealousy as I was ready to screw anything that moved and couldn't get anyone to even look at me." She snorted a bitter laugh. "It wasn't till we were at uni, flatting together in Randwick, that it happened. I remember I was at the kitchen table, my books spread out, and on my second wine for the evening by the time he strutted in. He sat down opposite with this lit-up look on his mush. 'What?' I said.

"'I've discovered my vocation.'

"Expecting some medical treatise, I prepared to be bored witless.

"He'd walked home through Centennial Park and been forced to stop at one of the loos. There was this man already there, sort of hanging around. The short story is he gave this guy a head job in one of the cubicles. 'And I was good at it!' he said. I was caught between horror at the risk he'd taken and something deep down, saying, *yup. You knew this all along.*

"He became quite the tomcat there for a while. Home late, if at all. God knows what he got up to, what he told me was only the tip of the iceberg, for sure."

"I'm always exceedingly careful," David murmured, frowning into his empty glass.

She extended a hand to pat his. "Don't fret, honey. After that first discovery period he got himself tested regularly. Calmed down a bit when he started as a registrar. I think the dignity of being a doctor went to his head a bit. And those bloody male nurses got to his other head. I used to hate him for the amount of action he got. Turns out he was cramming it all in while he could," she whispered.

He swallowed hard. Turns out so had he. His mind tailed off to a morning in his bathroom after a hard afternoon of painting.

He'd wandered in and found Martin shaving. Martin grimaced at him in the mirror. "Can barely lift my hand to my face. I think my shoulders have seized."

David wrapped an arm around his waist and breathed his shoulder in. "Hmm. I'll go easier on you today." He looked up. Squinted at the mirror. "Is there anything there to shave, anyway?"

An indignant look. "Less hair means I'm more evolved, you know."

David grunted. "Well, we know who the animal is. And I'm not done savaging you yet."

Martin laid his razor down and wiped his face, his grin cutting deep vertical lines in his cheeks. "You're never done. I love that about you, but there comes a time when I need to preserve the skin on my dick."

"You're just going to have to toughen up, Princess. S'gonna take a while to make up for all the time I haven't known you." He wheeled

Martin round, giving him an exaggerated leer. "And the one you say no to is the one you never get."

David cleared his throat and reached out for her glass. "Another?"

For the rest of the evening, there was an unspoken pact between them to keep it light and they spent the time trying to outdo each other with funny stories. He soon discovered that when he thought he had taken the conversation to its lowest level of vulgarity, Pamela only took this as a challenge to dive lower.

He poured a teardrop out of the vodka bottle and topped it up with orange juice. His throat was in dire need of salving after so much hard laughter. He cocked his head at his companion. "Are we going to cook something?"

Pamela's face askance. "Shit no. I don't *cook*. What do you think I was living with Fussy Britches for? We'll get some takeaway. Unless you want to go out."

While they waited for their Thai to show up, David ducked out and secured more vodka. Walking down King Street was a shock for him. He'd been in the sticks way too long. Skinny boys wearing stove pipe jeans sporting Mohawks, people of indeterminate sex with their arms around each other, bare skin a feast of tattoos and metal, people in thongs and singlets walking dogs, homeless people, people in smart clothes pouring out of restaurants and bars. Seeing the dogs did put a momentary smile on his face as he had a vision of walking Fang on a lead down King Street with him looking back at him with a *what the fuck?* expression on his face. Pamela was opening plastic containers on the coffee table when he walked back in.

"You're an evil influence, Pammy," he said, holding up his drink to toast her.

Her mouth quivered and she smiled. "Oh, hon."

"What?" He paused, glass in midair.

"Only Martin ever called me that."

He put his glass down and reached over to squeeze her hand. Not wanting her to cry, he grinned at her and deliberately sidestepped. "I'll be calling you worse than an evil influence in the morning, you just wait."

Later in the kitchen, he was staggering around washing up their plates. There was a loud crack and he arched backwards. A plate smashed on the floor.

"Bitch!"

Before he could even turn around, she'd retwisted the tea towel and done it again. He armed himself with a wooden spoon out of a jar on the counter and chased her round the living room. She turned out to be surprisingly agile.

"No. No more," she gasped, collapsing on the couch. "You'll kill me."

"But look what you've bloody done!" He whipped down his jeans and mooned her, two red welts glowing on his arse.

"Oh my," she croaked, her hand on her chest. "That's so much better than television."

It was getting on for lunchtime when he rolled off the sofa bed, his tongue feeling like a Moroccan tinker's inner sole. He splashed cold water over his face and head in the bathroom, and then made himself a cup of tea. The milk in the fridge poured out like junket, so he made himself another one, black.

Out on the verandah, he was comforted by the sound of Pam's gentle snoring.

The alcohol had done its work on both of them, and towards the end of the evening they were both feeling morose. It broke his heart to imagine the three of them there together, hooting with laughter, Martin smiling in a fatherly way at their childish vulgarity. In the early hours he held her while she sobbed, her makeup staining his shirt.

He looked at his watch. *Shit.* In only a few more hours he—and Pam, too, it now turned out—would have to front up at a solicitor's office in Woollahra. His stomach tightened at the thought. He wasn't sure if Pam's presence would improve matters or not. From what she alluded to last night, his parents had never been welcoming. He smiled. What a pair they'd make. The country bumpkin and the Goth-lite or whatever it was she was. He knew one thing about her. She could bloody well sing. At one point he'd mentioned the Sarah Vaughan CD and she said, "Yeah, I bought it for him." Without saying another word, she'd pulled in a breath and out came "*Summertiiime…*"

By the time she was exhorting him not to cry, he had tears running down his face. He'd get her to sing it again for him with both of them sober. There would be no alcohol tonight.

"What do you think about these?"

He looked up from tying his shoes to see Pam holding up a massive pair of zebra print leggings.

"Um—"

"Or these?" The same, but in hot pink.

"Come on, you're just shit stirring now."

"And why not, I say? Arseholes."

When she emerged in the zebra tights, it was with a long black stretchy dress over the top that fell to below her knees. He grinned, relieved. "You look nice."

"Ha. Had you scared there for a minute, didn't I." Then she looked him up and down and her face changed. "What's going on here?" She jabbed a toe at Martin's shoes.

His insides quaked under her critical eye. "I'm sorry, Pammy—"

"Hon, don't be sorry to me. Ever. It's kind of sweet that you're wearing his shoes. But the fact is they look ridiculous on you. Don't try to be something you're not. Get out those boots you had on yesterday. You're a he-man, not a ponce."

He looked down at the shoes and a bittersweet memory of Martin looking preposterous in his new hat at the saleyards flashed through his mind.

"I didn't want to go in there looking like I'd just removed the hay seed from my gob."

Pam patted his arm. "You're going to have all those hoity-toities in Woollahra spinning their heads on their necks when you walk past, my love." She leaned in and leered at him. "And there I'll be, giving them all the finger behind your back."

He sat in the car next to her, waiting for her to scrabble through her handbag. She held a packet towards him. "Mint?"

He shook his head.

"Do you have any idea why we've been asked to come along for this?"

"No, I don't, hon. Maybe he's made some sentimental bequests to us. Maybe you'll end up with his toenail collection from fifth class. You never know your luck. All I know was that he was set on donating his body to science."

"*What?*"

Pam paused with her hand on the ignition. "I'm sorry, David, I thought you would've known."

"No. I didn't know. We didn't actually sit up late at night talking about dying." Hot tears choked him. "So, you're saying he's going to be cut up by some first-year medical student or something?"

She placed both hands in her lap, her voice quiet. "I don't know, David. But it's what he wanted. He donated all his organs and from what you say, the conditions for harvesting them would have been perfect. There could be five or six people with a second chance at life today because of Martin."

He knew he was being precious, but he couldn't stop weeping. The thought of anyone touching him, desecrating his body...

Pam held his hand, saying nothing. He wiped his eyes with the back of his free hand. "I'm sorry. You must think I'm pathetic."

"No, I don't. You have more right to be upset than anyone."

"But what about you? Doesn't it upset you?"

"I've had longer to get used to the idea, hon. He used to go on about it at uni all the time. Besides. I told you he was quirky."

Chapter Twenty-Eight

They made the trip in silence, the only interruption when Pam verballed a driver in front of her. He was beginning to see how there was much more to Martin than he'd ever realised. Every new little fact cut deeper and deeper, showing him the interesting and touchingly flawed man he could have spent his life getting to know. So many questions he could have asked and didn't. Too focused on himself and the novelty of being loved.

They stood out the front of the house, looking up the marble steps to the front double door of panelled glass.

"They're in the business of looking intimidating, aren't they," he said.

"Oh, they're all the same. Men in suits acting important."

As they walked up the steps, it occurred to David that he had no idea how Pam earned her keep. He caught a quick flash of their joint reflections in the glass doors before she pulled one of them open, a twinge of suspicion hitting him. "Pam, what is it you do, exactly?"

They were now walking through a foyer, surrounded by expensive-looking paintings. She smiled demurely at him. "I'm an accountant, hon."

He stared at the back of her head as she walked up to the front desk. "You. Are. Shitting. Me."

The receptionist stared straight at him. "May I help you?"

They were shown into a meeting room set up with jugs of water and glasses.

"Stop fidgeting, will you?"

"What do you mean you're an accountant?" he hissed.

"I have my own business. I help artists raise funding, seed capital; coordinate joint ventures, corporate introductions. Is that okay with you? Or would you have preferred me to be a receptionist at a brothel?"

A short bald man hurried through the door, a stack of papers under his arm. He gave them an apologetic smile. "Hello, I'm Rupert Simes. You must be David and Pamela? Sorry to keep you waiting. Mrs James and her son are just coming through now, so we can get started."

A bald man with a bull neck and small eyes walked in. David felt Pam tense beside him. Brian shook the solicitor's hand, nodded vaguely in their direction when introduced, and sat at the end of the table, staring into space. A while later a tall woman, her hair in an immaculate French roll, stood nervously at the threshold. "Sorry I'm late," she whispered. She came and pulled a chair out next to her son, darting a glance at them both before looking for something in her handbag on her lap.

David couldn't take his eyes off her. It was like Martin had entered the room in drag. The same thin elegant body, the same dark deep-set eyes. It was a while before he became aware of the solicitor speaking.

He was talking about Martin's physical bequest and its details. David closed his eyes, grateful this wasn't his first knowledge of it.

"You may not be aware," he said, shuffling some papers, "but Martin came to see me only a few weeks ago to change his will. There was only one change, but it was a major one. I'll get to that in a minute. There are some minor bequests to go through first."

There was his library of medical texts, his golf clubs, and a few other personal things, all left to either professional bodies or friends who could not be present. His mother was the recipient of a Royal Doulton setting for six.

Brian shifted in his seat, the chair creaking under the strain of a large body.

The solicitor peered over his glasses at them and smiled. "Now to the financials. Through some modest and well-timed investments over the last decade, Martin built a portfolio of shares, some of which he inherited from his father. Its current market value is, let me see—" he ran a finger down a page. "—ah yes, a little over one hundred and forty-seven thousand dollars. All healthcare and medical stocks. This he has left to his dearest and closest friend, Pamela Wells."

A noise like a little squeak issued from Pam's throat. Under the table, David squeezed her hand hard, willing her not to cry in front of these people.

"And now we come to the changed items. Up until a few months ago, Martin had the bulk of his estate going to a selection of charities. He came to discuss the matter with me, and the changes were made. The flat in Paddington is of course encumbered with a substantial mortgage, but that should be adequately covered by his superannuation and insurance pay-outs. These he has left to his partner, David Mulkerin."

David's mouth went dry as he stared at the wood grain of the table in front of him. His partner. Now it was Pam crushing his hand. He heard furniture drag on the floor. He looked up to see Brian standing, adjusting the cuffs of his suit.

"Haven't you done well for yourself, Mr Mul-kerin. The merry-go-round stopped at the right time for you, didn't it? That property'd be worth over a mill by now. Not bad work for a few fucks, eh?"

He heard Mrs James' sharp intake of breath and Pam's voice in the distance telling him to sit down. He walked slowly over to Brian, not breaking eye contact, his fists clenched by his side. The expression in the shorter man's eyes changed and his cheek twitched as he took in David's full size.

"Now, gentleman, I think—"

David stood as close to Brian as he could without touching him, leaning right into his face. His voice was low and vibrated with emotion. "You repugnant piece of shit. Get out of my sight before you get one of your own thrashings handed back to you."

Brian's nostrils flared. "You bloody pervert. My solicitor will put a stop to this bullshit. Get out of my way." He pushed past David and barrelled out of the room.

David hung his head, sadness washing away his anger, until he felt a hand lightly touch his arm. He looked up to see those eyes staring into his. "I'm glad to have met you, David," she whispered. Then she drifted past him and left.

He turned round to see Pam standing right behind him, her face streaked with wet. He shook his head as if mystified and walked straight into her open arms.

They got in the car and neither of them moved. Eventually David spoke.

"Did you have any fucking idea he was worth that much?"

"No. Well, I say that, but…"

"But what?"

"Well, his dad wasn't exactly a pauper, y'know. And I knew he was earning good money and that he'd bought the house—a deceased estate—he had to do a lot of renovating. It was a wreck."

David shook his head. "It's embarrassing."

"Embarrassing? Why?"

"Because it was such a short time to be left—"

Pam's voice was urgent. "David, you were the first person he was serious about. Ever. Believe me. That's how important you were. It's why he changed his will. He always planned ahead. Would you feel more comfortable knowing he left it to Brian?"

He gave her a horrified look.

They held hands for a while saying nothing. Then he gave hers a squeeze. "A hundred and fifty thou, eh. What will you do with that?"

Pam smiled. "Do exactly what I advised Martin to do when I told him to buy them all those years ago. Put them in a drawer and forget them. By the time I don't want to work any more they might be worth something. And the dividends will be nice. I'll tell you something though."

"What?"

"If Martin was here, he'd be wondering why the hell we weren't heading off for a celebratory lunch."

"You're right." He grinned. "Somewhere with hot male waiters."

"Now you're talking."

He was staring at the menu with an untouched glass of beer in front of him. Pam was chatting away, but it was only background noise. A flat in Paddington. Fully paid off. It was insane. What had Martin been thinking? Then he recalled the key word: *partner*. That's how things would've been if he'd come to Sydney. They would have been a pair. A couple. Every night could have been—

He suddenly became aware of the breeze in his hair and the quiet. He looked up and found Pam looking at him with a sad smile on her face. "Haven't heard a word, have you, darl."

He shook his head and gestured at the menu. "Could you just…order for me? I'm not fussy."

Pam reached over and patted his hand and chuckled. "Yes, Martin said you were easily impressed."

He took a glug of beer and looked back inside at the white furniture and metal bar behind them. He'd never ventured into a place like this when he was in Sydney, that was for sure. Funny, but Pammy seemed right at home.

They were soon squeezing out lemon segments and slurping oysters.

"So." Pammy gestured at him with an empty shell. "Do you think you could ever go back?"

"Back? Back to what?"

She grinned evilly, waggling the shell more provocatively. "To women."

He grinned at his plate. "You are *terrible,* Muriel."

"Martin seemed to think he was a one-off."

"He was. In every way possible."

"So, the girls might get a bite of the cherry now."

He wiped his mouth with his serviette and spoke quietly. "Pammy, I can't even contemplate—"

"Oh, I *know,* honey. I'm just trying to lighten the mood. Sorry. Tactless Pammy at it again."

"No woman has wanted me for anything beyond a few squeezes to date, Pam. Probably one of the reasons Martin was able to open up my world. I'd never known what it was like before to…to have…" He couldn't go on. He looked up at her and she was watching him intently, her mouth trembling.

"Oh, I've got a pretty good idea how that feels, believe me." She flicked away a tear. "Maybe one day my Martin will come along…or Martina. Hell, I'm not fussy—love is love, after all—and you never know your luck in a big city." She gulped the rest of her champagne. "And hell, I'll be beating them off with a stick as well soon when they get wind that I'm rolling in it." She winked as she held up her empty glass, the sign for a young waiter to immediately hurry toward her.

Chapter Twenty-Nine

The weekend came and went. Pam went to work, leaving David to sleep in, mooch around, adjust. When cabin fever set in, he caught buses to the beach and Centennial Park and recalled what it was like to do exercise for its own sake. As he ran around the flat circle of tar blotched with shade, he marvelled at all the narrow-hipped women pushing prams, some jogging behind contraptions that looked like satellite attachments. What was this business about a birth rate problem? He dodged around dogs of all sizes, children on scooters, skateboards, and small bikes. Every time he passed someone coming in the opposite direction, he resisted the urge to smile or nod. He was in the city now.

Not that anyone would've noticed. Everyone seemed to be plugged into some kind of device and several people conducted loud conversations, seemingly with themselves. No time to waste or was it an inability to deal with the empty, lonely moment?

As he lay on his back looking up into thick layers of foliage, he gave up fighting and allowed his own feelings of pain and loneliness in. Every day was pulling him closer to the time when Tim died, when the only way he'd been able to cope was to shut down. It was only when Martin had come along that he realised how dead he'd been. And now he wished he was a different kind of dead.

Coming to Sydney might only make things worse. It was ironic, but living in a city was about as isolated as you could be. He would enjoy getting back to class and he could see that Pam and he would be great mates. But being with Martin had made him greedy.

There had been a moment during his run when he had fallen in behind a jogger with a tall, slim physique. He had slowed down his pace and watched him, imagining. When the man pulled up at a water bubbler, the unexpectedly different face had broken the spell and David had felt a slug of disappointment. And not long after, running past the playing fields, he'd seen a block of toilets at the back and wondered if that had been the place. Realised he wanted to have sex, badly. Imagined himself going in there, waiting for someone like Martin to come and offer himself. Could he close his eyes and do it?

He shuddered and rolled over, burying his face in the grass, shameful thoughts of Jodie now fighting their way in as well. What a selfish shithead he was, to have let that happen. Like he'd fucked his little sister. A sister who adored him. Who had once adored him. His leaving for Sydney would be best for both of them. Martin had called him a coward for running away from his problems, but this time it was the right thing to do. And yet, the thought of leaving her behind only increased his emptiness. It had been an ambiguous pet name that he'd called out when he'd come inside her, but she would've known. And yet now, with distance, all he could remember was the supreme comfort of holding her in his arms. Someone he knew. Someone who knew him.

Confused thoughts of Martin and Jodie jumbled around in his head with a mishmash of emotions ranging from sharp desire to shame.

He would call her.

Pam arrived home when he was fixing a salad to go with their steak. "I could get used to this," she said as she flicked through some post. While she read through a letter, she absently switched on the answering machine. The hesitant whispering voice that issued from the device made them both stop what they were doing. Without a word, Pam rewound the tape and played it again.

After the message finished a second time, the flat fell silent.

"Well." Pam threw her post down on a side table. She gave David a questioning look.

He was still standing there, dumbfounded. "I'd better call her back."

He'd drunk half a bottle of water in the air-conditioned restaurant waiting for her. When she appeared at the front door he rose from his seat. She looked the same as before. Elegant slim legs tanned to a becoming colour, a neat linen suit. Her hair was fine like Martin's, but honey blonde and immaculate. Their eyes met as she weaved through the tables, and it was like Martin reproaching him from afar.

She held out a cool hand to him which he held briefly before pulling out her seat for her.

She eyed him nervously as he poured her some water. "I— I didn't think you'd come. Thank you."

"How could I not come? Martin said you were the only one who counted." He swallowed. It bordered on pain to look into her eyes. "It's almost like being with him," he said.

She looked down at her hands, seeming to take this in for a moment. Then she spoke again. "I'm so sorry for the way Brian behaved. It was inexcusable. He won't be challenging the will."

He waited but said no more. He watched her long piano-playing fingers tear her bread roll to pieces. She looked away and blinked a few times. "Please, David," she said, addressing the next table, "just talk to me. Tell me all about your time together. My son's happy times with you."

He hesitated and then began where it all started. His cut hand. Martin's professional demeanour. Over entree, main, and dessert he told her almost everything. Even his own story, how much Martin had helped him by giving him love and acceptance.

He watched her dab at tears with a tissue and thrilled to her light laughter when he made any jokes at Martin's expense. She wished she had seen him wearing that hat. He watched her sip black coffee.

"Your smile is…his smile," he murmured.

Her coffee cup clattered down into its saucer as her hand raced to her mouth. He reached over and grabbed her free hand. They sat like that until her sobs subsided.

He inhaled her perfume as she walked back from the ladies' to her seat. Her eyes were glassy and puffy, but otherwise she had herself in check.

"Mrs James—"

She frowned. "Maureen, please."

"Maureen, how did things get so bad for Martin at home?"

The helpless stare she gave him over the arms of the waiter who had just that moment come to refresh her coffee almost made him regret asking, but he had to know.

"My husband…was a powerfully built man. Used to getting his own way."

David immediately thought of Brian's squat frame and piggy little eyes.

"He didn't have a high tolerance for weakness. Or what he perceived as—" She paused and looked away, pressing her lips together. Slowly she turned back to David and gave him a look of silent appeal.

It was then he realised. He spoke in a whisper. "It wasn't just Martin he raised his hand to, was it."

She shook her head.

They sat in silence for a moment. David saw that the restaurant was emptying out. He caught the eye of a waiter. "Brandy or whisky, Maureen?"

She sniffed. "Ah. Whisky please."

Over their drinks Maureen told David how things had changed once Brian had come along. The pregnancy had affected her health and Ken had grown impatient with sharing her attention with the baby. By the time Brian was three Ken was on his second affair and out of loneliness, she began her first. Then Martin had come along.

David gave her a steady look. "I see."

And he did see. He had been wondering what part of this monster's personality Martin could possibly have inherited, and the answer was now clear: none.

"I asked him for a divorce, and that's when it all started. I can't—I can't even talk about it."

"What happened to Martin's father?"

"He worked for my husband. Suddenly an overseas promotion was organised. An offer that couldn't be refused."

"Of course, he could—"

Maureen waved her hand. "You didn't know my husband."

David raised his glass to his lips, keeping his eyes on her face. "Did Martin know?"

"Oh, yes. He guessed. It started as wishful thinking, but he was a sensitive boy, and he knew me well. One night, after a particularly horrible day, I held him till he fell asleep and he said to me, 'Where is my father who really loves me?'"

David's bottom lip quivered, and he looked away. He felt Maureen's hand slide over his.

"It has a happy ending, David. He went overseas after high school for a gap year and stayed with his father, who was then in Amsterdam." Maureen's voice softened at the memory. "He came back a different boy. With his father's help he moved out of home and did not look back." Her eyes were shiny with tears.

"But you kept in touch?"

"Not as much as we wanted."

He thought again of that bullying son, realising he had probably assumed the family mantle in many respects after his father had died. And sadly, Martin's father had died even earlier. Only a few years after they had first met. All this Martin had never mentioned.

He walked Maureen to her car, parked in a back street. Standing with her beside her open door, her heels bringing her to his eye level, he was overcome with a feeling of longing. Without even thinking he had clutched her to him in a fierce hug. The fierceness was returned.

"Oh David" was all she said when he let her go. She wiped her cheek and soon he was standing there watching where her car had turned the corner.

For the entire bus trip home, he berated himself for never holding Martin long enough or hard enough.

Chapter Thirty

The pace of life picked up in that week before Christmas as the agencies he'd registered with started getting back to him. He attended interviews at various schools around the metropolitan area and by the end of the week he had mastered how to talk about the five-year gap in his resume with some degree of confidence. His best chance looked like being a maternity leave cover at North Sydney Boys High.

On his first morning of interviews, he'd been doing up his tie in the mirror that hung next to Marilyn when Pam had wandered out of the kitchen munching on a piece of toast. "Holy flaming—" She broke off into a fit of coughing. She plunged back into the kitchen and he heard the tap running.

"You all right in there?"

"Errgh. Yes." She emerged wiping her mouth with the back of her hand. "Is that what you wear when you teach?"

He turned towards her. "Depends on the school, but yeah, I used to. Been a while since I wore one of these." He jiggled the tie sideways. "Do I look like a hick with a suit on?"

Pam shook her head wryly. "I can't believe you're in any doubt. You make me want to do the HSC all over again, hon."

He looked at himself in the mirror, saw the uncertain face and the too-neatly combed hair. "I wish Martin could've seen…" He let out a big breath. He looked back at Pam wiggling the tie again. "He'd have been surprised to see me so serious and responsible." He tried to grin, felt it wobble, and gave up.

The last interview had been that day and they were now out at Pam's favourite Vietnamese restaurant. He watched as she twirled some noodles onto her fork. "So, you'll have another month to get yourself sorted before you start work. Where will you live? You'll have to give your tenants or Martin's the right period of notice."

"I can't count my chickens, Pammy. I might not get any of them, yet. Then I'll be looking for farm labouring jobs in Bullamakanka." Something he was beginning to think he'd be more comfortable with. The interviews had made him realise how long a time it had actually been. So much had changed.

The other big event of the week had been a formal inspection of Martin's flat. Pam had come with him to see the property. It was beautiful. Even though it was tenanted, Martin had let it fully furnished, so David was able to see his taste writ large. A spacious living room with a fireplace had a second-floor view into leafy trees on a quiet back street. He ran his hand along the back of the leather lounge suite, thinking it would have more than compensated for the loss of his cosy one with all the memories. There were two sizable bedrooms with built-ins, one with an en suite. The one that could have been theirs… And, even harder to bear, the large kitchen with island bench. He almost broke down at the sight of its chrome and marble efficiency, imagining all the meals they could have cooked and eaten there together.

Standing behind the glass of the shower stall, Pam had run her fingertips over the tiles in the bathroom. "It'd want to be nice," she mused. "He had to spend a lot of nights on my sofa waiting for it to be finished to his satisfaction. Bloody nightmare. If I ever buy a place, it will be ready-to-live-in."

He couldn't live somewhere so posh and said so. Pam shot him a sly look. "You should bring Jodie down. Get her opinion."

He had raised his eyebrows at her without comment. Over several nights and wines, he had spilled the story of what had happened, sparing himself nothing. Pam may as well know he'd been a rat.

"She sounds like a great chick," Pam said quietly.

"She's like my sister."

"In *your* head, maybe."

After dinner they headed toward the station along pavement that still retained the day's heat, watching the oncoming headlights glowing in the dusk. The streets were busy with Christmas party revelry and just plain dinner-goers like themselves. Every second person seemed to be holding an ice cream. They found the place down near the station and soon they were re-emerging onto the street with their own pastel coloured pileups. As they made their way back to Pam's flat, it occurred to David that in a week he would be back in his own bed.

He said this to Pam.

"Not before you meet the boys. You know I've been fielding calls from them since you've been here. They'd have my guts for garters if I let you go home without their getting to meet you."

David did know about the calls. Knew also that she had put these friends off as long as possible, sensing he needed the space, but the time had come.

"Yeah, well, we may as well get their disappointment over with. I'm just a rough country yokel as Martin once said."

Pam rolled her eyes, her mouth busy attacking her gelato. "Come off it," she said, when she could. "Besides, you've got to remember there's been no memorial service or anything. These guys are grieving and there's been no formal outlet for them to get things off their chests. They're all agog to meet you, sure, but it's also about needing to celebrate Martin."

He was quiet a moment. Too busy thinking of it all from his own selfish perspective as usual. Pam was right. He owed them in a way. He was the last to spend quality time with Martin. There were stories he could tell them. Laughs he could give them to ease some of the pain. Maybe he would get more than he bargained for and they might make him forget some of his own for a while as well. He sniffed. Okay, it was unlikely, but he needed to do it, for sure.

"You're right," he said. "I'll put my best face on. Martin would have wanted it that way."

Pam beamed up at him and threaded her hand around his arm. "Damned straight."

As they walked down King Street to the Thai Pothong she gave David's arm a squeeze. "You're going to be a highly desirable top surround by bottoms tonight, my love."

He pulled his arm away. "I am not a 'top'. You told them I'm not gay, didn't you?" He turned to look at her and she just raised her eyebrows and smiled back at him. He frowned. "You'll protect me, won't you?"

Pam burst out laughing. "With my life, darlin'."

He'd never had so many men kiss him in his life before. There were five of them, Graeme, Flynn, Scott, Mike and Craig, all of them nurses except Graeme, who was a doctor. He had a chance to observe them as they ordered their meals. They were all boyishly attractive like Martin, but none of them seemed to have his steadiness, his calm centre. Pam was in her element, flirting up a storm.

When the food arrived, Graeme lifted his glass and cleared his throat. "To our beloved absent friend."

"To Martin," they chorused.

"And to new friendships forged out of old," chipped in Scott, tilting his glass towards David.

Dinner was not the stressful event he had feared. He even enjoyed himself. Funny stories from their uni and hospital days showed him yet another side of the Martin he thought he knew; one story in particular about a prank with a stolen skeleton had him weeping with laughter. The only time he'd felt uncomfortable was when Mike relayed a story about a late night on the wards which had involved hiding in a broom cupboard. David was aware of the story feeling a bit truncated and furtive glances around the table being shot in his direction. He took a deep breath and drank his beer.

He enjoyed Pam having a good time more than anything, but he was finding it hard to imagine meeting these guys on a regular basis. He wondered how things would have panned out if Martin and he had lived together.

Graeme leaned into him and interrupted his thoughts.

He asked what David's plans were. "When you're settled, come round to ours for dinner. Alex couldn't be here tonight, and he'd love to meet you."

After they'd been talking a while, a comment of Graeme's about his work triggered a memory.

"Did you work with Martin at St Vincent's? Was it as bad as he said?"

"No, I was at RPA. You mean the court case? Yeah, it wasn't pretty. Soul destroying, actually. He had a rough time of it there at the end. We were all concerned for him. I thought he was going to throw it all away at one point. I think the time off helped…but what really helped him was meeting you."

David gave him an incredulous look.

Graeme responded by nodding. "No, really. Oh sure, he could hide things pretty well. He was very professional. But I could tell he'd met someone. Not just anyone either. Our phone conversations changed. He seemed less needy, more forward-looking. The black moods had been replaced by David-David-David." He laughed. "Mr Real Deal I started calling you. If I'd been single, I would have been downright jealous." He laughed almost to himself, but then his face changed.

"I'm joking of course. I was relieved. There was a buoyancy in his voice again. I didn't know who you were, but I prayed you were as serious as he was. You really…turned things around."

He reached under the table and patted David's leg, giving him a long look, making David tense, but the look quickly dissolved into tears. "I'm sorry." He rested his forehead on David's shoulder. "I just can't believe he's gone."

David patted Graeme's back awkwardly and realised the whole table had gone quiet, watching them. He saw all those sad expectant expressions and realised he should say something.

"It's great to see Martin had such good friends." He took a breath to steady himself. "It feels like—like he's actually been here with us tonight." He cleared his throat in an effort to keep his voice calm. "Martin said to me once that the people we love never leave us. They live within us." He placed his hand on his chest, saw a few of them nodding. He opened his mouth to speak again but could say no more.

Pam's hand reached for his under the table and gave it a squeeze.

As they strolled through the back streets back to her place, her arm once more looped through his where it now felt right at home, they smiled and reminisced about the stories told over the course of evening.

"See? They're a nice bunch of boys."

"Yeah, they seem friendly enough." They walked along in silence for a moment. "Are they all exes of Martin's?"

"Ohhh. Don't ask me to incriminate myself, now. Do you really want to know? It can't do you any good, can it?"

"No, I guess not. Stupid of me, but I can't help wondering."

"Well, they all liked *you*, I could tell. I think some of them were a bit proud of Martin for nabbing such an unlikely looking candidate in the depths of the coont-reh." He saw her grin flash in the dark. "They all felt sorry for him going into exile. He wasn't out there long and Flynn was asking if there were any nursing posts going."

He looked up through the foliage into the light-polluted sky as Pam fumbled with her key. No chance of seeing any stars here, he realised. Not like in the depths of the coont-reh. Back where he was headed very soon. He would have to brace himself.

"Pammy?"

"Yes, hon?"

"How would it be if I stayed for Christmas?"

The next morning, with Pam loudly asleep in the next room, he picked up the phone. He listened to the burr of the dial tone and began to wonder if they were all outside. It was nine in the morning after all.

Mrs Wilson picked up the phone sounding breathless.

"Is everything all right?"

"Oh yes. Those dratted cows just got into the yard again. Will we be seeing you for Christmas, Davey?"

He felt bad saying no. He always spent the day with the Wilsons, sitting around eating good food and drinking beer with the fans on full bore. Then he'd stay over to watch the opening of the Boxing Day Test with Dan and Peter. But the thought of all their unspoken questions and thoughts in the air was too much for him. Nothing had been said or even hinted at, and maybe nothing would ever be said, but it was too soon for him to face the thought of it. It had hit him, standing outside on Pam's back step last night.

"Well, the change of scene might do you good. Peter will be here until New Year if you can make it back." She told him how his cows were getting on. Then he heard her hesitate before saying, "Stephen Barry was moved out of intensive care last week."

"Oh?"

"Yes. He's paralysed from the neck down."

He felt no anger. Felt nothing at all. Not even sympathy for George and Ivy. What was wrong with him?

"There's some nice news though. Sally and Steve named their little boy James. After Martin."

He closed his eyes. Born on the day he died. He felt the exquisite pain of it but could still acknowledge that one day he'd think that was just beaut.

"Davey? Are you all right?"

"Yeah. Fine." He took a breath. Said he'd ring on Christmas Day. Relieved now that he hadn't had to speak to Jodie.

Long after Mrs Wilson hung up, he sat there with the receiver pressed to his cheek, his eyes closed.

★

He hadn't expected to hear anything so soon, but Owen called him on the last working day before Christmas for an update.

"Yep, there's been two." David could hear Owen's boyish enthusiasm coming down the line. "Both came through late last week. One more serious than the other. A bloke from Quirindi looking to expand his options…the other sent a rep up from Sydney to have a squiz. I reckon he's just a tyre-kicker. Time'll tell. Pity about the holiday interrupting momentum, but some people use that time to have a breather and look around. This rain's changed things a bit. Been fielding a few enquiries. Things are lookin' up. I reckon we might see you right before the end of January."

They exchanged some small talk on plans for Christmas and David hung up on the promise he'd come and see him in the first week of the New Year. He strode around the small space feeling he had nowhere to go. He should feel uplifted by Owen's chatter. So why did he feel even lower? He needed to sell. This is what they'd worked towards. Martin had wanted this for him…he'd been right. It would just take a long while to get used to it. With a farm came a whole identity; a whole way of seeing yourself. You didn't slough that off in a week…or maybe ever.

Another jagged lap of the living room and a pause to scan the contents of the fridge. He grabbed a beer out of the fridge and slouched into one of Pammy's armchairs on the balcony. She was at work and would be enjoying a Christmas lunch with one of her clients about now. He expected her to be pretty jolly when she got home…when she got home. He had a long afternoon ahead of him. It was only now, rubbing the bottle against his bottom lip, that he realised apart from his time in the park, he'd had precious little time alone with his own thoughts. And just as well. It had become a habit to smile on the outside while he felt like a gutted-out house on the inside. All the cheap fairy lights felt a bit disloyal to Martin in some ways.

As he took intermittent sips and the mottled-green light played over him, his thoughts strayed to Maureen James. She, too, would have to keep her pain on the inside. It would only draw contempt from her son; at the least, there'd be little sympathy. A sad Christmas for her then. He hoped she had a close girlfriend or two. He decided to give her a call and see if it was okay to meet her for a Christmas drink…maybe the night before. She was a grandmother after all and would have her day mapped out for her, perhaps. Decked out in her own fairy lights.

Then there was Jodie. Mrs Wilson hadn't mentioned her in their short call. He hadn't liked to ask…and once she started talking about Stephen Barry… He set down his empty bottle on the milk crate and steepled his fingers in front of him. She'd be spending her Christmas afternoon with *his* family, presumably. The fact that her presence or absence at Christmas went unmentioned seemed to render that definite. His stomach churned at the thought. Mrs Jodie Kelly…Mrs Stock-and-Station-Agent. At least she'd be comfortable. Soon be a few little cherubs for her to look after.

He pinched his nose between screwed up eyes. God. He hoped at least one would be dark and cuddly with her eyes. He allowed himself to imagine her walking up to him with this child—a girl?—on her hip and handing her to David while she did something. The child pawing and smacking David's face and gurgling away. Something tightened in his chest. God love her, she deserved some happiness. But thoughts like this made him realise he missed her company. She tolerated a lot from him; knew him better than…okay, maybe she didn't know him that well, but she did care for him a lot. He knew that all right. A fact he'd always dismissed as not worth anything…because *he* wasn't worth anything, but Martin had made him realise her value and given him an inkling of his own. Perhaps Gibbo man had also helped raise her stock in his eyes. And the way she had braved everything to come and look for him like that. She must have expected him to be dead. His courageous girl. And as much as he resented her not being Martin in those following days, there was no one else he could have tolerated in his house but her. More pain in his chest. Sadness. Regret. Shame. Loss. All he needed was an olive on a toothpick and he could shake it all out into a glass.

Pam had presented him with what looked like a rather expensive tie, after he had prised open an eye to see and feel her squashing him into the back of the couch. He watched her face as she quickly shredded the paper he'd laboriously stuck together the night before. She seemed pleased with his choices: Miles Davis and some Dean Martin Christmas tunes. The latter went straight on the player while she busied herself with some champagne and orange juice in the kitchen.

On his second Dutch courage he picked up the phone and listened to it ring.

"Hello?"

Felt a jolt. "Oh, I thought you'd be…off somewhere. It's David. I…Merry Christmas."

"Where did you think I'd be? Pretty sad that you already think you need to tell me who it is." Her voice distorted slightly. "It's David. Yes, okay—Mum said to tell you your yesterday-today-and-tomorrow has busted out into bloom."

"Oh. That's beaut. Mum'd be pleased. Wish I could see it."

There was a pause down the line.

"You *will* be seeing it soon…won't you? Before Pete heads off?"

"I'm not sure. Owen reckons he has a fish on the line. I don't want to get excited about it, but I said I'd come and see him."

"Oh."

He was then passed round the family. The more he exchanged wishes, the emptier he felt. He knew he should be there. Something felt false and wrong.

He hung up the phone and knocked back the last of his drink. Sat there and stared into his empty glass.

"Another?"

Pam was leaning against the kitchen doorframe watching him carefully.

"Maybe some food?"

"Food? We're goin' out for Christmas brunch, aren't we?"

He laughed and shook his head. He set his glass down and walked over to her, feeling his throat tightening as he thought about what he wanted to say. What he needed to learn to say more often. He slung his arm over her shoulder and pulled her in for a hug, mumbled into her neck.

"Thanks for this."

"Oh darlin'—"

"No, I mean it, Pammy." He ruffled his hand in her hair and wobbled a loose teary smile. "I love you for it."

★

The woman who opened the door surprised him. Her hair fell softly around her face and she was shorter. Linen pants and no shoes revealing bright-pink toenails.

He smiled and quickly thrust his gift into her hands. A brightly coloured bag with a Johnnie Walker label visible from the top.

"Oh, that's lovely, David, please come in."

He followed her down the hall into a sitting room where classical music was playing. Felt an immediate stab of memory. Saw Martin looking back over his shoulder. *If you're willing to take a punt, that is.*

Maureen made no sound as she glided around. "Come out onto the balcony, David, I've set us up a cheese plate for supper with a few prawns. Is that okay? I don't know about you, but I don't have much appetite left after all the Christmas eating."

He looked out over the railing. They were on the tenth floor and he could see Bondi Beach in the distance. Close enough but not too close.

They chinked glasses and he thought how much more relaxed she looked than the other times he'd seen her. Maybe some liquid Christmas cheer had done her good.

"Some time with your grandchildren today?"

"Oh yes." She beamed. "I love them, but they are boisterous company. Glad to come home."

"I—I saw the flat."

She cradled her glass in the palms of her hands. "What do you think?"

"Spacious. Elegant." He raised an eyebrow at her. "*Posh.*"

She laughed and the sound lifted his heart. "Yes, it is, I suppose. He has—" She stopped. She looked at David and took a sip of wine. "My son had very good taste." She took an even breath and glanced into the flat. "He helped me pick out a few things here too."

His eye caught the glint of some framed photos on a table past the kitchen. "You'll have to show me those later," he murmured.

"Of course. There's a lot I'd like to share with you. So many memories. *Good* memories, David." She looked at him anxiously. "I probably left you thinking the other day—"

He waved his hand. "It's okay. We both have a lot to wallow in…and through. And maybe…not many people to help us do it."

"No."

They were both silent for some time and he was aware of the distant sound of traffic wafting up on the breeze.

"So, do you think you will…move in? It would be a shame to sell it."

"No, gosh no, I couldn't sell it. That hadn't even crossed my mind." He saw her shoulders give a little. "I need to get a job first. Then I can figure the next thing out."

She nodded. Handed him the dish of prawns.

He stared at the fat orange-and-white crescents on his plate.

"Oh Maureen." His shoulders began to shake uncontrollably. "This isn't how it was meant to be."

Chapter Thirty-One

He'd left Maureen in the early hours of Boxing Day morning. They'd talked and cried and talked some more. Between them they had kept Martin alive for hours and that awareness made it hard for them to part. Finally, he had stood in her doorway with a taxi awaiting him downstairs. She had taken his hand, and kissing her fingers, pressed them into his palm. "Make sure you stay in the light, David."

Since then, her words kept slipping into his mind at random times. She was right. He'd read somewhere that love was the death of death. That's what he had to focus on now. It was the only energy source that would keep him out of the dark.

And there was still plenty of that. The first day back on the farm brought him down hard. He barely noticed the fresh green of the paddocks. The house was stifling, having been shut up in the heat, but it would have felt thick and close regardless. Everywhere he looked he saw Martin's absence. By late afternoon he could no longer stand it.

The cicadas were zinging as he approached the tree line and there was a hot breeze lifting the grass and leaves. It was good to be in open space with no people. He took big lungfuls of air as if it might clear out his internal lumber room. Even in the shade he felt the cool rivulets of sweat running down his temples and the stickiness of his shirt as he lunged in large strides up the hill. He followed the route that he and Martin most often took on their hikes.

Soon he was easing himself down onto the shelf of rock that had been their favourite viewing point, forearms resting on his raised knees, just staring at nothing. Fell into what felt like a meditational space where he lost awareness of his surroundings, focusing on holding or being held. Conjuring into his mind Martin's scent as the breeze flirted with his cowlick and tickled David's cheek. The texture of Martin's shirt against his arms, the bumps of his spine pressing into his chest. The leanness of his legs as David ran his palms down a jeaned thigh. The secure comfort.

The heavy ache built in his chest with the layering of detail and the intensity of his memories. Tears ran down his face at intervals, more as a release of feeling than from grief; he was so submerged in the memory of each of his senses it was like he'd created something real.

A currawong let out a loud caw in a tree close by, making him jump. Hours had passed and the shadows were collecting around him. He wiped his face and took a series of slow deep breaths. He became aware of the trees around him and the golden light shining through their branches; the deepening blue of the sky and the clouds with their pinkening edges. The ache had passed and was replaced with a sense of euphoria, as though he'd had a palpable fix. Enough to sustain him for the next while.

He made his way down the hill slowly, feeling stronger, more capable. He could do this.

★

That night he had the luxury of sleeping in sheets that still gave off a faint smell of his lover if he searched out the right spots, although he came across the false trail of Jodie several times. He woke in the night with his arm falling on nothing. He lay there in the dark, clear-eyed, imagining Martin breathing next to him. Thought about all the facets of Martin's character that he had discovered too late, that would have been the pleasure of his life to unwrap over time. Imagined silly trifles like leaning on a shopping trolley while Martin inspected packet labels, snapping fresh sheets over their bed on a Sunday morning, standing around in the foyer of the Belvoir ready to go in for a play, coordinating chores like car repairs over the phone with both of them at work, scrubbing out that capacious bloody shower stall. He considered Maureen and felt the pain of what her life must have been like, how they would have brought her into theirs. The life that he had been on the brink of having and how different it would be now.

How different.

He thought about the things he wanted in his life; what Martin had shown him was possible. A partnership based on trust and love, how good it felt to have that bedrock of security. Knowing that you were *known* by another person. The shared history of experience no value could be placed on. Martin had shown him what it was to love, but more importantly what it was like to *be* loved. That he, David Mulkerin, was lovable.

He had a lot of healing to do before he could consider such things, but it helped balm his heart to know that in the far distant future it would be there for him. It would be out there somewhere.

★

The next day he started on the series of jobs he'd come home for. Things had happened fairly quickly in the first few days of the New Year before he arrived. He dropped into the solicitor's office and signed the papers for the sale of the farm which had been rushed through as soon as the Christmas break was over. Dan had congratulated him on the timing as there was no more rain on the immediate horizon and the green would not last long. He saw Ethan and confirmed his financial arrangements. Now all that remained was to pack what he wanted and sell the rest. He contacted a few locals about the machinery items, advertised some other pieces. Sold his cattle.

He brought a load of empty boxes home from the Co-op and was surprised at how little he wanted to take with him. His mattress and frame, his computer and desk, and the rest all boxes of books, kitchenware, and clothes. The local school had appreciated the donation of his piano—he would buy a decent second-hand weighted keyboard that was flat-friendly. The wrench was the lounge. He couldn't justify dragging something so large and shabby all that way, and yet discarding the memories it held was the hardest decision he made. He told himself it was about moving on, but his heart wasn't listening.

The days leading up to the holiday weekend were hot and solitary except for the odd person dropping in to inspect an item or take something away. Every few days he walked up to the top of the hill, but he was managing on less as January wore on.

Also in that time, he drove out to the cemetery on the Gibson road. He pushed open the rusted ironwork gate and listened to it cry out and then bounce *chank-chank* behind him. Noticed a new grave in one of the aisles, its most recent flowers already fried to a crisp. Richard Barry. The realisation didn't make him look back.

It was getting on for early evening, but still close and hot. As he approached Tim's grave, he slowed his pace. Lifted his hat and ran his hand through his sweaty hair, wedged it back on again. He stood in front with his head bowed for a moment. When he looked up, he cast a glance at his father's grave alongside and wondered if his presence was causing him to roll over in it. He looked back in front of him and shook his head.

Ah, Tim.

He squinted up at the sky. He'd have been what? Thirty-four now? Struggling to keep the farm going himself while he, David, lived it up in Sydney? Or would he have had more practical sense and given it up at the first chance. His mouth quirked to the side. "At least you wouldn't have had Penelope nagging at you, mate. She'll get her bag of lollies." No more to be said there.

He sat down on the edge of the grave. Talking half to himself, half to Tim. Tim knew all his goings on already, no new news to tell. Just chewing stuff over. Straightening things out with him. Taking his leave.

A few days before he was due to go, he went over to the Wilsons' for a final dinner. The conversation was just the normal family-style talk, although most centred on David and his plans. He'd already told them that none of the Sydney jobs had come through, but the agency had tentatively run a last-minute offer past him. Orange High School. Six weeks. Starting the week before Easter. He'd said yes.

That yes had caused an internal calibration that squeezed out the doubtful empty gaps. It was a long enough appointment to get him back in the saddle, but short enough that he wouldn't be gone too far for too long. He'd be back in Sydney before the chill started setting in.

Jodie had remained fairly quiet over dinner, although he pretended not to notice. When she got up to go outside, he leaned into Nellie and indicated with a flick of his head towards the door. "She okay?"

"I think she's finally realised you're going." Nellie gave his arm a squeeze. "She won't know what to do with herself."

"What do you mean by that? Isn't Gibbo man keeping her busy?"

Nellie closed her eyes and quickly shook her head as Jodie walked back through the door. Nellie got up to serve the pie that had been left out to cool. It was hard for him not to search Jodie's face for clues as they all made busy with scraping their bowls. Not that she was making any eye contact with him anyway.

Dan came out to the car with him to see him off. Nellie was watching from the verandah. Dan shook his hand and pulled him towards him in a half hug. "We're going to miss you, son. I'm glad your place will be occupied though. I hope this Collins bloke turns out all right. I'll be here to give him a hand, anyways."

David held his hand up to salute Nellie. It felt right. He needed time and open space. He needed to drive long distances and be with his thoughts.

Winter was a long way away.

Epilogue

Winter had come and gone. David's extended placement in Orange had ended with the last snowfall. It was time to move on. The gods had smiled on him and the principal of his old school, South Sydney, had been in touch. He was ready to give it another shot.

The drive to Bruce took the best part of a day, but he had energy to spare. He'd stayed in touch, but he'd never been much good with regular phone calls. He would've emailed, but the Wilsons weren't connected. He'd written a letter to Jodie. He'd tried to keep it light, the single page full of all the things he couldn't say. She'd sent him a postcard from New Zealand.

It felt like home, sitting at the table with Nellie and Dan, drinking tea and eating sponge cake. Chawing and talking.

Jodie was at work and wouldn't be home until teatime. But he knew how to fill in the remaining hours. It was a long circuitous route from Dan's, as there were a lot of rocky outcrops in the way, but he eventually found himself on that rock shelf he loved. Strange to think he was now trespassing. The rock was cold and damp under his arse, but the pleasure of sitting there with Martin outweighed all. He rubbed the year-old scar in his palm as if he were conjuring a genie.

All too soon the light dropped, and he returned, the Wilsons' outside light guiding him home. His time on the hill had left him feeling peaceful and full. He could face Jodie now. He could.

When the front door opened that evening, his heart started banging in time with her footsteps down the hall. He started to raise his beer bottle to her in a salute, but his hand froze in midair. He jerked up from his seat at the table and strode towards her.

"Oh, Jodie-girl," he whispered. She stared back at him with large eyes. So large in her thin face. His consternation overrode his caution and he wrapped her in his arms. "Where's my curvy girl gone?"

She wriggled out of his grasp, forcing a smile. "There was plenty to spare."

He frowned as he looked her over. "You were always just right. Are you well?"

"Fighting fit."

Nellie herded them to the table, and he was glad of Dan and Nellie's unbroken stream of conversation as it gave him plenty of cover for observing Jodie. It was like she had sunk into herself and it broke his heart to look at her.

After dinner had been cleared away and it looked like she was going to skive off to her room, he said quietly out of Nellie's hearing, "Grab a jumper. Come and sit outside with me for a bit."

She gave him a wary look.

"Come on. I'll be gone before sparrow's fart tomorrow."

She nodded and returned with a shawl wrapped around her. She took a seat next to him on the front steps. They sat for a while saying nothing, the clear cold night absorbing their thoughts. The distant moan of a cow broke the quiet.

He reached over and took her hand. "I've never seen you look so unhappy."

"I'm fine." She glanced at him. "Really."

"Is that right."

"Yes."

"Your mum says you've been lonely. Not been—"

"I'm *fine*."

He let out a long breath through his nostrils.

"Well, I'm pretty fine too."

She squeezed his hand. "I'm glad to hear it."

He rubbed his thumb over the back of her hand, feeling the small angular bones.

He thought about how much he'd missed her, how he'd ever break through these battlements between them now. Wanted to ask if she'd ever consider living in Sydney. Maybe use his place as a stepping-stone to…something else… But his nerve failed him.

He cleared his throat. "The flat's looking good. Had the painters in last week." He watched as she pulled her shawl closer.

"Feels weird going back to the same place, the same job, after all this time. Like I'm going backwards."

"You've changed too much for that."

"For the better?" The rising inflexion in his voice annoyed him and he took a deep breath.

"I think so."

"And you? Have you…changed?" He was aware of his anxiety levels rising, waiting for her to answer. Eventually she just shook her head.

Not daring to speak, he pulled her hand towards him and pressed his lips where his thumb had been. Then he placed it back in her lap.

"Say you'll come and visit." His voice had gone hoarse.

He focused on counting elephants waiting for her to reply. He made it to twelve.

"I suppose I could."

He pulled off down the hill, the dogs seeing him off to the gate. Once he was on even road, he started up the CD player, letting "Flame Trees" wash over him. All he needed now was courage, and the rest would come.

Acknowledgements

The support and encouragement writers receive in their long journeys is often hard to gather up in a short space, so the following acknowledgements are by no means complete. First and foremost I must thank Helga McNamara who patiently and generously midwifed the initial draft of this work over a three-month period way back in 2014. Your wisdom and humour kept me inspired.

And speaking of wisdom and humour, Scott McCosker. I hope our frank and wide-ranging conversations over jigsaws and wine are allowed to continue through a few more decades yet.

I am grateful to my initial readers, Shawn Hollbach and Trudy Whitcombe, who gave their time to provide feedback and moral support. Sample chapters posted on Literotica.com received generous feedback and encouragement from John Selleck et al.

Nicola O'Shea provided an invaluable assessment of an early draft with insightful follow-up conversations and advice. Denis Corke reviewed the manuscript and applied his copy-editing skills and literary wisdom to save me from more than a few oversights. Any remaining, are of course, all on me. And on that note, I'm very grateful to the good people at NineStar Press for helping me realise this dream, in particular Elizabeth Coldwell, for her support, patience, and good humour.

The Iranian poetess Dr Kamand Kojouri made my day by generously granting permission to quote from her wise and beautiful work.

I would also like to thank Ann Morris and Terry Peters for the generous provision of a peaceful location to contemplate and complete my work, and my godson Mitchell for calmly and methodically taking on my knotty IT difficulties and winning.

And last but certainly not least, my mother Paula is owed everything for getting me to love stories and reading in the first place. It is the gift that keeps on giving.

About Alicia Thompson

Alicia Thompson grew up on a farm in country NSW. She has a Masters in Creative Writing from UTS along with some financial and accounting qualifications. She has worked as a bookkeeper, photographer, editor, adventure tour leader in the Middle East and China, business analyst, writing teacher and general herder of cats. Her published work includes numerous book reviews, travel articles, and short stories. She lives and works in Sydney. More can be found on her website www.aliciathompson.com.au.

Facebook
www.facebook.com/aliciathompsonauthor

Instagram
www.instagram.com/aliciathompsonauthor

Medium.com
@AliciaThompsonAuthor

LinkedIn

www.linkedin.com/in/alicia-thompson-7b3b278

Also from NineStar Press

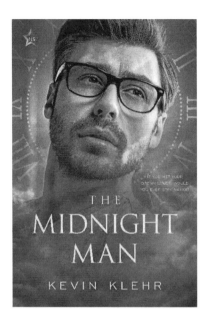

The Midnight Man by Kevin Klehr

Stanley is almost fifty. He hates his job, has an overbearing mother, and is in a failed relationship. Then he meets Asher, the man of his dreams, literally in his dreams.

Asher is young, captivating, and confident about his future—everything Stanley is not. So, Asher gives Stan a gift. The chance to be an extra five years younger each time they meet.

Some of their adventures are whimsical. A few are challenging. Others are totally surreal. All are designed to bring Stan closer to the moment his joyful childhood turned to tears.

But when they fall in love, Stan knows he can't live in Asher's dreamworld. Yet he is haunted by Asher's invitation to "slip into eternal sleep.

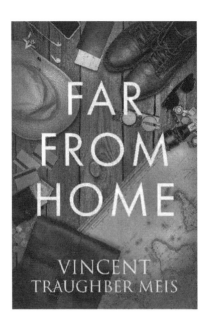

Far From Home by Vincent Traughber Meis

Far from Home is a collection of twelve short stories, taking the reader on a journey from the desert sands of the Middle East to a forbidden Caribbean island, and many points in between.

Though two of the stories are set in the U.S., others find gay people dealing with gayness in Saudi Arabia, Bahrain, Spain, Turkey, Cuba, Mexico, and the Netherlands, places where the characters are physically and psychologically far from the comfort of home. Most of the stories focus on Gay men suffering alienation, confusion, violence, and loss in the eternal search for love while they travel or live in other cultures.

The overall focus is on LGBTQ people as they venture out into the world.

Border CTRL + ESC by Ivy L. James

In the United States…

Mariana Mitogo is struggling to make ends meet. Then, out of the blue, she learns she's to receive a huge inheritance that would erase all her debt. The problem: she has to be married for six months to receive it, and her dating life is nonexistent.

In Spain…

Santiago de los Reyes, Mariana's Internet friend, has drained his bank account to support his family. Desperate to get his mom the heart surgery she needs, he interviews for a better-paying job that would take him from Madrid to Virginia. When he's offered the position but can't get a work visa, Mariana offers a solution that benefits both of them—a fiancé visa and a quick wedding.

If anyone finds out it's a green-card marriage, Santiago will be deported. Mariana would face a colossal fine and jail time. Good thing they're committed actors.

But as Santiago and Mariana pretend to build a life together, the lines blur between charade and reality. Will they dare to choose the love that feels more honest every day?

Border Ctrl+Esc is a lighthearted friends-to-lovers marriage of convenience between LGBTQ+ Internet friends (a demisexual woman and a bisexual man).

Connect with NineStar Press

www.ninestarpress.com

www.facebook.com/ninestarpress

www.facebook.com/groups/NineStarNiche

www.twitter.com/ninestarpress

www.instagram.com/ninestarpress

Printed in Great Britain
by Amazon

69088529R00189